Ashes to Angels

A Novel

By Natalie McCollum

ASHES TO ANGELS. Copyright © 2021 by Natalie McCollum.
All rights reserved.

Published in the United States by Kindle Direct Publishing.

Cover painting by Chris Fullam.
Author photograph by Charlie Gast.
Cover design by On Waves' Design.

This is a work of fiction. Names, characters, places, and incidents are either the product of the author's imagination or are used fictitiously, and any resemblance to actual persons, living or dead, is entirely coincidental.

All quoted material has been used either by permission of the original author and/or has been meticulously credited to the artist and used under the "Fair Use" section of the Copyright Act of 1976.

ISBN: 9781481805803

To the lovers I didn't have to love.

Contents

Part One:
Across the Universe the Sky – Is – Falling.

1. Gravity's Child   5
2. The Junkyard Love Song   13
3. ER: Rock Opera for a Busted Angel   22
4. The Deal, The Dealer   31

Part Two:
The Trouble with Poets

5. Caffeine to Mortality   41
6. Angel-headed Hipsters   51
7. Drunken Bar Poetry   59
8. The Fight Scene   78
9. "Porphyria's Lover" Makes a Circus   84
of the Sun
10. "Yes, Asher: I Like Fire and I Like Veins."   93
11. Iced Roses and Psychosis   105
12. Your Red Right Ankle   108
13. The Anti-Saint Valentine's Day Massacre   119
14. The Busted Lovers   125
15. The Prison Diaries   129
16. "St. Teresa Came to Me in Dreams"   132
17. "I Kissed a Drunk Girl"   137
18. A Beautiful Man with a Guitar   154
19. Slumming   163
20. Canal St.: The Balcony Scene   170
21. The Whoroscope: Angel Reads   187

Her Zodiac
22. "Sorry I Missed Church; I Was Busy Practicing Witchcraft and Becoming a Lesbian."   190
23. Burning the Commune: "Escape from Mantua"   198
24. Alms for the Poets   206
25. Id (The Twelfth Voice)   215
26. "She's Been Calling Me Again"   219
27. Bleeding Lessons   223
28. If Wishes Were Whores   230
29. Video Killed the ~~Radio~~ Porn Star   232
30. In Defense of Strippers: An Inquiry into the Nature of Band-Aids.   241

Part Three:
Shakespeare, Tattooed.

31. Auryn Pleads for Her Wings   247
32. The Playlist   254
33. Auryn: "I Don't Know, It Must Have Been the Roses"   261
34. Asher: "It Must Have Been the Mushrooms"   267
35. Like a Loaded Gun: Some Say It's Love   271
36. Pawning the Wings   275
37. The Rape of an Angel   278
38. Angel Dust: Bleed Like Me, O Mortality! 289
39. *Pulvis et umbra sumus*, or Dust.   295
40. Ash.   298
40 ½. P.S.   309

ASHES TO ANGELS

Prologue:
The Late Great Poetry Journal

Ashes to Angels
Extended Version of a Story:

The Novel
By the Poet.

[Note to Self: This is purely and corruptively a work of Fiction; as such, the Literal can STOP HERE. This book is about the form love takes between two crazy people. They have violated the line between Fiction and Poetry, among other things. From here on out, all things considered must be poetry. *That is,* IF you made it this far, and/or have not lost your sanity and contemplated selling your own soul for less dangerous reading material. This disclaimer protects the writer from any and all metaphorical damages incurred by the reader.]

Read at your own risk.

NATALIE MCCOLLUM

~n. (for narrator)

Ergo: *Here we go round the prickly pear,*
Prickly pear,
This is the way the world ends
Not with a bang but with a whimper.

*T.S. Eliot "The Hollow Men"

Before (T)romeo and Juliet,
There was Tristan and Isolde.
But before Tristan and Isolde,
There was
Asher
and
Auryn.

ASHES TO ANGELS

Part One:

Across the Universe
the Sky – Is – Falling.

If I Should Die Before I Wake...
...Merrily, Merrily, Merrily,
Life Is but a Dream.

NATALIE MCCOLLUM

ASHES TO ANGELS

Chapter One

Gravity's Child[1]

Auryn hit Earth just as Asher hit the brakes.

She landed at a crossroads, the place where suicides are traditionally buried and vampires are born.

It was the day the sky was falling. Across the universe, Galileo discovered that you cannot apply natural laws to the supernatural. She was a girl. With wings. Best time ever. The girl who fell from the wasteland of angel dust and ash landed six feet under the sunken rainbow, wearing Laceration Gravity and stocking feet, with no promises to keep but miles to go before sleep. With all the virgin suicides happening in literature these days, "cremation enjoyed a rise in

---

[1] "The very fact that . . . the new Humanism [recognized] that the Divine had come to Earth as a flesh and blood human being, who experienced the dualities of joy and suffering just as we do, meant that the angels . . . could not (without *falling*)" (emphasis mine). Malcolm Godwin, Angels: An Endangered Species, page 249.

popularity."[2] She was the poet's envy.

There was a girl who fell out of the sky, they say, a love story drop-out, horror story knock-out, delinquent daughter of a poison love, no sleeping pill to anesthetize the wing amputation, just gravity's law of laceration. Her name was Auryn.

Wings I was born missing
Angel of Harlem cut them off
in the womb, knowing I would
Only use them to stitch myself
in the tomb.

But the angel, meanwhile, was left in her own manhole, one far deeper and more impossible to scale back up than the cut-off chords of the song, wingless, soulless, and suddenly a child of a lesser god. No longer whole, there was a void, but that void was a man.

She hit earth just as Asher hit the brakes, and she fell flat on her face in the middle of the intersection, *nearly* causing an accident at the yellow light, not *nearly* the red light.

"I'm on a roll, I'm on a roll this time, I feel my luck could change…" he'd told his cigarette shortly before therapy. Mornings were so depressing. He still had this song stuck in his radiohead by the time he bailed out of the therapist's cell block and was jamming the

---

[2] "Mrs. Lisbon, however, objected to this idea, fearing it was heathen, and even pointed to a biblical passage that suggested the dead will rise bodily at the Second Coming, *no ashes allowed.*" The Virgin Suicides by Jeffrey Eugenides, page 36. Emphasis mine again.

ASHES TO ANGELS

key in the ignition of his little red moped. Usually a master of persuasion, the ashes seemed to indicate otherwise. "It's gonna be a glorious day. I feel my luck could change."[3] His melancholy tone was unconvincing. He was soaked through to his bare skeletal fibers as he hadn't thought to take a rain jacket, or even a poncho, sinister and shroud-like though it may be, and as the tiny chain slipped through his wet fingers a third time, a definitive "Damn it!" escaped his bleeding lip, – *this is what it sounds like, when doves cry, fuck you Prince,* – which he had bitten too hard on the way home, trying to keep from drifting in the smoky ruins of his own neurotica. Self-inflicting pain had worked, it always worked: he remembered exactly how he got here, but it had cost him some pain and added a shot of warrior-like rogue to his already disheveled appearance.

She did not remember exactly how she got here. Head trauma. All she knew was the sky was falling.

Asher thought he had hit a pedestrian who appeared out of nowhere, not realizing there was a naked angel stuck to his fender and causing quite the commotion in the middle of Lower East Side's busiest intersection. Asher got off at the scene of the crime; he'd seen a flash – something yellowy like sulfur – he'd heard a clash – like kryptonite on wings. He bent down to have a look. Yep, that was one naked angel. Because a naked angel is a wingless angel, with or without soul, or so the saying went. He did not just break an angel. He hit the brakes, not her. You don't just go around hitting on random girls out of the blue. It's not everyday you got a broken angel on your hands and at your feet.

---

[3] "Lucky" from the album *Ok Computer* by Radiohead.

NATALIE MCCOLLUM

Last Call—with or without Wings

The world is calling for angels.
But all it gets are moths beating in cracked
    street lamps after hours at 2 a.m.
They are you and me and everyone
   who has loved dangerously
     and cut herself on ragged emotion.
Beings higher than us are down on their knees
    crawling toward hallucinatory redemption,
   dragging their skins in half-truths
     too thread-bare to save this shabby soul.
And the place we cannot see up there
   is all out of winged people.
They've fallen into earth's ashtrays
   and fraternized with mortals.
So maybe we don't have to Imagine, John.
We have no heaven in exchange for no hell.

Those wings, those heavy, heavy wings infested with human matter and laden with the stuff of poets, were an (un)found object that shed an unidentified mixture of faerie dust and ash at the gentlest shaking or the slightest touch, and the burden of soul had fallen off in two halves at the shoulder, split at the cross section of two evils bookending a faith that died before Jesus came and leaving the rest up to dispute, as to which fraction of the story to remain untold, the superhero that tripped and fell or the superstar missing in action between them.

This dirty city…if it's not gray snow falling on shit, it's feathers littering the dust. Pulvis et umbra sumus.[4]

ASHES TO ANGELS

Asher slammed on the brakes with shocking acuity for someone who hadn't nearly come down, certainly not falling as fast or as far as a girl out of the sky – yeah, he'd gone to his therapist high, and she was on to him like a police dog trained to sniff out ticking bombs, that bitch – but Lucy in the sky with diamonds was causing quite the ruckus as people on their way home in rush hour spilled coffee on the dashboard, sacrificing their precious five o'clock fix to spare some half-dead looking little vixen with ashen gray feathers leftover from last year's Halloween costume ringletted through her auburn hair like the ancient warrior princess Judith herself. Angry fists graced the mob converging at the LES's busiest intersection; some punk with blue hair, watching the spectacle as he pulled out of the gas station scene, had the audacity to bite his thumb at the other punk on the moped who cut him off just to avoid hitting a bird or a plane. For a moment Asher envied that he hadn't conjured this scene himself – where were those raving fans, the voices when you needed them? There's a song for that, "Somebody Save Me" – then he jerked back to life – and death – realizing he had a rare opportunity to play the superhero, if only he played the chaos just right.

Amid pandemonium, everyone seemed to have forgotten the sole cause of their outrage. The tiny soul survivor of this one-man act was shivering, cramped almost coma like before his front wheel, in the spotlight of his burned-out one headlight. She was so encrusted, like antique silver jewelry just unearthed from the crypt, with the dust of the road, the polluted air through which she'd fallen, and the smoke of the

---

[4] From the Latin, *"We are but dust and shadow."*

exhaust that the formerly duck-down feathers sticking out of her tousled hair now just looked like a bad case of dandruff. Wherever she had come from, she certainly hadn't washed in days; the waif looked like she'd lived in a refrigerator box shoved down the fire escape a few too many times. She was shuddering, presumably at the noise, and cringing at some as yet unidentified pain, which Asher found the cause of when he coaxed her out of her defensive fetal position, not unlike wrenching a scared vicious injured animal out of the iron jaws of a clamp set by a fox hunter: a solo long white feather, razor sharp and silky dense as a swan's thrust crudely into her protruding vertebrae, somewhere south of a soul and third rung to the right of the spine. It stuck out crooked from her backbone, waving jagged and ghastly like a stripped mummy with but a single bandage flailing shamelessly in its wake to retain what scrap of dignity it could while streaking, skinny dipping, or at least flashing the public.

"I broke an angel."

It was quite the sight such as no police officer ever hopes to meet when Asher gave his license, registration, and insurance information to the officer who seemed to materialize out of someone's cell phone: a broken angel lay at his feet with tread marks from the tire imprinted across her forehead. Asher, having finally wrested the imp out of her foxhole, practically smoking her out with a stalled engine, stood there holding the limp body in lieu of evidence like Dracula's slut buried alive under the bed, among other night things. But the officer, with night fast approaching, did not find her to be human: he thought Asher had merely hit the decorative lamp-post in the crosswalk median, sending the Victorian architectural cherub flying headlong off its pedestal and smack into the cement, thus accounting for the minor but unsightly dent in his fender, and finally framing the arbitrary naming of things by the city-commissioned artist: "Our Lady of Sorrows."[5] Asher wondered for a half moment if he should fight for her, the girl, the arguably real mortal being he held, draped helplessly in his arms, but the officer took him for a freak when he requested checking for vital signs or calling the paramedics, and once he started to protest, as he KNEW the fans in his head would do, the man would suspect his incoherence to be a matter of drunkenness and get him on a DUI. The delayed reaction to the signal light was indeed a matter of drowning his post-therapy sessions in scotch, but not his coherence. The voices were always clear on that point. So that was beside the point. Asher didn't need *yet another* misdemeanor on his already sullied record, so he summarily sacrificed the girl to avoid getting framed. The officer wrote him up a ticket for "failure to yield [slash] running a red light" (*It was mellow yellow!*) with a verbal warning about public vandalism, and sent him on his way to the junkyard to properly dispose of the remains. "Heh, she's **your** responsibility now," though the cop qualified his bad joke with a promise that part – the broken angel – wouldn't appear on his record, just the *near-fatal* accident he (*SHE!*) almost caused in the busiest intersection of history. Asher laid her down in the grass of a clearing not too far away from said dump, and proceeded to decide, in private away from the public stage and likely scaffold, what, in fact, to do.

---

[5] My Chemical Romance.

ASHES TO ANGELS

Chapter Two

The Junkyard Love Song

"Excuse me, miss, but – you're beautiful."

She lay there like a corpse, a crystallized virgin mary frozen in a block of ice shrouding it like cling wrap to her pathetic precious rosary. There was no ecstasy of St. Teresa in this little virgin whore. She needed a transfusion and a transverberation or somesuch other shock therapy performed by a vampire, Armand the angelic-faced one himself. On second thought, Asher checked for a pulse: her sign was vital, but her hands were cold. What the fuck, she had seemed alive under the moped's shocks and brakes, likely shot now owing to this. "Damn you, little vixen, if I have to get *another* bike repair I can't afford…" Asher muttered under his breath as he turned her over to have another look and more careful assessment of the original wound: the satanic swan's quill with its horrific abscessed tooth-and-nail white shadow fluidity, – "Who knows how many horror movies have been spawned from that kind of obsessive thing," Asher mused unaware, and shivered involuntarily in the steamy night – was solid gone. All that remained as evidence of the flight of fantasy / fight to the death was a long bloody black X down the length of her bare back, like someone had reversed the reflex and scratched black nail lacquer on a white chalkboard. She was marked out like a map by a treasure in her chest buried alive.

> *i thought*
> *you thought*
> *[someone] thought*
> *i had moved on*
> *i had finally buried*
> *my crippling hang-ups*
> *i did bury my love*
> *hung it on a nail,*
> *then nailed it shut*
> *in earthen boxes.*
> *gravely marked your site*
> *with you my crutch,*
> *but it seems in hindsight*
> *i buried you alive.*

[*Asher, what are you doing, man, you're in a fucking landfill looking for a dead rainbow!*]

"Where's the crime in looking for love in a junkyard? It'll never give itself up. Too many screaming voices, raving fans."

> *because it is embedded*
> *in the crux of my soul*
> *nights it is my vampire*

ASHES TO ANGELS

rises up from its pyre
bites me with desire
out of measure
out of pleasure
so that i wake up
screaming your name.

[*Coma poetry – This must be what going mad feels like.*]

"You can fake it for the papers, but I'm on to you."

little girl in pretty boxes
upheaves her ancient
burial mound –
ancient because
    i have buried you
    many times around –
    many times because
    you have been in all—
    been all– my past lives
    before this one,
    but it's this one,
    i cannot dig you
    out of i dare not
    for by rejecting you
    i am also ½ rejecting me.

[*She's gonna say it's so damn hard to date a rockstar.*]

"Go to hell, you freaking angel-headed hipsters!"

At the sound of his words, the warmth of breathy respiration seemed to revive the dead, and she stirred on command.

[*Oh you speak to me in riddles and you speak to me in rhyme*[6]

NATALIE MCCOLLUM

/
my body aches to hold your breath, your words on borrowed time!]

" 'Cause I'm your superhero."

Irregardless[7,8] of the friction poeticizing fiction somewhere between the lines, hot with fresh ink, of the above heated verbal exchange, she, meanwhile, was writing this on her forearm, down the length of the bone with the white demon feather that had been otherwise missing, leaving a bottomless black hole in place of a spinal tap. The piercing rendered the $100 hole a self-medication, priceless artwork by the body piercer meant to rival any self-induced euphoria via starvation by the hunger artist. If she couldn't talk, she would write, the cheapest form of therapy and the trouble with poets who talk too much. She stopped, her thought unfinished, her sentence incomplete. Her grammar needed medical attention. She had missed her first period in months. The self-editor in Asher took over the possessive case: he grabbed the ballpoint quill from her clenched fist, and jabbed it

---

[6] Sarah McLachlan, "Possession"

[7] ***usage*** *Irregardless* originated in dialectal American speech in the early 20th century. Its fairly widespread use in speech called it to the attention of usage commentators as early as 1927. The most frequently repeated remark about it is that "there is no such word." There is such a word, however. It is still used primarily in speech, although it can be found from time to time in edited prose. Its reputation has not risen over the years, and it is still a long way from general acceptance. Use *regardless* instead.

[8] (Footnote to the above footnote [Solenote]: At least, according the esteemed Merriam Webster in the year of somebody's lord 1993. *Long live the dicktionary.*)

ASHES TO ANGELS

desperately into her pores, like a paramedic performing last-resort makeshift first aid, and the stabbing thrust and release, back-and-forth action of the sharp object, right there in the middle of a junkyard, south of Manhattan, made her downy nervous system lined with featherbed dandruff and dirty snowflakes and cigarette ash all hold steady in a frozen moment transcending time, space, and history: she took off her

> mortality like clothing
> like strippers
> like saints stoned
> looking up shooting up
> pain shooting like a star
> and saw choirs of angels
> numbing the pain like a drug
> laced with self-denial,
> narcotic euphoria,
> meditational mutilation
> heightening the senses
> to hallucinatory 4th dimension
> where wingéd people woke up
> screaming aloud a prayer
> to their secret gods in 4th person
> and all other cases of 1st, 2nd, and 3rd
> deferred to that POV which was
> the voice of god Itself.

And finally she began to bleed.

But not out of the hole: like a disowned dead relative of Bloody Mary Queen of Scots herself, this little matchstick girl, one royal name short of a kidnapped warrior princess, cried red. It dribbled down her cheeks, the double trickle mirror images on either side, but like Anastasia's murdered kin those dark eye sockets encrypted eternity, her black eye make-up smeared so bad it looked like she'd received a naughty but nice shiner, and Asher figured only a good dose of alcohol, a white Russian, would revive this hypothermia. The bar was three blocks away.

Running out of options, in desperation he looked up from his unsolicited charge and his gaze fell on the gaudy, ridiculously oversized statue erected by the Jesus Freaks over St. Mark's Place, an intimidation technique no doubt to scare this ghetto Verona into last-minute penance and to recant on its unwilling death bed in the hotbeds of punked-out Lower East Side. This unspeakable thing was locked in a stare-down with the blatant billboard across the way advertising hot pagans: Madam Mab, star cross'd card reader, psychic hotline 867.5309, area code somehow (666) in a (212). *Someone get me to the doctor. And someone call the Nurse. And someone buy me Roses. And someone burned the church.*[9] This imposing Mother Mary, sputnik-haloed by a tiara of barbed wire antennae masquerading like an alien on Broadway, out of place but not so out of touch, gleamed with fire from her eyes – her eyes penetrated prismatically into the darkness like the glare from headlights, entrancing him with the spectrum of the rainbow, the colors undetectable by the naked human eye. He followed their lead – one eye infra-red, the other eye ultraviolet, regardless of retinal damage to his own unprotected pupils looking directly at a solar eclipse, a Halley's Comet 1000 years[10] too early seen unknown and known too late, – he followed the Saint's ultra-violent

───────────────────────

[9] My Chemical Romance
[10] Last seen February 1986.

ASHES TO ANGELS

eyes in this time of trouble down the highway, watching the gruesome spiked telephone poles loom up along the way from exit to exit, all stuck with tacks and poster pins and looking the part of a veritable chain of crucifixion crosses illuminated with background strobe lights from the very same lamplit gothic angel architecture Asher purportedly hit. *Someone get me to the doctor. Someone get me to a church. But I hear you anyway.*[9] I could hear you, but I couldn't speak! *Well I thought I heard you say I like you.* He dragged his rotten romantic roadkill straight to Roosevelt Hospital across the way from the gothic cathedral hoisting her stoned imposter on display like a sideshow freak suspended between the twin spires of the Dakota. "I felt so symbolic," he would later say, in defense of his decision to leave the scene of a crime – with the victim, not the "body" – in tow. "She's *not* dead."

"The Junkyard Love Song by Asher"

>i met you in montauk
>riding the guard rails
>with that girl nicknamed
>Suicide
>standing at the water's edge
>waiting for the water to receive you
>canal side
>you said it was Mordren
>who wrote this poem high
>but i took out your soul that night
>on the café terrace with van gogh
>memories on a mudslide
>in a station of the metro
>we saw you in the deepest part

the darkness up to the heart
on your branded waist
you stood there cold and bare
in your bewitching disgrace
i gave you a charred letter
and a black rose while
sleeping on the subway
you put off your mortality
like clothes
under the shower of lamp-post lucidity
moth-eaten angel dust where heaven is fire
i wish i chose hell
do you know under your spell
sometimes i still hold your hand
at night lying next to you
though we're miserable apart
for some reason we can't stand
to be together--
it's better to end it before we start.

(by Asher. The Emporium. 10 January.)

[*alternatively: 12:00 am Wednesday 11 January. "The Junkyard Love Song by Mordren" sitting high in the car by the canal outside Auryn's apartment.*]

(Auryn already knows this. She is the poet, the poet's Muse, and the poem. Asher doesn't know this.)
Vampires will never hurt you. They'll never hurt you because I won't let them. I won't let them hurt you because I'll beat them (and you) to it.
Asher. Missing. Not here to defend himself. . . . . ∞

ASHES TO ANGELS

* * *

THIS IS THE FUCKING BEST DAY EVER.

So Asher and Auryn first met as a freak accident in the aftermath of a bike accident.

When we met in the emergency room. And in our beds.[11]

Their relationship started at the end: bedside, in a hospital room.

---

[11] My Chemical Romance.

NATALIE MCCOLLUM

Chapter Three

ER: Rock Opera for a Busted Angel
(*Angelus Occidentalis*)[12]

FACING UP

The last visitor left.
You closed the door and smiled at me.
I watched you cross Room 515 through
the flowers in vases, and your face
looked just like your face, smiling
down at me in my stupid green issue gown.
I felt myself want you
through the plastic tubes,
the vines around, across, and above me.
I felt myself want you

---

[12] The genus of a number of angel species and sub-species found in the monotheistic religions of Judaism, Zoroastrianism, Christianity, and Islam.

ASHES TO ANGELS

>Exclusively. Even pain faded
>into the scenery as you leaned in
>to kiss me. And I met your kiss
>>with my lips and we were both
>>folded into it,
>>into that clean, clean folding,
>>that soft longed-for kiss
>>across the side rails. That particular kiss
>>in its delicious oblivion hoisted us
>>above the suffering body.
>>We felt that long transfer of soft
>>for softness, that kiss lifting us
>>above the basement drawers
>>where we would finally face up.[13]

>*– L.B. Thompson*

Asher looked up from the poem he was reading with detached interest and somewhat condescending criticism in an expired issue of *The New Yorker* the moment she stirred. He had as yet not even seen her eyes. All he had to go on was this tattooed tramp or dirty daughter from the labor camp that, post-impact, he had laid down in the grass of a clearing nearby on the road to Harlem and watched while she wept. But she was willing, she had that going for her. Just not her eyes.

If poetic canon decreed the eyes a mirror of the soul, and popular culture designated closed eyes an indicator of death, then this radical was subverting both fact and fiction. To her, it seemed she feared her

---

[13] Reproduced as originally printed in The New Yorker, June 16 & 23, 2003, p. 140. Torn out of a university health center's waiting-room coffee-table copy.

soul would escape to the afterlife if indeed she opened them. So she resisted even a fluttering of lashes like a butterfly avoiding the net, in an inverted defiance of death. Or so Asher the poet interpreted it. Or what was otherwise uninterpretable in the absence of a muse, or at least the presence of a makeshift one on his hands, lying limp and shackled with hospital I.D. band diagnosing her condition as **Temporarily Out** of commission at his very feet, which he had propped on the bedside rail while he read. So she began to wash them with her tears. Saltless. It wouldn't sting, but it wouldn't clean and disinfect, either. Soul-less. An atheist's perfect woman. From the most unlikely place of spiritual perfection.

Asher was growing increasingly conscious that he was in the same medical institution he had just left. *Well I felt I couldn't take another day inside this place.* In a funk, Asher looked up with clearly exposed annoyance at the moment she pushed those impossibly long flyaway wisps of red from her scratched cheek and strangely scarred forehead (she must have received that ghastly indentation from the front of his fender where he found her in a contorted position that could only have been self-disentangled by a Houdini prodigy before he peeled her off the crooked license plate) and the force of tears forced the opening of her lids to induce like labor the penetration of undesirables, light and facing up to reality, and instead of the expected frightful blood-shot red to match her head, he saw the sky that had clouded over with purple so photogenic as to be unphotographable only moments before she fell to the ground within hours of impact. *From silent dreams we never wake.*[14] His first reaction was to hit back

ASHES TO ANGELS

when hit. *We'll wake up dreaming.* Instead he grabbed the cold blue steel of the bed railing. He clenched his fist and caught his breath: this was no force of gravity, this was no rainbow, and this was certainly no child! This woman was the religion he had forsaken; an atheist's heaven erotica. He was losing his religion before he even got some, and with each shocking stab of the light penetrating into the r.e.m. cycles of her purplish-gray irises, she was losing out on both sleep and purity before she even had a wet dream.

She started, sat up gasping for air like a fish just given a lung transplant, and coughed up a bit of black bile. *I could hear you breathe with help from the cold machines. Every hour on the hour, they drew blood.*[14] She looked up at a crucifix that could have been hung by Van Helsing himself, affixed grotesquely on the wall above the visitor's chair, and asked for a bloody mary. That was the last time she saw Jesus. They brought in something sweet and tangy and orange instead. Fire over ice. Sugar on the rocks. Lots of it. She started drinking.

Vampires will Never hurt you. Deprived of salt, she felt the sugar course through her veins and infuse her peppermint stick bones with life like a famished anorexic vampire, or vampirish anorexic in need of nourishment – a blood transfusion or an NG tube – after being nailed shut in an earthen box and pinned to the heel of a golgothic cross she had climbed herself – in order to see better during the live filming[15] of the romantic religion being born via public staging of history's most notorious and controversial suicide –

---

[14] My Chemical Romance.
[15] Check out the premise of <u>Live from Golgotha: The Gospel According to Gore Vidal</u> by Gore Vidal.

and liked the view a little *too* much to come down from her high. The alternative vegetarian fare in lieu of a catholic cannibal communion satisfied her craving for carbohydrates, staving off the onset of ketosis, and resurrecting in its wake a ½ vampire, ½ angel with a whole lot of explaining to do.

"I'm sorry I broke you."

The patient sensed the importance of this first moment, and that she not let it go on a spook-impulse, and so she quickly reached for his arm before he could shut the door in her face.

"Wait," she pleaded, "I'm not a hallucination. I'm for real; I've come all the way from a, uh, another life just to see you. Please don't turn me down."

He stopped a moment to look at her suspiciously. At this narrow window of opportunity, she delved in.

"I know all about your, well, *condition*," she enunciated *tactfully*, as if *completely* unaware of her own very physical relationship to the word, giving off the darkly comical effect of the resurrected dead dispensing survival advice to the dying with one foot still in the grave, "and I know you see things sometimes and the world tells you it isn't real, the reception you get is something of a rejection note stating that you're 'Not believable as a human being,' but I represent a rare moment of reality for you." (She cringed somewhat at this morbid sales pitch of sorts, wishing for the first time that she had *not read something* – so many scripts were bound to get warped in her literal rendering of the literary). "You *do* believe in angels, right?" she abruptly cut off her introduction, which she had spent over two millennia perfecting, opting out to wing it instead with a note of suspiciously girlish hopefulness. She skipped ahead without waiting for the dreaded reply telling her what she already knew. "Well, I've waited centuries to ask you this—" she paused as if to compose herself before firing off the grand debut and long-awaited utterance of her over-rehearsed eternal line, "—Would you like to go out for coffee?"

At this point Asher was a bit amused with this stranger, and her animated unpredictability jumping around from one to another fiery flowing vein of thought. *From mortality to caffeine.* It went straight to his head:

though it is not readily apparent at all times, the U.S. as a cultural entity has not outgrown its roots as a Christian nation—so why not lift a term from the Book of Genesis to organize our class: Pedro. Your words are bolstered by the idea that many aspects of experimental manipulation and training activities of animals can be positive experiences for animals, and should not be summarily excluded as a component of a facility's environmental enhancement program. But try not to get carried away. Let me remind you *Anaphylaxis* is a term coined by Richet and Portier in 1902 as a direct challenge to the prevailing dogma that the immune system was always a good thing which guarded against attack (*phylaxis*). Asked by Prince Albert the First of Monaco to investigate the toxicity of jellyfish stings, they showed that repeated challenge with miniscule amounts of antigen, far from guarding against disease, sometimes induces life-threatening reactions. But you said it best when you said nothing at all: We *must know that we have been created for greater things, not*

27

just to be a number in the world. We have been created in order to love and to be loved.

Mother Teresa-

Heinz

Kerry

It

Through.[16]

Clearly, Auryn finds it absolutely necessary here to interject, and inject, *a translation of the above mental contortions:*
The broken angel had just asked out a schizophrenic poet while she was hooked up to an IV in the ICU of the hospital.

Come see the angel fall and the poet go mad!

"*[A ward of the] state has called for me by name, but I don't have time for [her]. . . .*"[17]

---

[16] "Mike Boblitt responds to Natalie McCollum's 'Synchronicity,'" Eng 693, 10/13/05.

ASHES TO ANGELS

He decided, even though he did not consider himself a nice guy, that he would appease her just this once and see what she would do. If anything, he was curious and wouldn't mind a good laugh right about now. So, taking his cue and playfully acting the role of the hot date, he grabbed his black motorcycle jacket and gloves with the cut-off fingers from just outside the intensive care hallway, and mock responded, "Okay, babe, where to?" At that the angel nearly lost herself in giddy girly discomposure and had to steady her fluttering heart – a new experience for her and probably not advisable in her as yet medically unstabilized state – with a dose of magical realism as she watched him walk out the door. "It's gonna be a glorious day."

Asher decided to go the quicker route and take the subway home from the hospital this time, to avoid déjà vu run-ins with madwomen and having to deal with *two* broken angels on his file, and at that he thought wryly, *so, hit an angel, get a date. Or rather, hit* on *an angel, pick up a girl.* He marveled at how the light changing changed everything, not just the flow of traffic – *indeed the flow of fate.* In the blink of a light, the blink of an eye, an endangered species mortalized like a blip on the heart monitor screen. In an instant, a split second going the wrong direction down a one-way street, was a pair of split wings. Time grabbed you by the slit-wrist and directed you where to go – and *how* to go: two-by-two, not waving but drowning in a double suicide. Split infinity down a one-way street wrecked in a head-on collision with heaven's dropout and a yellow light's burn-out. How ever did the ancients fit it all in? No

---

[17] "Lucky" by Radiohead. Subject and pronoun gender changed.

room in the end.

He was just passing the motel's **No Vacancy** sign that could usually be seen blinking from the Brooklyn Bridge at night, but this time he blinked twice and looked again. It said: **Get a Room.** He smiled grimly to himself but nodded in masterful synchronicity with the flash. *All in good time*, he thought with the precision of a pop artist and the sense of timing of a con artist – *patience IS still a virtue even if used for unvirtuous purposes.* The perversion of virtue was as close as the next exit, the next flashing yellow light. Red or green, heaven or hell, it could go either way. They just wouldn't let gravity get in the way next time. The *woman* would get the right of way, and the child would get the right of passage next time. Wednesday's child was born on hump day by immaculate conception and natural selection: spreading the wings in lieu of spreading the legs and falling out of sky from the cosmic womb-space was gravity's girl.[18]

---

[18] "Before modern science appeared in the 16th and 17th centuries, and with it the newly discovered Laws and Forces of Nature, angels were supposed to have moved the stars and the elements. Gravity was not a law of nature but an active angelic intelligence." Malcolm Godwin, Angels: An Endangered Species, page 7.

ASHES TO ANGELS

Chapter Four

The Deal, The Dealer:

Sell me your soul and promise me your firstborn.

Wing-clipping, coupon-clipping; is there really a difference?

*Ashes, ashes,
We all fall down.*

Death Sold Here.

He could tell right away that it was his guy – this made the fourth victim in three months. The man considered himself an artist, a Jesus Christ making women his dead disciples. The young woman was completely naked, her legs were spread wide-open and blood was still trickling from her ravaged vagina. Bruises were beginning to form on her neck, arms and legs. The man that did this enjoyed the violence of the rape – it wasn't the penetration that got him off. He loved hurting his victims.

The young woman was around 20 years old with

blonde hair and green eyes – she fit the profile. The detective knew before turning her over that he was going to find lashes on her back. Whoever did this didn't use just any whip, but one that was twisted with barb wire to ensure that when he struck his victim's skin it would rip and tear. The cross was laid at her feet – it had an emblem of a heart on it and was wrapped in flowers. He did this with all of them, as if he was leaving a romantic gift at the feet of his sleeping lover. Under this the detective knew he would find a note. He moved the cross and sure enough there it was. *"Jesus wept."* What a sick motherfucker – this one had a serious God complex. He checked her vagina for semen and didn't find any. He hadn't expected to – the ritualistic rape for this one wasn't about getting off. For him it was a way of possessing them, claiming them, making them his – they were his disciples.[19]--*AP News*.

It was shocking when the angel responded to the advertisement in the personals and met the dealer face to face. She had never expected to have such a run-in with her banished half-sister, but the demon twin was just as startled that her first responder to an SOS in satanic verse was a holy whore. She had to get her bearings and adjust her strategy a bit. Then, as she realized the sheer genius of the situation she had stumbled upon, she was consumed by a thought "Of insidious intent / To lead [angel] to an overwhelming question…": It was about to be Christmas in hell. Or,

---

[19] Although quoted within the context of fiction, the passage is the original work of a colleague of the author, who uses it here for fictional purposes with permission. Luke Horn wrote this piece in response to his interpretation of the author's tattoo.

ASHES TO ANGELS

the Nightmare Before.

So the dealer bluffed a premeditated answer to her leading question: "Because, Auryn, the only ones *not* at risk are the ones who have already risked it all. It's just a game, Auryn. The world plays it and loses it like a bad hand of cards."

"Poe, remember when you played 'Black' with me in the casino on New Year's Eve, and at midnight we hit the round of three's – avatar, you dealt. And you got me a six. And a six. And a six."

"This is true. You were **Temporarily Out**. Banishéd baristas working the graveyard shift put up that neon sign, which flickers iridescent blue like an electric star on fire, when we run out of devil's food. So I stole it, my dear PoEtGuRl, on the chance that good poets borrow, great poets steal, so the credo goes."

"Don't exploit Eliot."

"I come from parents wanton, a childhood rough and rotten. You come from wealth and beauty, untouched by work or duty."

"Don't diss The Decemberists."

"Well, I can't help it, I can't help where I've been. You've seen. You're part me, being of the Sixth Choir. You've done the rounds on the perilous borders between the first and second heavens. You Powers think you're immune, but even St. Teresa[20] said those damnable human souls are subject to you guys and your risky business staving off demons who are your own step-brothers and sisters. Don't deny it."

"Poe, you – you 'dirty daughter from the labor

---

[20] Originally St. Paul said this, according to the research presented in <u>Angels: An Endangered Species</u> by Malcolm Godwin. I have "swapped saints."

camp.'"

"Likewise."

"Oh? Oh? How dare you!"

"Done. I dare you."

"How so?"

"I dealt the cards; here's the deal. I dare you to switch places with me – swap your soul for mine, a little 'soul-swapping' we'll call it. You give me your wings so I can bust out of this slum, and you get my fallibility so you can mix it up with the mortal."

"The mortal?"

"Don't act smart. You may be angel, but you're not immune. Otherwise you wouldn't be a Power. And you *know* you sure as hell can't switch Choirs to be a Ninth, the humans are hopeless enough without having a drifter adulterate the Order already closest to the human species. Akasha will *never* allow that, the poor wretched fool. What a *Slumus Lordicus*[21]."

"You are *such* a plagiarist."

"You read too much."

The demon twitched, antsy. This was so ghetto. She fidgeted and fingered the pair of scissors she held under her lacy black nightgown. It was somewhat hard to conceal under such skimpy attire, and she actually longed for the modesty and coverage of those heavy long wings, so feathery and ashen they practically bled faerie dust leftover from Neverland, and she could still hear the wailing oracles of Greece, "Great Pan is dead!" She seethed with indignation still hot to the touch. Whoever the church fathers feared always ended up demonic. It was fucking human nature to satanize anything misunderstood. St. X-tian Peter re-

---

[21] Short nonfiction by David Sedaris.

ASHES TO ANGELS

visioned pagan Peter, preventing Wendy from ever finding Neverland, which became by extension a kind of hell for the lost souls of child suicides, Peter Pan being the teen angel of death Wendy fell for. Peter was the boy trying to help these unsightly souls escape the bodies, but the bodies were hanging on in very unorthodox fashion. Thus boots and shoes all over Europe were filled with coal and smoldering ash rather than food, let alone angel food cake, a traditional favorite of the damned and the devils alike, on the Day of the Dead. Poor John and Michael, in spirit of their spritely namesakes, became child martyrs and saints venerated by their playmates on All Saints Day, November 1, and blamed for the mark of Hook's hand on the forehead of every youthful soul damned to eternity in Never Never Land on All Souls Day, November 2. The only consolation she could swipe was the chapel sign. The snotty jerks had put in all caps, "YOU THINK ITS HOT HERE?" to try to scare and humble penitents during mock Xmas in July. With all the skill and craft of a hooker, the grammar nazi had prostituted art and switched around the letters to re-direct the lost boys,

from

"SIGN BROKEN – STOP IN FOR MESSAGE"

to

D $_A$ M ^{A} $_G$ E^D G $_O$ ^{O} DS – ENTER <u>HERE</u> TO *GET SOME*

X-tian or no, men were men, and if you blow it, the pimps will come.

Yes. She rubbed her hands. She hooked her thumbnail around the scissor legs. At that, she gazed clean through the angel: she would manipulate her like men. Exploit the angel's own faerie dust to manifest the mortal "Ashes to ashes, dust to dust" and thusly get her hooked on the most addictive morphine in existence, LOVE.

"And I think you read into humans too much. This poet guy or whatever. What's his story? What can you possibly offer him? Those wings are so loaded with purity they'll drag you down. What did Emily say, before poets took to signing away the copyrights to their souls? 'My life had stood a loaded gun.' If you want him, you've gotta cut 'em. Or he'll shoot you down."

(She again fingered the scissors stuck in her black garter holding up the fishnet tights.)

"But I'll fall."

"Precisely."

Two pairs of eyes, one a purplish-gray iris and the other a sick rose, stared back at each other with equal intensity of ultraviolet and infra-red rays.

"Akasha'll never spring for it."

"Likely not."

"I don't wanna fall like that."

"That's *enough,* gurl!!! Get off your Ivory Tower, Auryn! It's a neverending story, and anyway herstory *is* the greatest story never told! Give it away!"

"What?!"

"Cut! Cut! CUT CUT CUT!!!" She started to chant, a cross between Wiccan witches and Gregorian monks, with all the self-help gusto and motivational force of a financial counselor pushing her worldly sister to cut up a bunch of tempting credit cards that would otherwise her trendy weakness and ticket to debtor's prison, *posthaste*.

But the demon didn't even have to jump the angel before the fabrication kicked in. Auryn grabbed the blades from between her sister's thighs, accidentally jabbing them into the leg as she lunged, and like a heroin addict careless of contaminated needles, she snipped off the airy burden in three cuts: one for each wing, and a third down the spine. It left a streak like a raggedy seam, leaving her soulless and no longer seamless, merely a limp and limping Raggedy Ann doll stuffed with fluff and a candy heart. But at least the cold deed was done, like perverting a fairy tale; it left the sickest sweetest taste in her mouth; and suddenly the sky was falling.

Such things as guitar strings and angel wings:

Before she hit, the demon, now avatar, finished off the job with her own branded trademark, sticking ball point pens and guitar stings into the girl's lower back, which left the numbers of the three cards dealt in a row in "Black," the joker's runes carved like a very crude tattoo. The mark of the handicraft of an avatar. Little goddess was now mortal. Angel was sewed up with a screw-up. As the girl fell through negative space, she didn't happen to look up through the dried blood from the scissor-Hook indentation on her forehead that matched the accidentally-on-purpose scrape on her sister's leg and notice Poe had tied on her wings with guitar strings plucked from Ani DiFranco's own acoustic, had "tied that sucker back on with a string" to her tattered, moth-eaten negligeé. All she saw was a ~~rem~~ dream sequence of very Charlie Chaplinesque freeze frames, like watching a replay of her own death in slow motion. She would look at compromising sequential pictures of it afterward, on

NATALIE MCCOLLUM

Separation Sunday in the line-up of mug shots of the Supernatural suicides committed in front of mirrors – Adia, Luca, Mordren, Raven, Auryn – or on Sunday Bloody Sunday, the soundtrack to the horror movie which spawned those dirty daughters of Bloody Mary as manifested in the million-dollar Scream, whichever opened for the end of the world as we know it. A MUST-SEE: but what is the going price for souls these days? All that damn inflation, all that fornication.

Part Two:

The Trouble with Poets
is they drink too much.

NATALIE MCCOLLUM

ASHES TO ANGELS

Chapter Five

Caffeine to Mortality

"So why did you break up with your ex-girlfriend?"
 He took her to a place called the Emporium.
 "She wanted me to do something scary in bed."
 So the coffee affair with the…didn't she say she was an angel?…was weird, but he was beginning to think ` maybe he wasn't having delusions after all. She was a little quirky but sweet and well meaning in a *para*normal sort of way. That kind of intrigued him, what with his psychotic fraternizing with the otherworldly in recent years. But if only she weren't so…good. Angelic. He snickered wryly at his own ironic thought. So it was, street smart dates book smart. The angel and the outlaw. Maybe he wasn't so unwell — life itself was a flirt with the desperadoes and the deranged.
 "I don't want to fall to pieces, I just want to sit and STARE at you."[22]

"What-the-fuck."

Catching herself late on the barbed wire of pained consciousness that she had spoken uncensored thoughts aloud, Auryn tried to recover her too telling tracks before she had damaged what had not yet even been there for the damaging.

"Oh, uh, I mean, that was just a line from a favorite song. So you're a rockstar?"

At this rising chance to strut his rasta wear like the glam rocker whom only the hysterical raving mad fans saw in his suicide poem, – [poor rockstar without a record label!] – Asher perked up and completely forgot his skittish knee-jerk impulse that she was trespassing into dangerous territory he wasn't about to commit to.

"Hell yeah, I'm more popular than Jesus now. Well, almost. Once those damned Beatles hand it over. Stubborn spoiled dead guys. Haven't written anything new in years, and they're still getting write-ups." Asher lit up a cigarette as he casually rifed through the latest *Newsweek* lying on the coffee table with its big 10-page spread on the anniversary of the death of John Lennon, defiantly proclaiming, "Lennon Lives!" on the facing page opposite a full-length black-and-white photo immortalizing the mass mania swarming the gothic Dakota in Manhattan just moments after the fatal crime.

"But the one – McCartney? He's still around, yes?" Auryn stabbed timidly at a subject she wished she knew more about. Like a blind shot, it at least struck somewhere within range on the dartboard.

"Well sure, and so are a whole lot of other band members living in the shadows of their former glory.

---

[22] "Fall to Pieces" by Avril Lavigne.

ASHES TO ANGELS

This is like a Shakespearean drama almost. Each person has something to be totally miserable about because of the way they were put into this play.[23] It's a tough line to walk. It's like walking on a dead man's grave,"[24] Asher mused, blatantly yet smoothly lifting half the thoughts from a line he was half reading in the article with the side of his mind drifting like the alleged wings he still itched to line up for questioning.

"So…what are you, really? I mean, come on, you have to admit you don't look like an angel. They're supposed to have wings, right? Where are yours?" He scoffed extra condescendingly in excess of what was necessary for the bite to be unmistakable and the sting to be felt. His eyes sized her up and looked her over with practiced shrewd subtlety as if groping for a reason to do so in the absence of wings. Subtle but obvious. Asher the skeptic; he knew he had her backed into a corner impossible to navigate out as an M.C. Escher drawing. He wanted to see her falter. To his surprise she started to reply, though she must be winging it. He sat back with idle amusement, though clearly listening intently. This oughtta be good.

"The trouble with mortality is caffeine, Mordren," she began.

He jerked up his head. He'd heard a voice. Only the fans and Muses said things like that. Things so randomly obscure, and so disorienting in the beautiful disconnect of utter poetic chaos, no sane and rational person would have the brilliance to utter such sweet unspeakable names, in every sense of the word, except

---

[23] Direct quote by Yoko Ono, as printed in "Lennon Lives" by Jeff Giles, <u>Newsweek</u>, November 28, 2005, page 63.

[24] Direct quote by Paul McCartney, as printed in "Lennon Lives" by Jeff Giles, <u>Newsweek</u>, November 28, 2005, page 72.

the word itself.

As if reading his thoughts, nay, writing them in blood on the page of his throbbing temples and then stealing them, in true poetic form, from the screaming fans calling for an encore from a rockstar whose lyrics idolized an imposter and immortalized the source of all human thought, she silenced them with a statement irretractable as mortality itself:

"The trouble with poets is you."

She then launched into an explanation only a scholar in the field could have rattled off the top of her head, because—

"I know every poem ever written." It was a stark contrast to what came next, in rare form:

"The crux of your disturbance, Asher, with me, this 'Auryn' persona, is this: As a schizophrenic you are in a double bind. Your senses tell you one thing – I am seeing an angel – yet your belief system tells you another – as an atheist, there is no such thing. The dynamic between us, Asher and Auryn – our inability to accept each other's existence, or seeing is NOT believing – is itself schizophrenic. 'This double-bind situation is one of the roots of the psychological distress found in many schizophrenics….When confronted with such a double bind a person can simply block out the unacceptable part [me, Auryn] or the habitual response to it ["You never *looked* like an angel"[25]. A similar principle seems to be in operation when a witness blocks a memory of encounters with angels, spirit guides, demons or even extra-terrestrials.'"[26]

---

[25] "Angel of Harlem" by U2.
[26] "Part Two: An Endangered Species": Chapter One, "Eye

ASHES TO ANGELS

To which Asher, prosaically speechless, could only reply in verse:

Sitting unpublished in this joint
Shacking up by the wayside of 5th
Making love to my 5 o'clock fix
I think, it's too damn cold to go this alone
So I'm provoked in the places my soul
shows through my peppermint-stick bones
--organ donor
        --flower child
I wonder why I was born in the 80's
  'cause I'm still a Swing Kid
lost somewhere between 1920 and the Beats
  with you and Kerouac

AP censored the human story
  on the pretense of a lost cause
But rain hurts more in December
    when light is too thin to attach to you
like it should—on the 24th we believed we could
  change raw emotion into words you see
  by the sign of mercury or a half moon—
    those eleventh hour desperations
on nights of ancient witchery
  I was fire and you were water
saying chants at Midnight Mass in Camelot, so

If you find it, they will come
  Do you want:
    Scandal at the World Series? Or
    Sex and candy on Hollywood's biggest night?
But somehow the world didn't end
  --or I didn't die as promised
or so I thought one could find heaven

Witness" pages 153-54 of Malcolm Godwin's <u>Angels: An Endangered Species</u>.

>   --by drowning and waving
> (that freak accident off Route ∞)
> Guess I should stop drinking this
>   'cause I'm just a writer, same as you,
>   and that's all we really need.
>
> *~Coffeehouse Muse*

To which Auryn promptly replied, in the voice of another published mortal: "That's because it's hard to counteract the validity of sensory impressions. We are designed to believe in them."[27]

"No power in the verse can stop me!"[28] In spite of his defensive volley in this meeting of the minds, Asher still twitched uncomfortably. He used avoidance tactics to focus the attention back on her. His therapist, had she been sitting in on the discussion, would have recognized that his mind game only defeated his own purpose; it was merely a projection of himself onto ethereal Auryn, like a film projector using her as a screen for images of his subconscious. "So did it hurt to fall from the sky? Or did you just get kicked out of the casino in hell," Asher, still the caustic skeptic, cut into the pretty little piece of flesh as if de-winged weren't deranged enough. "I mean, pardon me, miss, but that's one sweet ass to hit the cement. Ouch."

"How am I supposed to fly without any wings?"— missing his vulgar sarcastic emphasis accidentally on purpose. "Do you realize that I just sold my soul by cutting off my wings?"

---

[27] Susanna Kaysen, Girl, Interrupted, page 140.
[28] From Joss Whedon's TV series Firefly.

"No problem. This thing called a 'soul' you speak of – who needs one? Souls are like…" he was about to create a very loaded simile by referencing a body part that clearly only the human anatomy called for, when he caught himself on what so far had only shaped up to be a metaphysical being peering at him over the edge of a huge wide-rimmed mug. He decided he could only speak for himself, at this point. "A soul is like my appendix. I'll never use it." He sat back and crossed his arms.

She stared at him. "You think my wings aren't real. Just because you can't see them, you don't believe they exist."

"Actually, nothing really exists." Asher didn't fight the accusation; he flaunted it.

She sighed, her suspicions confirmed. "Because existentialism in excess means the dream is dead." She slumped forward, her chin propped in both hands. She gazed up at him through the unruly locks suspended from the top of her head like marionette strings. Her sad puppy-dog eyes searched Asher's gray-green orbs as if performing a retinal scan to decode a password. Don't just let it be; Let me in!

"Sometimes, I 'forget' that I'm supposed to be an angel girl, and lapse into this pseudo-human state. But, I've never even had a real boyfriend."

"What do you mean, you've never had a 'real' boyfriend?" No one's dating her? What's wrong with her then?

"Well, Peter Pan and I have something of a history together. Wendy suspected that he was into someone else, and she jabbed her needle into his heel and cast a shadow over his wandering eyes. He couldn't see me anymore; we were meant to be, supposed to be, but we lost it. I was almost Auryn Pan. So much for my happy ending: Wendy always hated me – she was always jealous of my wings, because the only way she could fly was with Peter's fairy dust, mooched off that firefly or whatever he toted around for a familiar. I'm convinced Wendy thought my wings were attractive to Peter, and they were stealing her boyfriend. Anyway, he wasn't a real boy, though. He was a Lost Boy."

"I think you mean Pinocchio," Asher chuckled, amused at her fucked-up fairy tale. *She's either a pathological liar, or…my therapist is about to lose some business, 'cause I'm not the one with the problem!* "He wasn't a real boy. Made of wood." Asher rapped his knuckles on the table.

"Yes, yes, and I suppose you buy into that whole 'wood floats, ducks float' propaganda? 'She's a witch! Burn her!'"

"I love that movie."

"Huh?"

"Monty Python. You just quoted a line from the witch hunt scene."

"I don't know what you're talking about, all I know is that I need more than a coin-operated boy. The instructions say I can even take him in the bath, but I already have a rubber ducky. And all that clean laundry at the coin-op is starting to make me feel too sanitized, like I'm living in a hospital, not the Milky Way. It's too clean up there." She jabbed her thumb upward into the space of nowhere in particular. "And besides, doing laundry really turns me on. You know…all undressed and nowhere to go." She folded her hands pragmatically. *She didn't realize what she was actually saying by screwing up the line.*

"Are you saying there's no sex in heaven? Huh. Figures. It's up. Sky. North." She wasn't taking the bait. "There's Sussex, Essex, Wessex…" he trailed off suggestively, but she still wasn't following the intended pun. "Nossex. No one would wanna live there." Smirk. He was hacking into another layer on something to the effect of damaged goods from a virgin forest, when the blank look on her face reeled him back in before he got carried away on his own stolen line. "Oh. Um. Celtic. Ancestral. Family thing." It was a lame joke anyway.

At that she relaxed. "Oh, I'm Celtic too. My sister is Bloody Mary."

"Eh?" Asher jerked his head up, spooked. "She's dead. Been dead for years. Maybe your ancestor was Mary Queen of Scots." He stressed the proper verb tense with all the ridiculosity of a poet instructing his own muse.

"Oh, no, no. She actually just died last week. Didn't you see the last episode of *Supernatural*? They got her, but not before she cut my wings off." The angel looked down self-consciously.

"I don't watch the WB."

"Oh. Well, she's loosed from hell now, and running around in my wings, so if you run into her, tell her they suit her well for a prostitute." Auryn couldn't resist taking up some of that bite she had come to associate and take at face value with Asher.

"Your sister's a whore?" Asher was sold and hooked now. Hmm, I have bought the mansion of love but not yet possessed it and although I am sold not yet enjoyed…Oh trespass sweetly urged, give me my sin again! "Your sister's a whore, and your mother's a witch? How does that make you an angel?"

"Well, angels are just the by-products of witches copulating with demons. Lilith, my un-biological mother, ditched her first date, bewitched her bedmate, and the succubus spawned me the love-child instead of the intended Christ child. So thousands of years from now, if X-tianity never happens, it's because of me, not Eve. It's got nothing to do with forbidden fruit, and everything to do with slutty saints."

"You just insulted someone I hate by referencing something I love."

"Well there's no such thing as a saint without a past." Auryn cut-and-pasted her philosophy straight out of TV shows when it was convenient.

He tried not to sound too eager to ask the next question in quick succession. "Does it…run in the family, perchance?" One ellipsis should be good enough. "'Cause I'm afraid all I can give you is a reputation."

It was. Auryn was naïve enough to be nice enough to be naughty.

ASHES TO ANGELS

Chapter Six

Angel-headed Hipsters

Love started as a crime: Asher technically still had a girlfriend, albeit a "scheduled break-up," when he started to fraternize with a girl who claimed to be a de-wingéd angel.

Asher took her home after the "date" – against better judgment he let his new little whim tag along to see the Commune and meet some of the residents. She had seemed so captivated by the Mantua crowd that he wasn't really surprised when she showed up again at the Commune the next day. Dorian and his consort were sitting on the front steps of the old brownstone, a pair of dealers and swingers counting their tips by day. Random pieces of furniture, including a poppy red futon and a rainbow beach chair, littered the sidewalk along with some water-stained packing boxes filled with books spilling onto the street past the parking meters. It looked like someone was moving in or out, it was hard to tell. Adia and Luca were nowhere to be seen, but a few discarded syringes lay scattered near the trashcans in dead giveaway of their recent activity. Auryn nodded to these off-beat residents of the Mantua Commune, Bed-Stuy on the J train, according to the slip of paper on which Asher had scrawled his address, and tapped the knocker on the door. Marley answered. She was wearing a bedsheet. It had a hole burned in it from her dangling joint. "Izzy's not here," as soon as she saw Auryn. Auryn shook her head, inquired after Asher. "Oh," there was visible relief in the lesbian's expression, "you look like one of her little punk rocker friends. *Ein Moment*." With a rustle, Marley got Asher, along with her ashtray. "Punk fairy wants to see you," she was saying as she returned from the murky inner chambers, trailing Asher in her billowy cotton wake.

"Is there a difference between fairies and angels?" Asher leaned in the door frame holding a large plastic Dixie cup of wine. "Oh, right – fairies come with wings," he jabbed more good-naturedly than in the coffeehouse scene. With a huff, Marley tossed a corner of the sheet over her shoulder like a toga and receded into the shadows of the dimly lit house in a flourish of paisley. He looked down at her feet. "Fairies wear boots," he persisted. She stomped in defiance. He took that for affirmation. "I'm going for a walk on this lovely black sabbath. Care to join?" They made quite a pair, masquerading up and down the sidewalk together, the darkly garbed gentleman escorting a pale little sprite of waning innocence.

Unfortunately, they ran into Raven. His live-in ex-girlfriend was still there, packing her things after a somewhat ambiguous break-up. "Auryn, may I present to you, her ladyship Raven." Asher bowed low with a swoop and a clownish grin, then, "My only love was a chimney sweep," pragmatically as he lit up a smoke. He winked with goodwill at Raven, as if conjuring the song for his ex-lover in place of an olive branch or other peace-pipe offering. Raven was moving back to the House of Vervain to live and work among her own kindred spirits and psychic professionals. But the crafty Raven, in a moment of opportunistic exploitation, laid down her knapsack and feigned a friendship. She mock warmly slid her icy fingertips across Auryn's shoulders with the affect of a sympathetic girl friend and gently pushed Auryn aside, out of Asher's earshot.

"Now, for my alternate reading," began Asher's psychic and psycho ex, playing the angel – *there's nothing real about this poet-snatcher, this patron saint of liars, except that she is the favorite figment of her own imagination.* "There is another voice that creeps into his—" she tossed her head toward Asher, leaning idly against a telephone pole, taking another long slow drag, somehow completely unaware of the pow-wow going on between his newly christened ex and his newfound "play thing" as the former viciously referred to the girl with the angel complex— "head. Every once in a while, particularly on pages 33-37 of <u>Freakery: How to Become a Writer</u>. I highly recommend it. I don't associate it with either Asher or you, Auryn, not even the other fans already mentioned. That's why I think she's the real narrator…" Here Raven summoned all her powers of the Sight to assume the form; in the manner of an actor this alien on Broadway got into character with her lost alter ego. Like a necromancer, she continued. "This narrator has loved Asher prior to Auryn coming along and taking him away. This narrator is younger than Asher, she probably knew him from classes in college (but maybe never talked to him too much), which explains the references to graduation, a note on a teacher's door. Because this narrator is missing Asher and lost, trying to figure out what she did wrong to lose him, she created this myth of an angel falling for him and taking him away – and really, an angel is the only being that could lure Asher from her (she'll rationalize) – but she doesn't know the whole story, so she has to make all this stuff up, invent conversations (which will appear in red ink) and imagine a conflict that will break them up because he didn't really want Auryn anyway, he wanted her (narrator) all along."[29] Raven crossed her arms in front of her chest and leaned back to watch the effects of her final fantasy, leering at Auryn. The girl seemed unfazed. Like all things, the origin of Auryn was an open text inviting interpretation. If Raven wanted to cast her as a reincarnation of her own troubled affairs, let her. Let men burn stars[30], while she's at it.

Asher shuffled over, apparently curious as to what, praytell, a Raven could be imparting to a being higher than herself. Everyone knew angel wings could out-do 13 different ways of looking at a blackbird, let alone a raven.

"Now, don't scare her!" Asher scolded Raven for her witchy meddling. "She just got here post meridian – I don't want her running off all wingless like that."

At this bit of information, the ever-perceptive Raven pricked up. "You mean…she was at the Commune last night? She was running loose around

---

[29] Page 4 of "Ashes to Angels – A Response" by Brian Leingang, 2/15/06
[30] M83

here while you and I had break-up sex? On our last night together? How long was your little hoodrat friend here?!" She shrieked in utter disgust and slapped him across the face.

As Raven snatched up her bags and her ego, she flicked a last bit of the bone she had to pick with Asher caustically over the chip on her shoulder. The flint struck by the first nick of the wrist and spawned a bonfire just in the nick of time before the last dying ember flickered out. "This one goes out to the one I love. This one goes out to the one I left behind: You are a very bad man!" The huntress sent a flaming arrow of grievances against Ash like a tree, the charred history trailing in her troubled wake from the bedsheets to the ashtray.

At this, Asher rose from the tree stump he had been sitting on, and called after the departing fury, "Yeah? Well, I hope your rules and wisdom choke you!" He stretched to his full six feet height, threw back his head, and whether it was an S.O.S. sent after the vanishing figure, a subverted effort to save a soulmate swept away in her own burning desire to hate the man she loved, or more of a cry to the universe to let men burn stars, a plea of defiance, it was lost on the exhale; nearly coughing up a lung, this time he incriminated his accomplice in the turn of a single word: "WE HOPE YOUR RULES AND WISDOM CHOKE YOU!!!" He sank to his knees like he had just witnessed the death of a very grave man on the sandy stage of Sycamore Grove. Auryn went to him. She had never seen him cry, but he was sobbing now. He gasped, choking on his own rage, "We hope – that you choke – that you choke—" His whole frame shook with the backfire of his own curse. His hands were on the soft yellowed leaves of grass. Her hands were on him. She summoned all her strength to try and raise him up. If she could just get him to his knees, then to his feet – in a surge of freak adrenaline, she got him up into the air where he could breathe and the sky could fill his lungs. A paper bag would help subdue the hyperventilating, she knew not how she knew this bit of mortality. But as the angel hoisted the fallen man to his knees, the sky seemed at once to fall and open up, and with a shiver she felt them – she had the old sensation of her wings descending back upon her back, reclaiming their rightful place on the seam of her spine like the return of the king, Richard resuming his corrupted throne after Robin Hood, the Prince of Thieves, stole from the rich and gave to the poor. You send your thieves to me, silently stalking me dragging me into your war. They were there, she knew it, she felt it, she breathed it. And she realized, in a moment lucid, he did too. Their faint outline hovered in the negative space around them, wrapping their safety and guardianship around the two shaking forms sunk to the ground, not waving but drowning, drowning the two shipwrecks in the beautiful wreckage of their own trespassing. We sing sins, one of them said, neither one knew not which, give me my sin again! The forbidden boundaries crossed, like two households, both alike in dignity, except two halves equal a cross between two evils – Give me my wings again! – from ancient grudge break to new mutiny, where civil blood makes severed wings unclean!

In synchronicity with the split-second climactic god-sighting when all thought erases completely and the mind experiences in the black hole a momentary flash of star-bright clarity, she heard Asher utter a Headboard Heartbreak and with the fading of the

ASHES TO ANGELS

wing-span, she saw in their de-effervescing wake The Ecstasy of the Busted Lovers[31]:

> There's our bed. What a mess.
> Banged on the twisted wrought-iron
> You got me the best.
> If love is blind, you see I would have
> Dove head first in hindsight,
> Coming down from reality for a dream
> High on 4-20, no less than 69 tonight.
> You've got one hand on the wheel
> and one hand on the slow curve of my back—
> If I don't feel like I'm losing you,
> If I don't feel like I'm using you,
> Why do my arms ache from holding on
> with my nails dug in your neck?
> What a beautiful wreck
> Has derailed our bed,
> Busted us giving head,
> For a love that started as one man's crime,
> This joint trip has sure fucked with our mind.

In the spent exhaustion of their shared neurotica, they came down, they got up, and brushed off the dirt. Auryn wondered if he knew she had stroked his skin, because There are teeth marks to be sure. Maybe

---

[31] [a]Ecstasy of Saint Teresa, by Bernini, sculpture of a saint pierced by a vision that caused agony and ecstasy similar to orgasm, A.D. 1645-52, Santa Maria della Vittoria, Rome.

[b]"We're down in the hollow, leaving so soon, Oh Saint Teresa, higher than the moon." Joan Osborne, "St. Teresa"

[c]"From ancient grudge break to new mutiny, Where civil blood makes civil hands unclean." (Act 1, Prologue, lines 3-4, Chorus)

[d]"O I have bought the mansion of a love but not possessed it and though I am sold, not yet enjoyed... Oh trespass sweetly urged! Give me my sin again." (Act 3, Scene 2, lines 26-28 and Act 1, Scene 5, line 109, respectively.)

we're best close to the ground. Maybe angels drag us down. I wonder which part of this will leave the scar?[32]

"What did you see?"

"I could hear you, but I couldn't speak."

"Saint Teresa came to me in dreams."

"When I drive the sharpened object in, choirs of angels seem to sing."

"'Cause I don't know if I can stand another hand upon you, All I know is I should."[33] Raven peeked back over her shoulder from afar, "She would love you more than I could, she who dares to stand where I stood,"[29] her whispered song carried on a wind current of momentary human weakness and wisdom.

And it was in that moment, Auryn thought, watching Raven's back, an electric chill running down the spine in her own, that I realized what I'm in for: I'm about to be thrilled to fantasy one too many times.[34]

---

[32] "Faithfully Dangerous" from The Home Recordings by Over the Rhine.

[33] Missy Higgins, "Where I Stood."

[34] Lyric: "I've been thrilled to fantasy one too many times." Song: "I Just Died in Your Arms Tonight." Band: The Cutting Crew.

ASHES TO ANGELS

Chapter Seven

Drunken Bar Poetry

"If They Don't Show Up at a Scheduled Time,
How Will the Muse Know When to Find Them?"

Auryn was late to the show, sold out. Security refused to let her past the media and the cameras, with their bulbs flashing every angle. There are angels in your angles[35]...the ubiquitous camera seemed to croon, mockingly, like a mockingbird, above her missing ruffled feathers. She cried to Asher over the screaming crowd inside, but couldn't get through the idyllic mob, waving her arms, hands reached out toward him over the talking heads. This bar was called The Embassy, and at the gate of The Embassy, their hands met through the bars. "I don't know, Asher," she choked in response to her mishap, "the sign just said, LEAVE YOUR WINGS AT THE DOOR."

In hushed tones, he instructed her in the ballad: "Alley back of the fire escape. Meet me on the vast veranda, my sweet untouched 'Cassandra.' And while

---

[35] The Decemberists, "Angels in Your Angles"

the seagulls are crying, we'll fall while our souls are flying!"[36]

The punky angel knew what was happening to her the more she got played by Asher and his cronies; she could feel the purity of her former existence slowly being snuffed out of her and running down her legs like hot wax. She couldn't deny it pricked her conscience like prickly fruit, when her thoughts drifted up to the higher days gone by. The righteous babe with the universal record label, she would walk in a room and all the world stop to stare, she mesmerized all who were caught in the glare of the spotlight that followed wherever she'd go, did it light up the emptiness?[37] But she felt that to make up for it, at least she was keeping ideals. She wasn't becoming a slutty angel, she rationalized, getting drunk on nightclubs or one-night cheap hotel rooms. Really, all they did was go out to the coffeehouse on the corner of 5th and Main and just talk the evening away. Really, everything was going according to plan, which took the past twenty-six and 2/3 years – it was August, after all – to write, unwittingly, without realizing the incrimination she was branding not on her forehead, but on her arsonist heart. Really. She told herself. Really.

She was beginning to think what she had done was paying off, as she and Asher were getting closer, and maybe this wouldn't be a bad trade-off for mortality. She was beginning to find reason to believe in the evolving goodness of human nature, the upstaged

---

[36] "We Both Go Down Together" by the Decemberists. Name intentionally misquoted to confer the Cassandra complex.

[37] Slight paraphrase of "Drifting" lyrics by Sarah McLachlan.

antihero to human spirit, so beaten down to pulp cliché by now. She was existing at the hot spot of an emotional high until the night that Asher came up with his own idea of how to spend the evening.

"You mean, you want to go to a strip club? That one on the other side of town?"

"Dance club. Alley Cat. It rocks. I haven't been there in forever. Used to spend every Saturday night there before I went schizo." Asher raised his eyebrows up and down suggestively.

"Um, I, uh…" The angel stuttered, not knowing how to respond to this unexpected spitfire. She hadn't seen this coming. She thought she had fallen on an open book, landed on the same page as Asher. Now she was seeing him as the member of fallen humanity that claimed not to have started the fire, but that had been burning all along. She had only fanned the fire by fantasizing him to be a name, not a number, among the millions of other mug shots of human third-time offenders, cocky pre-dawn insomniacs, and repeat denials. Suddenly, she was no better than a mortal: it was a self-predatory revelation, the kind that stops you in your tracks.

"I thought you said your sister is a stripper. Doesn't she like, work there now?"

Witches had burned at the stake for this, but so had Joan; she had been there, watched with ill-begotten cathartic side effects, much like the Virgin had witnessed her own morphling, a product of the metaphysical*morphosis* of natural conception, hang on nineinchnails. Suddenly, she wondered if angels weren't just a pseudonym for witches whorifying sainthood, or saints prostituting witchcraft. The dividing line between the two seemed about as clear as charred edges in the aftermath of banned book burnings during a mob hunt. All Hallows' Eve and All Saints' Day were back-to-back, according to Roman calendar tradition, after all. What was to stop one party from criss-crossing over timelines to the other? Upon this last, that chronic panicky feeling of uncertainty over her irreversible decision gripped her and she faltered. As much as she wanted to do anything to keep him, she just wasn't ready to commit an uncommittable.

She decided it would be best to be straightforward – literal, for once – on the chance that he would understand and change his mind. So she explained her feelings and tactfully tried to persuade him to an alternate course of action for this not-so-silent night.

At this, Asher felt a flame strike up inside of him. What had he expected, spending time with an angel? It's a wonder she wasn't thumping a prayer book at him, rather than thumping on him. Suddenly he realized he had mixed feelings: he really wanted to go to the club, but he wanted her to be there with him to share in the wild, beautiful, scandalous night. Her goody two shoes irked him. Where was his angel in devil's shoes? Who cut the playlist? "Not you too?" When she asked him why he wouldn't like to spend a night building a mystery, counting the stars in multiples of three from the window of the coffeehouse, rather than carousing with the revelers of the world, it set off the impending fireworks inside him and he exploded like Roman candles. "I'd rather dance with the damned than suffer with your saints," a line he hadn't known he'd had dormant inside him but sure as Dante's Inferno, it felt damn good to vent his volcano.

At this point, Auryn realized they were having their

first fight, a fist fight with bits of wonder lost in abstraction, in which their serious differences were showing through the fantasies she had created of him in her mind she left carelessly back in Andromeda's windswept alleyways. She wanted to salvage their relationship, in a backwards way to correct for not salvaging that mind, the medium of her existence comparable to the human body.

"So, are you with me?" Asher started to walk away, his hands shoved deep in his pockets.

"I don't even know you any more," she hurled back, as she flinched at her false start.

He scoffed. "You don't even know me yet. You've only known me for like, six weeks." He had a point.

"I've known you for *like*," she mocked his irritating grammar, "26.666 years, if Time be willing to waste its digits on the measure of a man."

"Oh? And just what, praytell, is the measure of a man?"

"a single temporal
one-night stand called
humanity...or maybe
just what is
the measure
of a man."

He considered this. "I do believe, missy, you're actually scared of us, then. Accordingly, I have a proposition – a modest proposal, if you will: I dare you. No, I double dare you. No, no, I double dog dare you." By this time he was right up in her face, staring her down imposingly. She self-consciously clutched at her throat, her fingers reflexively brushing at her open neckline further on down. She blinked, half expecting to see Poe in Asher's shoes because the dare could've been The Deal all over again. It smacked of déjà vu. Her ultra-violet irises eclipsed his own Aquarian green in a microcosmic imprint of the Lost Planet Earth biting the hand that feeds, the Sun who can't resist trying to re-open a sore, a fire spot infecting a black hole, and for once, womb ecology came out on top. You send your thieves to me, silently stalking me, dragging me into your war. Would you give me no choice in this, I know you can't resist, trying to re-open a sore.[38]

"I don't know who you are, Ash. I don't know if I'm fighting fire or water, so leave me be, I don't want to argue, I just get confused and I come all undone. If I agree, well it's just to appease you, 'cause I don't remember what we're fighting for."

He lingered in the distance like a lost puppy. She materialized by his side. "You're right: I don't know who you are, but I—" Here she drew in a sharp breath. "I'm with you."

*   *   *

"Aren't you going to drink?" Asher said, eyeing her over a tall foaming glass of Guinness. The question sounded derogatory. She'd just finished someone else's Bloody Mary, her first drink she'd scavenged from some dude named Dorian or Damien, something to that effect. Her first time at a bar, she didn't approach, not knowing what to order. Now, with the spiced tomato still pricking her tongue, she wondered why she'd wanted one in the hospital so bad.

"I'm going to need to see some I.D." The disgruntled bartender cut in gruffly, leaning over the

---

[38] "Time" by Sarah McLachlan

side of the bar and eyeing her with a different sort of suspicion. "She doesn't look a day past sixteen. How'd you get in here, anyway? Doors were at 9:00."

"Actually," Auryn drew herself up in composure to realize her full height – all five feet 1.5 inches of her – the half inch being very important – "I'm no less than 26 human years old, same age as him," pointing to Asher, who shot her a disgusted look. *Don't implicate me! You're already on my record, and there's still that warrant out for that ticket you cost me. So far, neither of us has paid off.*

The burly bartender wasn't buying it. "What are you, supernatural?" He snorted. "I don't have time for cutesy little games, miss. I've got a show to run. Now hand it over or I'm kicking you outta this joint for loitering." At that, he lit up a cigarette and puffed away, taking little or no care to spare her the growing impatience on his face as much as the smoke wafting into hers.

At this point, Asher was thoroughly feeling the A.D.D. and itching to settle this absurd poker game with all the foxy finesse of a seasoned con artist. So he bluffed.

"Hey, babe, you forgot this." He smoothly lifted a card from his ratty tweed coat pocket and slid it across the counter to a stop in front of her space. He chuckled, fakely fondly. "Silly girl, what would ya do without me?" Auryn glanced down at the photo before her. It certainly looked like her. Auburn-reddish hair. Purplish-gray eyes. Pale complexion. Only – the scissor-Hook scar on her forehead was conspicuously absent. Was the demonic indentation from her struggle with the Anti-Soul to catalyze the fall and its corresponding fallout perhaps unphotographable? Inconceivable! But, come to think

65

of it, she had never been photographed. Were supernaturals so immaterial as to be on (sub) par with their evil Other half, those nefarious necromancers and naughty nymphets in keeping with the vampire tradition? Poe had told her plenty of ghost stories growing up, those sultry sleepovers on hellishly hot summer nights when Auryn had illegally ventured over to the Dark Side of the house to stake out her sister's bedroom. According to vampire lore, it seems the nocturnally disturbed, those wingéd waifs and Ladies of the Night, couldn't be photographed by their bloody lovers on account of their rather *delicate* soul-less condition.[39] This was a direct consequence of the Dracula precedent: poor unsuspecting Stoker had no idea his fictional creations were to become larger than life, spawning an entire race of beings separate-but-equal to their human counterparts, whose "early camera is one of the many modern gadgets in the novel. Stoker's working notes contain a reference to Dracula registering as a skeleton on photographic film, an effect omitted in the finished novel."[40] So this can't be me. However, Auryn also knew from the reliable source of her schooling in folklore tradition, that a vampire casts no reflection because s/he has no soul, and furthermore, vampires can have erotic contact only with humans, not with each other. That's why I had to fall for a human down here on post-postmodern Earth, not one of my own wingéd people.

---

[39] "And maybe the reason vampires don't die is because they can never see themselves in photographs or mirrors." Chuck Palahniuk's Haunted on vamps, page 144.

[40] Direct quote of a footnote by editor Nina Auerbach in the Norton Critical Edition of Bram Stoker's Dracula: Chapter II, page 29, #2.

ASHES TO ANGELS

A fact she had yet to reveal even to the Dealer, let alone risk incrimination by admitting it to herself in her own bugged mind. Someone could be listening in. There were so many loose wires, some brain hacker could easily take advantage of the private collection of time-sealed documents where she stored every poem that's ever been written in a file called her "Brain Trust." Another secret to her power of the Muse, no power in the verse would stop at anything to keep dead poets DEAD, a misleading tourniquet circulating among the Un-Dead a revelation forbidden even more than a forbidden relationship across boundaries of im/mortality. Better to fall than to crack.

But, surely her dealings with the demon half-sister didn't make her by default a half-vampire as well? But as she scrutinized the ambiguous photo more closely, the image seemed to alter slightly, in the undetectable way, subtle and barely perceptible to the untrained eye concerning matters of the supernatural, and the color tone took on a rosy surrealist hue, like gazing at the world through a pair of those old funk sunglasses celebs were spotted wearing when they didn't want to be recognized, rendering everything in sepia red, black, and white, from the gauzy tutu skirt and tight corset-laced bodice to the grotesque theatrical porcelain doll make-up and spiked dog collar around her neck, making her come off as something of a demented ballerina, maybe something from *Swan Lake*, because suddenly, out of nowhere – her wings appeared!

They just effervesced on the plastic, and they were undoubtedly hers – the ones she cut off. With scissors. Stunned into a lapse in self-awareness, Auryn dropped the card, which clattered guiltily on the bar, and blurted out, "Poe?!" She pinned Asher with her startled gaze. Snatching the card back up before the bartender could get anything other than a brief look, Asher slipped it in the little velveteen coin purse around her neck, patting it for safekeeping as he mock gently reminded, "You left that at the club the other night. How many times do I have to tell you not to be so careless with your belongings, babe, especially on the bad side of town at some hole-in-the-wall. Identity theft runs rampant – it's like an STD in this Day and Age." He shook his head at her, keeping eye contact with the bartender. "She's a wild one, that girl. Would rather dance with drunkards than sock hop with the sober. 'Do a little dance, make a little love…'" The red herring wasn't working on the bartender, who was no straw man himself.

"All right, Casey, I've had enough of your sunshine smart-ass. What hole-in-the-wall?" He was about to be offended that this punk rocker wannabe was dissing his joint. He hadn't gone to bartending school for this crap.

"Um, The Hole-in-the-Wall?" Asher took a shot in the dark.

For once, his menacing scowl lit up something other than a cigarette. "Oh? Ned Pepper's?"

Asher took his lucky break and ran with it. "Don't get me wrong – I highly respect bartenders. I mean, knowing how to mix all the drinks, just so, and then having to deal with all the drunks. Big responsibility." Smooth talker.

The bartender slapped a stamp on her hand. "Fine," he huffed, completely wasted of the whole affair, "she's your responsibility."

Why does everyone keep saying that? Nonetheless, Asher grabbed their two beers produced by the bartender mainly just to get rid of them as he hastily ushered Auryn into the ever-increasing crowd. He never faltered once to a dead-giveaway as he confidently tossed back over his shoulder in lieu of a token for a tip, "No problem. I know her like the back of my hand." Then directing his steely penetrating gaze privately into hers, "With a stamp that says I paid to get in." With the ominous force of the words, Auryn looked down at the back of her hand as if on cue, the left one where the blue ink should have left its mark on her skin, but – the stamp wasn't there! It had either dissolved on contact, or...it had never set in. The pigment dye of the chemical was unable to bond with the non-human properties of non-water based cells of non-carbon based life forms. But no one – not even Asher – had seemed to notice, or care. What was visible to the naked unaided human eye was immaterial and of no consequence as he pulled her by the wrist and directed her into the thick of the crowd, hoping she would blend in with the mob in the mosh pit. Under the spotlight. Center stage. Good luck with that.

Presently, a drunken Dorian swaggered over. He nodded indiscreetly at what he distastefully referred to as Asher's "pretty little piece of flesh," not so much out of eyewitness account as his hopeless romancing of a pop Shakespearian cult spin on the talk of the town, or what the rest of them were calling Asher's newest "hot little item." The former bit with irony, considering precisely the amount of "flesh" composing a supernatural being with possible vampire wirings was yet to be determined.

His propriety utterly dissolved in libations, Dorian ripped right in, biting off more than he could chew, as usual. Other than his shady dealings in marijuana and a few other illegal drugs, he was harmless, depending, of course, which side of the coin you were on. More often just annoying in the way that some species of insect feed off their host outside of a symbiotic relationship. "So what are you guys, anyway? Together, or just sleeping together?"

"Fuck off, Dorian. Don't you and Jo Pitts have, ahem, 'business' to attend to?" Asher raised his eyes suggestively at his own dealer, in reference to his sketchy little lady partner-in-crime.

In true gnatty fashion, Dorian refused to buzz off while his own tipsy buzz was still going strong. "So she's fresh meat?" (continuing his own raw metaphor), "a free-for-all?"

"Excuse me," Auryn piped up, "but, I'm right HERE. I'm standing right here. You can speak directly to ME, not through me like I'm not even visible." She stomped her foot, once for each clause of the last sentence for special emphasis. Auryn couldn't understand why Asher would neither claim nor disclaim her. Asher couldn't understand why she had such a visibility complex. He rolled his eyes. Supernaturals.

"Oh, she's a free-fall, all right." Above the growing noise of the crowd and the opening band, Asher misheard the drunk's slurred question. Even though Dorian was not only his dealer but beyond that a friend, all this interrogation was making him nervous and he wasn't up for questioning. He grabbed Auryn's wrist and guided her again through the crowd. A little too forcefully. She shook her wrist free. He stopped short and faced her. "I'd play along, follow my lead, and do what I tell you," he hissed in her ear. "I just saved your wingless ass tonight. Without those wings, you've got nothing to cover you. Not even a cover

ASHES TO ANGELS

charge."

"What do you mean, 'wingless'?" Auryn produced the photo I.D. she still had, but he waved it off.

"Sit tight, stay quiet, and DON'T give out any more information than you have to. I'm up." He motioned toward the stage, which had just cleared for the open-mic portion of the night. "I don't want to find you causing any more trouble until I'm through with you here. Remember, you're MY RESPONSIBILITY." He nodded accusingly toward the bar. With that, Auryn found herself engulfed in a sea of objects, a dizzying swell of screaming strays, loitering lushes, and genuine artists hoping to hear some good ol' drunken bar poetry. Tonight was no exception; they were not to be disappointed by what was to come. Asher was going to give these people what they came for.

> you wonder why you are still serving coffee.
> still serving the coffee you should be drinking to help you
> dehydrate yourself of that novel people say you're writing,
> drinking to help impair that insomnia the novel tells you
> it's inciting, that expression of anxiety called writing.
> you wonder why your life must be over-simplified
> and under-justified by a viscous and ectoplasmic
> stream of thwarted desire and delayed gratification,
> an oozing slime of the sublime seducing,
> what you spit up on the page makes words not love,
> a laxative written down in ink and blood,
> inducing relief by indulging in grief,
> and you wonder which is dirtier: what came up or what went down.
> until you start to feel suffocated by deprivation,
> though you wonder, irritatedly, with gutting disgust,
> and fanciful distrust of your own vague situation,

why every girl you meet falls for you.
because the only alien on broadway you ever seem to crave
must always become a ravaged, war-torn emotional landscape
staged on some thorny horny tragedy of Shakespearian proportion.
you wonder, just once, just once, why couldn't Romeo
wait a few more seconds, just one more second
is all you're asking for – you don't ask for much
and you're not hard to please – so please,
why couldn't the poor lucky bastard wait one more second
to swallow the poison before Juliet awakens?
had he no more words to stall for time and bargain
with the bard's reason and iambic rhyme?
you sit idle and listless across the outdoor café
with your coffee companion, sharing a lazy hazy Verona mirage
an afternoon siesta and a tinted pair of funk
wire-rims to avoid recognition by the mob,
he lights up a smoke, shuffles scraps of papers he calls poems,
the wind ruffles through the pages of words you call home,
and he breathes deep, exhaling upon your existential countenance
true poison: "well, poison is as poison does:
it still is and will always be – poison."
somewhat transcendentally, you agree all too transparently.
and so, you wonder why the dehumanizing cliché to which humanity
has defamed its humans cannot save the last romantic from erosion
jaded human experience, the realist the skeptic the atheist

the greatest force in the Universe, if Love be that curséd verséd
cliché, then why cannot it save itself
by the very content of that cliché
from the very nature of cliché?
must the Force be reduced to a self-defeating force-feeding?
must it be kept alive at the point of its executioner's blade?
do philosophers come up with theories just to be famous,
get quoted in books, and get laid?
and if the spirit is broken, the mind is cut open,
does the body even care if it's taken as token?
how do you convince the world that your affections lie elsewhere
when, in fact,
they don't believe those affections have an elsewhere to lie?

you wonder why, X years later, you are still writing the same poems.
you wonder why you are still writing poems about things
that don't exist until you write poems about them.

The rowdy audience hooted and hollered. Lights flashed. Lighters flicked and flashed. Including Asher's. He lit up, took a long slow drag, then powered on as if with renewed energy, inspiration, and gusto. The emcee tried to intervene, expecting him to have finished with the prior – according to the schedule on the nightly program, his first poem should have been his last. But he just kept going. Page after page after page, he tossed hand-scrawled scraps of paper over his shoulder, discarding them in between drags on his cigarette poised dramatically in one hand, reading on and on the words that just kept coming and coming almost magically from the sheets flared in his other. And when they ran out, he didn't: in a sing-songy, almost lyrical voice with an unmistakable born lilt, Asher took his hearers on a Spoken Word rendezvous, speaking of fabulous places, creating an oasis, weaving a verbal palette of riddles and rhymes, a sheer orgasm of language as it ravished the audience in phantasmal captivity below him under the revolving kaleidoscopic lights of the disco ball moon. I'm more popular than Jesus now…until the bartender complained.

"Let go of the mic." Asher wouldn't let go of the phallic symbol broadcasting his rising stardom: "Passion or coincidence once prompted you to say, Pride will tear us both apart. Now pride's gone out the window, cross'd the rooftops run away, Left me in the vacuum of my heart."[41]

"Get off my stage." Asher hadn't gotten off yet, and he wasn't about to leave until he did.

"Leave, or I'm calling the police." Asher slugged the menacing bartender in the right eye.

Chaos erupted in the mosh pit. Bodies were flying, a levitating violence of bumping, thumping, and grinding in an effort to swarm the stage, friends and enemies alike, but no one could tell the difference. They say there is a fine line between love and hate, and everybody had crossed it. Like the Menu of Daily Offerings hanging by a rusty crooked nail above the ravaged liquor cabinet, it was the "Same Ol' Shit": this bar fight was the third city brawl. The police arrived on cue, like a brainwashed sick comedy act, blaring their bells and whistles and waving their no-less-than

---

[41] "Ordinary World" by Duran Duran.

phallic hand guns, while in the heat of the writhing, sweating, shrieking mass, an angel stood to get broken again. The same policeman who found her as the vandalized architecture Asher hit paused a moment, as if torn between déjà vu and time warp, but before he could place it, Asher, who had caught sight of the potentially dangerous development and wicked turn on his already messy record, nabbed her with enough time to spare for his own official banishment, or (r)ejection proclamation: "The poet Asher, pseudonymically known as Mordren, is hereby banned from performance at this fine joint UNTIL FURTHER NOTICE."

Hanging on to his tattered cabbie by a mere thread, Asher panted as he and Auryn made their getaway down the deserted 2 a.m. streets, darting from moth-eaten lamp-post to street lights lucid as angel dust. "So tell me," he managed between breaths, "tell me, 'cause I seem to have forgotten: how did you manage to slip through the cracks and get in there in the first place?"

Her answer was lucid and loaded with moths and angels and such things that fly or fall depending on whether they keep or cut their wings: "I don't know, Asher: The sign just said, 'Leave your wings at the door.'"

[White space]

Asher skidded to a stop, turning on his heel to face her again and halting her in the process. "What wings." He gestured abruptly with terminal emphasis as if in exasperation to say, "What now?" It was not so much a question as a demand. She shoved the questionable photo I.D. at him.

"Where did this come from? And why is she

wearing **MY** wings?!"

Asher scrutinized the fake I.D. as if seeing it for the first time. He began slowly and pragmatically, keeping it cool. "I don't see any wings." Pause. "I don't know any more than you do. This was found at the scene of the accident. It was all you had on you. Hospital needed something to admit you. Caught on the bloody tip of a wi—" He stopped short, realizing too late he'd said too much. She moved up to him invasively, getting herself directly in his face by the light of the moon, the same moon under which they had just danced only hours before, now a bad moon on the rise. If anyone could read a liar, it was the poet's muse.

"You see them," she whispered conspiratorially, her voice dripping with vice and venom. "You see them, and you know where they are. You know EXACTLY where they are." She backed away. "You're the reason I haven't got any," she accused like a pregnant woman blaming the man who knocked her up for her subsequent discomfort. She could tell right away that it was her guy. "And you're the one who's gonna get me some. I want them back – pay up, or put out. Until I get the goods delivered to me, you aren't gettin' any for the damaging." With a suggestive sweep of her hand over her figure, she spun on her heel and sauntered tauntingly away, down the street, stomping in her combat boots and chains, swinging her hips in mock defiance of the fact that she could, without the overbearing coverage of wings to save her ass, her modesty, and her newfound pawn with which to manipulate words – and men.

ASHES TO ANGELS

Chapter Eight

The Fight Scene

She was kicking the vending machine.

Asher stopped dead in his tracks when he saw the little vixen, going at it on the glass encasement, beating her tiny white fists to a pulp of fiction on the cold blue steel. She seemed to want something.

She was screaming all sorts of bloody marys alternating with hail marys just to see if reverting to her desperate origins would still have any effect. Apparently, it didn't; the Skittles wouldn't give. Over the Rhine was too poor and rough a side of town even for Gravity's Child to partake of the simple rite to taste the rainbow.

She then resorted to kicking the base of the slot. Various students walked by, casting sidelong glances not quite excusing her by reason of insanity, but definitely wary of their own precarious position in the goth girl's silvery slivered path of destruction.

She eventually found her way to the public restroom, on pain of banged up wrists calling for immediate sanitary attention before calling more attention to her fitful scene, and emerged from the bathroom, raw knuckles swaddled in wet brown recycled paper towels of 33% post-consumer content, having washed them first in a pink liquid soap foaming at the mouth of the dispenser bearing a label signed like a waiver that it would not kill 0.1% of the germs. She sulked and slinked into the cafeteria, opting instead for a vegetarian burger which reeked suspiciously of leaked juices from neighboring hamburgers on the communal grill and adulterating a mound of salad in red wine vinaigrette.

Izzy and Marley met up with her at the condiments bar, pawing through the various plastic utensils.

"Auryn! How are you? I mean, how are you?" Izzy asked, knowing that Auryn would never answer with simple conversational pleasantries; despite the law of metaphors, angelic beings did not abide by the law of censorship in any sense of the word. The impossibility for them to fake it meant they were relegated to make out fairly well as collective soul a traitor to themselves, betrayed only by a bloody kiss-and-tell.

"I NEED A KNIFE!" Auryn's answer hit ground before the question could find space. "Human beings make me want to carve their names in my wrists and bleed out from every name so that whoever finds my body can read who is going down with me!"

Marley misinterpreted Auryn's extremities, getting off on the technicality that there ARE NO FACTS, only interpretations; she was of the Nietzsche school of thought.

"Wow, what a great new line, Auryn! So symbolic of the man. I'll bet the carpenter will hit the wall, you're always such a step ahead of him, poor bastard…hm, always a step-father, never a Christ.[42]"

"Sweetie, you're such a fucking brilliant doll," Izzy praised Marley's diva intellect. The lovers smiled amorously at each other. Suddenly, it wasn't about the words.

Auryn wasn't there; she was already brushing past Izzy and Marley and blowing them off with an inadvertent double entendre.

"Can't now, girls; I've got places to go, people to do [in her frenetic lucidity she is known to confuse her direct objects]…You know, so much to do, so few people to do it for me." [Ahem. Again.]

She began to pace-prowl the basement halls. Her feet hurt from the high heels of the heavy trench boots; devil's shoes off-the-rack were a deal when it came to poor college students, cheap beer, torn jeans, and the sell-out economics of signing away one's firstborn, but they were a bitch to wear for any extended due date.

This time, she accidentally (on purpose) walked into the men's restroom. She marched right past a row of urinals, intent on flushing her soggy mess of a meal down the toilet, including a very disturbing side dish of phallic-looking baby carrots. When she had emerged from her dirty deed, she paid no heed to the guys that had just come in, though she did pause long enough to write some obscenity in black Crayola marker, the one aptly named "burnt marshmallow" if inhaled deeply enough, on the inside of a stall door as a public profession of her current opinion of Asher's new rating on the jerk-factor; he was always an over-achiever.

---

[42] In the words of a real-life Damien.

ASHES TO ANGELS

I saw the best minds of my generation destroyed by
    madness, starving hysterical naked,
dragging themselves through the negro streets at dawn
    looking for an angry fix,
angelheaded hipsters burning for the ancient heavenly
    connection to the starry dynamo in the machinery
of
    night
who poverty and tatters and hollow-eyed and high sat
up
    smoking in the supernatural darkness of cold-
water
    flats floating across the tops of cities
contemplating
    jazz,
who bared their brains to Heaven under the El and saw
    Mohammedan angels staggering on tenement
roofs
    illuminated,
Who passed through universities with radiant cool eyes
    hallucinating Arkansas and Blake-light tragedy
    among the scholars of war,
who were expelled from the academies for crazy &
pub-
    lishing obscene odes on the windows of the skull,
who cowered in unshaven rooms in underwear, burning
    their money in wastebaskets and listening to the
    Terror through the wall.[43]

"Asher! Ash!...*Mordren!*"[44]

At the sound of his pen name, Asher stopped mid-step. Only the fans knew his pseudonym, but this

---

[43] Allen Ginsberg, from Howl, Part I, lines 1-22.

[44] A bastardization of the name of King Arthur's bastard son, Mordred, an ambiguously evil character of misunderstood motivations, arguably the victim of hasty generalization concerning the nature of villains.

small voice screaming world he clearly knew apart from the idyllic mob.

He turned in his fugitive tracks and froze. Auryn.

"Asher, why won't you speak to me?! Look at me, LOOK! AT! ME!" She caught up to him, nabbed him by the jacket sleeve, and jerked him around a corner like a mugger when people started to stare. "You listen to me, Asher, you listen to me!" She jabbed her tiny forefinger into his chest with all the emphasis she could like tiny swords. "You are NOT going to get away without finishing the job. I paid you well. The stamp – I paid to get in. The speeding ticket – you paid to get off. Now finish what you started!"

Asher wasn't amused, nor was he in the mood. Something new was on the cusp; new shit to write. He had a poem on his mind.

He took an unconcerned drag off a cigarette he'd apparently rolled himself, held it deep in his chest to let it "marinate" like marijuana from a bowl, then gracefully blew the smoke in her face with all the metrosexual charisma he could fake. His answer convinced her the stuff had to be laced.

"I'm sorry, I can't fix you. Touché." He touched the rim of his threadbare plaid cabbie, profoundly.

She staggered back, took a surreal moment to process what he had just said, so careless and yet so weighty, too stunned to collect her thoughts and fire back a characteristic mouthy retort before – suddenly his mouth was on hers.

She pushed him back with both fists, stumbling back in ecstasy herself, though not before meeting the boyish thin red line with equal intensity and clearly not resisting the overture.

"You insult me, and then you kiss me?! Insult

heaped upon insult!" She slashed back. She stepped back up and kissed him violently in her own turn of aggression. "There! Now a taste of your own bitter medicine! How do you like that!" She hissed, hoping to scare him like a rabbit into his little foxhole where the other dead poets waited for their delinquent group member to complete the circle, join the society, finish the story.

He licked his lips. "Good."

NATALIE MCCOLLUM

Chapter Nine

"Porphyria's Lover"[45] Makes a Circus of the Sun

"I know who killed me."

"You can't be dead if you were never alive," sneered Asher.

"I'm alive now," Auryn countered. "I was just never human."

"So you're the Undead. You're related to the vampires or something. Maybe you got bitten, but somehow never turned. Ever thought of that?"

Auryn shrank back; her fingertips went instinctively to her soft white neck. She remembered the night in the club, when Asher produced a fake I.D. and her image failed to appear in the photo. Had she no soul? Suddenly she couldn't remember if she had ever seen herself in a mirror. Come to think of it, her fall from the sky had landed her at a crossroads, where her physical manifestation had nearly died in the path of oncoming traffic. She had nearly been buried alive in

---

[45] A poem by Robert Browning.

the dust and smoke of motor vehicle exhaust on the spot, like all proper suicides who were buried at crossroads. And then it hit her: according to legend, suicides buried at such places became vampires.

<u>Girl, Interrupted</u>: "Suicide is a form of murder – premeditated murder. It isn't something you do the first time you think of doing it. It takes getting used to. And you need the means, the opportunity, the motive. A successful suicide demands good organization and a cool head, both of which are usually incompatible with the suicidal state of mind.

"It's important to cultivate detachment. One way to do this is to practice imagining yourself dead, or in the process of dying. If there's a window, you must imagine your body falling out the window. If there's a knife, you must imagine the knife piercing your skin. If there's a train coming, you must imagine your torso flattened under its wheels. These exercises are necessary to achieving the proper distance.

"The motive is paramount. Without a strong motive, you're sunk."[46]

Auryn looked up from her reading. "I should have known I was DEAD as soon as I fell – why did I feel so alive on the way down?"

<u>DIY DIE: A Handbook</u> had reprinted various mortal accounts of their attempts. Mainly the successful ones, of course, since this was a handbook aimed at instructing. This posed a literary controversy. It exhumed the old fiction writers' debate about the dead narrator construct. How much verisimilitude

---

[46] "My Suicide" from <u>Girl, Interrupted</u> by Susanna Kaysen, page 36.

does a post-mortem point of view actually suggest? Necromancy seemed the only loophole in this circular argument with a dead end. Conversely, the immortal's obsession with suicide!? "Here comes that story again – all about that television show: 'Sex and Love: How Dangerous Is the Difference?'" In the poet's head it went like this: Here's this girl who believes she's an angel without wings – it's a little neurotic, potentially schizophrenic, but there is something **so hot** about a girl who would *jump*. My dating history is with "safe" girls (except Raven); maybe I'm ready to play it not so safe, to take on a girl with a little history [hystery] herself. There's just something about Auryn.

"But all vampires were formerly humans, and I'm not mortal now, so I can't be a vampire who changed back, either!" Auryn's revelation shook him out of his own reveries.

"I don't know what you are then," he shook off her hand clutching at his sleeve. "Insane. Like a madman laughing at the rain, a little out of touch a little insane – it's just easier than dealing with the pain!"[47] He winced as her tiny claws dug into his shoulder on another attempted grasp.

She relented and put her hands on her hips. "You mean, like you?"

"Well, it takes one to know one, kid, I think you got it bad."[48]

According to Wikipedia, the basic message of the Veronika book went like this: "Collective madness is called sanity," and collective sanity is just mental conformity. Girl interrupted with her own etiology: "I

---

[47] "Runaway Train" by Soul Asylum.
[48] "Lua" lyrics by Conor Oberst of Bright Eyes.

am sane in an insane world." Apparently, the title was adapted by Danish metal band Saturnus in 2006, as they released their third studio album titled Veronika Decides to Die[49].

She looked up from Asher's notebook computer. "Is there a record store around here? I want to find this music."

He peered over her shoulder at the screen's content. "I'm not familiar with that band, but if Village Vinyl doesn't have them, nobody does."

They took the subway from Brooklyn to Lower East Side to East Greenwich. At one end of their car, a bachelorette party of giddy girls was getting started early. It was hard to tell if the bride-to-be or the giant blow-up penis was the center of attention. Auryn couldn't help noticing Asher's gaze straying toward the more suggestively dressed girls. When he didn't notice that she was noticing him, she kicked him in the shin. "Ow, hey, what was that for?" It worked. He finally turned his head back toward her. She merely crossed her legs and folded her arms across her chest, staring straight ahead, her little pointed chin jutting out. He was still rubbing his leg waiting for her answer when the train lurched to an abrupt stop and sent Auryn flying off the seat in the onslaught of boarding passengers as the doors flung open. Asher swiped her from the path of the stampede just in time, as the car became shoulder-to-shoulder standing room only. The slutty bachelorette party was no longer visible. Wrapped around the pole, Auryn stared up meekly at Asher's glare. Nonetheless, he hovered protectively over her, partly out of necessity for lack of personal space. They rode the rest of the way like that until

---

[49] Veronika Decides to Die, the book by Paulo Coelho.

their stop, and then he unwound her from the pole and whisked her onto the platform, up the stairs, and finally, into startling daylight above ground. Auryn let the incident, and her annoyance, stay below the sidewalk grates rattling with the thunderous roar of the subterranean flying dragon.

Though it was late afternoon, and the sun was slipping off its high pedestal, the stark shift from the cool darkness underground to the brightness outside caught Auryn off guard. She shielded her eyes and asked Asher if he had any sunglasses.

He slowed his trot and peered at her cloudy eyes. "What's wrong with your eyes?"

"The light hurts my eyes."

"It's practically twilight."

"I don't know, but it hurts my skin, too." She now wished she had worn a few more layers, instead of trying to compete with such fashions as had attracted Asher, and extracted the voyeur, on the train. He shrugged off his canvas jacket and handed it to her.

"Anything else, your highness? Perhaps you'd like my skin as well." Auryn tried to smile at his sarcasm, but inwardly she winced at the irony. Yeah, she'd love to have his mortal layer. That was the whole point.

She relaxed again when they found the record store and let the overwhelming stock of music distract her. Asher drifted to his own favorites while Auryn scoured the boxes of used albums for the Danish group. She paused a moment when a band name caught her eye: "Auryn." The album was from 2005, and the band hailed from an obscure midwestern town called Dayton, Ohio. According to the inside jacket, their namesake had origin in the film, *The Neverending Story*. But somehow, the part where anonymous writer (call her #5½) forgot to write who begot whom – did a band named Auryn write the angel of music into being, or did a schizophrenic poet named Asher compose a lyric that morphed, or mutated, into a living breathing poem of blood and ink – that part got lost or whited out for reasons that couldn't be helped as much as love and its look of violence in the mythology. She considered this a while, until Asher's voice from across the store interrupted her reveries. "Hey Auryn, I found it! That metal band you were looking for." He scooted around other browsing customers and display racks until he got to her section. He handed her the record. "The Veronika one, right?"

She nodded and put back the Auryn LP. "Thanks." She turned over the Saturnus in her hands. He was clearly proud of his obscure victory.

"I have a sweet turntable too, so it's cool they have it on vinyl 'cause that always sounds better than CD's." He flashed one of his by-now classic charismatic smiles. "I'm an old-school junky."

He even paid for the record, so she didn't want to ask him to front her namesake as well. Perhaps she should see this movie, this *Neverending Story*. She would ask about that later.

As they stepped back onto the street, they were accosted by a curious-looking clown. Rather, a street performer, one of a colorful group of buskers prancing around the Village, promoting the upcoming Cirque du Soleil. This particular performer looked like a classic mime, with the black and white face paint, the striped boatneck shirt, the black knickers and suspenders. He danced around Auryn, offering her the flower from his suspender. It was a big red poppy, and when she buried her face in it to inhale its bewitching scent, he feigned shyness and put his gloved hand to his cheek as if trying to hide his blushing. Auryn was charmed with the act and continued playing along, taking his hand delicately like a teacup when he offered. Asher just stood there like a zombie, watching the whole display with apparent disgust. Auryn amped up her own act when she saw the jealousy register on his face. What a lunatic, getting jealous of a fake suitor. She played the poet's envy a while longer, marveling in this unexpected new sensation of revenge, until suddenly he snapped out of his stupor and yanked her out of the mime's embrace, just as she was twirling a ballroom dance version of a pirouette. She spun out of the mime's hands and stumbled into Asher, who blocked her fall with repossessive intent. "Stay away from my girl, you Freak!" Auryn could tell by the way he said it, it was freak with capital F.

"Asher! He's just acting!" she scolded, but he wouldn't have it. She watched horrified as he took a swing at the mime, who remained in character. You had to admire his dedication to the art. Auryn tried to plant herself between them, but that ill-fated move only resulted in Asher snatching her poppy and pursuing the perturbed mime as he nimbly backed away. "Asher, stop it!" she pleaded, aware of the attention they were attracting from passersby, but he plucked the petals one by one, mocking "She loves me, she loves me not" and ending conveniently on "She loves YOU – *not*!" He threw the last petal at the retreating mime, who was safely rejoining his fellow performers as they continued on their way. She stood sobbing in a circle of discarded petals.

"You're the freak! Like you assault a mime!"

"I didn't 'assault' him, I merely defended your honor. I saved you. Isn't that what you want?

ASHES TO ANGELS

'Somebody saaave me, I don't care how you do it, just stay, stay, c'mon. I've made this whole world shine for you.'[50]" He held an imaginary microphone as he winged the lyrics.

"Saved me from what?!"

"I saw the way he was looking at you. The perv. You can't trust clowns. He's prolly a washed-up circus act who had to register as a sex offender after molesting some kid at a birthday party. Never ever trust a scary clown." He crossed his arms in front of him pragmatically, shaking his head to the rhythm of the syllables in "never ever."

"First of all, I am not a child, and second, that's a mime! You're fucking deluded!" She bent down and started gathering up the scattered petals.

"Um, what are you doing?"

"He gave me this flower. I'm keeping it."

Asher threw up his hands. "Fine. Go ahead. You want him? Fucking run. Run after him. Run away to the circus. Glamour him with your fantasy fallen-angel-who-cut-off-her-wings story. I bet he'll dig it."

She threw the dissected poppy in his face. "The things! You say! You're unbelievable!" She flung off his coat and chucked it at him. It was dark now. "I wanna go home." He reached for her arm, but she jerked away. "Don't touch me."

* * *

She secretly regretted taking off his jacket though on the train ride home. Now the sun had gone down, it was cold. He noticed her shivering two seats ahead

---

[50] "Save Me" theme to the CW's "Smallville" written and performed by Remy Zero.

of him in the nearly vacant car, and he got up and draped his jacket over her bare shoulders then returned to his seat. She didn't look up, but she didn't protest, either.

ASHES TO ANGELS

Chapter Ten

"Yes, Asher: I Like Fire and I Like Veins."[51]

She wanted to stay in for the day. The daylight had been irritating her skin. And though they were even, they were still sore at each other. Asher went out to "take care of some things," as he said in his usual vague, sketchy rhetoric.

"Come ride with me through the veins of history. I'll show you a god who falls asleep on the job."[52] But she refused his advances. Deliberately misleading, she told him she was going to bathe and shave her legs. She had heard of some conditions called XP and Porphyria, and she wanted to conduct a little experiment in secrecy.

Her diary lay open, ravaged, brutalized, torn, and vandalized with the contents of her head transcribed on the blank page like graffiti:

---

[51] Text message. Name changed.
[52] "Knights of Cydonia" from the album Black Holes and Revelations by Muse.

I guess, at some submerged level, at the very core of
the apple core, there will
  tries to jump off the painted railroad bridge in the District
always be some remnant of the feelings that have
been, to witness the
 her retort: "How am I supposed to FLY, without any wings?"
remains of loving [insert name of whomever I am
currently strung out on],
  (passive-aggressive jab at Ash, for whom she cut them off)
at least a tiny smoldering ember that could easily be
reignited to
            (for whom the bell tolls)
bonfire severity, smoldering at the highest stake
whether it be love or hate,
  *and she's not getting the payoff she thought she had coming by
            simple cause-and-effect*
because when it comes to me and him,
there really isn't much difference between the
beginning and the end.
                    ~Auryn

She signed the note and tucked a corner under her black-and-white cameo, which was all the fake I.D. card really amounted to, a gothic picaresque of her wings and the otherwise unphotographable anatomy of a vampire. She flinched at the stigma. If only she could bleed. If only she knew how to bleed. That would show them. She couldn't be more than half bad. She was only half the cross between two evils. She had angel wings, after all. Not even Glinda the Good Witch of the East could boast those.

Turning, now, to the scene at hand, in cameo. Only

a few things left to do. She flicked off all the lights in the outer rooms. She slipped like a shadow translucent and lucid into the softly lit chamber, the crime scene, her suicide cell, her play grave. Only the blinking light bulb hanging on a chain from the ceiling glowed with a false sense of security, carving out the orb light like a barren womb: come into my warm, engulfing interior, the womb-space beckoned, come into me. Playing both the victim and the vampire, she responded like the Undead un-born: she descended into the bright shadows of her death nest, child bride of Nosferatu, hovel of Frankenstein's voyeur vicariously staking out his humanity, a foxhole, a black hole stuffed with fluff and the entrails of cloud nine lined with a silver that is in fact a bullet etched with the exchange of empty vows, I brought you my bullets, you brought me your love, the assurances of a vampire kissing his lover, "Vampires will never hurt you," but are you kissing or cutting, my dear? The difference between a vertical and a horizontal cut is the same as getting horizontal.

Her head filled, like Coleridge, with ancient witcheries, she lay back in a bathtub lined with candles and candlesticks, some already flaming darkly brightly in a ritualistic spiraling twist in on their own eventual demise, some holding steady in mature defiance of this same fact, and others snuffed out in the wake of their scent-sual counterparts of pirated pyromania, incense sticks jutting and penetrating the smokescreen put up behind a salvation in suicide: "Yes, Asher, I like fire and I like veins." She fanned the fire with her premeditated note, the one written on the palm of her hand in that fermenting purple that always bled through in place of the actual iron&wine red on deathly grayish white zinfandel water-based cells recycling oxygen, oozing through black membranes printed on carbon copy skin thin as newsprint yet un-biodegradable as immortals come. Scrawled across said palm, THE GIFT IS NOT LIKE THE TRESPASS:

> Dear Ash,
> I --- --- .
> (Sorry, I ~~don't~~ didn't live by rules.
> Else this would be a suicide note,
> not a love letter. Maybe
> they're really just the same thing.)

She couldn't write any more than say the three words. She couldn't get past 1/3. As the equal other half to Asher's tattoo poetry, the call to his response, all she could do was leave a place for the unspeakable 2/3 and hope to god that his feelings got in the way, because, if I loved you, I would have to kill you. If it's not vampires, it's love.

Ohhhh. She moaned at the slight shock of the first flick of the wrist, a sleight-of-hand trick she learned from the tattoo artist who wrought his runic rhymes with knives, not needles, a veritable ancient mariner. It was only a small slit. Nothing mortal. Not even deeply horizontal. Still a long way to go before she could slash half off the price they're asking for mortality. The going price for souls these days had skyrocketed with all the inflation but she didn't put much stock in a market where people sell their souls for a bit of paper, a share of arbitrary manmade numbers, and a quantum physics theory on some code-cracking addict's pattern to the universe that really just proved the existential atheism of a societal infrastructure built on consumerist numerology.

ASHES TO ANGELS

She sucked in a slick breath. The next flick of the razor blade once-removed from its protective dispenser caught her off-guard like a vampire feeding off his lover, slowly killing her with his love. This blade, his teeth, it was consensual, she convinced herself. It was good for her poetry. For Ash's. The ban at the bar would lift soon. He'd be back in the spotlight where he belonged, larger than life was his fiction, and though he could fake it for the papers, she was on to him. She would deny it to people's questions, that he's killing her, because he convinced her this IS love: it hurts and kills. That's how mortals tell the difference. Vampires bite and so does love. The 80's rockstar said so. If she was immune to vampire bites it didn't mean a thing without that sting, just a troublesome side effect of an angel trying to date a vampire ambiguously misconstrued as a human, and a vampire taking their mortal enemy as sexual partners, by consent, mind you, my dear arch-nemesis, but clearly a slurring of the bleary blurry lines between friends and lovers composing musicforthemorningafter in a violent ballet of tattoo poetry and symphonic sex. But mortals can't be immune to love. If love could be lethal as her own attempt at mortality (the born-mortals speak of this thing called suicide) then she could bleed. She could commit love suicide and become mortal, part Ash, half blood, and then he'd love her. She was convinced of it. There was always a price. The mermaid sold her soul in the form of her voice. The angel cut off her wings and prostituted her soul to a demon. To each her own; mythologies are relative.` Now all she had to do was get herself to bleed. All stakes were raised to the one through her heart, and it meant everything: her human-ness, her virgin biology, her defense against the demonized wings from ever returning to steal away her chance with the poet, her capacity for the fallacy of human love. Surely, if she could write, she could die; and if she could die, she could love – and be loved. The question was simply, how to die.

in the dream I had four days later, (call it 26-27 June), I accidentally slit my wrist. I looked, and I hadn't realized it: I felt no pain. conversely, I felt no love. every action has an equal and opposite reaction. I just saw a thin red line running parallel to and in-between some veins on the wrist of my tattoo, writing down the bones of the hand I write with.

Rather, the question became, how do you inadvertently attempt suicide? The poetry journal lay open, loose pages strewn around the bath chamber like ashes in honor of the dead, so she continued her scrawl.

(you're afraid that you won't be able to slit your wrists "just a little bit," and you're not ready to die unnaturally. yet.)

That was the enraging impossibility she played with like matches, tearing out pages, setting off a fire made of Ash. She also set off the fire alarms. It was a domino effect. Sunk in the stagnating water, she swooned on the intoxication of her own soul-less spirits, willing it, willing that purple ink dripping out of her wrist to turn water to wine to blood. Uttering a drunkard's prayer, reaching for the half bottle of whiskey perched precariously on the bathtub rim, she slipped on her jutting hip bone and plunged into the bath, missing the bottle and hitting an especially long candlestick. The black stick candle, like a long finger, in turn pointed accusingly at its target, a set of tiny white votives all in a row preceding a thick red stump candle, and thus went the fireworks display, ring around the roses, pocket full of poesy, ashes, ashes, they all fell down, each hitting the next for fantastic fatality. The erstwhile bottle of alcohol, tipping with tipsy doom, shattered on the tile floor, spilling its contents just in time for the falling candlesticks and their hot-tempered flames to find intemperate pleasure in the matching of fates, a cross-fire made imploding stars. Let it bleed. Let men burn stars. She was seeing them.

Someone saw her. An unsuspecting bystander actually broke the bystander effect. It came upon a midday clear in the clear voice of a little girl: "Mummy, look! That girl's on fire!" The ringletted golden baby doll pointed up at a tiny second-story window overlooking the busy street.

The harried mother, lugging shopping bags and tugging at the little girl's hand with all the urgency of the Mad Hatter's rabbit on his way to Wonderland, looked up in haste and alarm, but saw nothing of the specter plastered against the tiny quadrant window, her wings hovering two-thirds too close and one-third not close enough to be seen. "Honey, what did I tell you about little white lies? You don't yell 'fire' on the street."

The little princess was undaunted. "But she is wearing wings, mummy. Why doesn't she fly?"

"Come now, Angie, we're late." The mother sidestepped a pothole and pulled the hyperactive imagination in ribbons and curls behind her. "If we're late, we'll miss it, and then what a shame to be all dressed up and nowhere to go."

"Is that what angels look like?"

"No, love, they can't be angels without wings."
"Do they burn like that?"
"She must be a witch, not a nice little human girl like you."
"And what do they do to witches?" the little girl named Angela asked, innocent of popular culture and the Hollywood love affair between horror and satire.
"Burn them!" The mother finally gave in to the fairy tale and in so doing killed off its characters.

From Auryn's vantage point, the dreaded condition was sealed by the words of the mortal; the ambivalent possibility now rendered finality with the direct quote from the source. The ones who bleed are the ones who lead, when it comes to fame. Natives of the end of the world splayed all their raw misgivings on the front of *The New York Times* under the caption: NO TIME FOR THE END. A poet-journalist looking for his big break answered without fear of infamy:

> Christmas 2000 in the city found me
> Camped on the curb with nothing but my
> music and a copy of *The New York Times*
> with the child's return making headlines
> I played for him till my fingers cut red
>
> The notes ran like water from my wounds.
> It was the end of the world
> and no one knew its real name
> The wolf and the lamb got lost
> Somewhere between 5th Avenue and infinity
> people rushed past on subways 'cause
> they didn't have time to stop for death
> like Emily warned before poets took to
>
> Signing away the copyrights to their souls.

ASHES TO ANGELS

So I huddled in my morning jacket
lined with fake dirty wool
rubbed my hands together
in last year's borrowed gloves
Nodded to the homeless guy
over there reading Dickens
and started this song on my guitar
as my way to help the unwell earth
Cope with the best and the worst

while my beggar pal wished me good things.
As we parted, I thought I saw an angel
who had fallen down here hail a taxi
and say to me over her crooked wing,
"See you in the next life, my friend."

Auryn, meanwhile, trapped inside the steaming flaming bathroom cubicle, found herself vaguely soothed in spite of her apparent photosensitivity; the fire cast cool shadows decorated with the rosary and a string of pearls and a crucifix turned upside down above the sink and incense still burning and turning with the smoking ruins of the synthetically induced apocalypse now. Like saints and mystics, angels and addicts, she felt a poem coming on, the stuff of muses and such things as guitar strings and angel wings…

Dear World:

In the middle of the burning bathroom, she took out a fresh slip of paper and began to write.

World stop hurting me, you.
Don't fuck with my heart, too.
The world keeps telling me what's best for me,
People think they know better than me
Poets think they can instruct their own muses,
What the gut, what's the good, where's the sense,
If wishes were horses they'd fly if pigs could.

> *But – It's my heart! Only I can know*
> *What my heart is telling me and no one else,*
> *because it's not in anyone else's chest cavity*
> *–but mine! This is the time when I most feel*
> *like cigarettes, to watch all my beautiful*
> *heartache go up in smoke.*
This is when I feel like slitting my wrists,
just enough so I can watch the blood ooze
out slowly to mirror the feeling of my soul
bleeding out of my skin, like a tattoo,
fresh ink under the needle, out of the pen.
You feel like you must have been a wounded
animal in another life, because all you want
to do is crawl into a cave, drag your limp soul
into a dark deep crevice of a rocky cliff or crag,
and just lie there in physical relief while you let
Your Self bleed at will for a while,
And die a little bit.

Like the writer, the suicide note had survived its own intent. Like the writer, the things they carried out included all scraps of evidence pertinent to the ensuing police report. They wrote her off as a little matchstick girl, then melted at her innocent ode to a bit of careless candle wax, and finally sloughed her off as a maniac faking her own death. Ash found it and hit the wall.

"How can an immortal commit suicide?! You're either already dead or faking mortality! You can't die, you can't even *bleed!*" She caught his reference to the Red Right Ankle, said with somewhat nasty concession to a flare-up of his earlier atheistic disdain for the concept of anything with claims beyond humanity. She summoned herself. He was, after all, an atheist in love with the divine.

ASHES TO ANGELS

"I was only trying to bleed
because if I can bleed like a mortal,
Bleed like you,
then I can *be* a mortal,
be like you.
And if I can be mortal,
I can have human biology too,
and if I can be biologically human,
I can logically sleep with you.
And if we sleep together,
You will love me better.
Right?"
Pause.
"I was not trying to die;
I was checking for vital signs,
Looking for Signs of Life –
signs of mortality –
Signs of love."
(As an afterthought,)
("I did not *mean* to commit suicide
I did not *mean* to do it by your side.")

Asher's face clouded over and his brow furrowed in grave recognition of the gravity of the situation. For once, words were too much for the poet. "Will we burn in heaven, like we do down here?" Asher's question to Auryn was more of a snide comment as he pocketed the charred note and walked out the door in the wake of her retort:

"The poet becomes a seer through a long, immense, and reasoned derangement of all the senses! All shapes of love, suffering, madness! He searches himself, he exhausts all poisons in himself, to keep only the quintessences!"[53]

"Come ride with me through the veins of history…" he started mixing up a shot of Adia and Luca's junk hoping to relax her with an erotic high. "I'll show you a god who falls asleep on the job – how can we win when fools can be kings?"[54] He mused as he hit and pushed off into her wrist. "Don't waste your time, or time will waste you."

She clenched her fists and beat them against the burnt bathtub wreckage, pounding out a song on notes of narcotics some wiseman has yet to choke up.

---

[53] "As Ginsberg wrote in his journal, they experimented with drugs to facilitate their discovery of a new way of life that would enable them to become great writers." Quoted from an Introduction by Ann Charters to the 1991 Penguin Books edition of Jack Kerouac's On the Road. Auryn's lines are Ginsberg's *sans* exclamation points.

[54] "Knights of Cydonia" by Muse.

ASHES TO ANGELS

Chapter Eleven

Iced Roses and Psychosis

"Like a bed of Roses there's a dozen reasons"
for My Chemical Romance.

"Can you take me higher? Fly me over yesterday!"[55] Dreaming off her despair over Asher's hostile critique of her ambiguous suicide attempt and its attendant note, she was a writer whose manuscript just went under the editorial red pen. "The first time I was high, I thought I could fly." When I peaked, I realized I had the exotic desire to cut myself to feel higher, to release those endorphins with the agony and ecstasy of pain, like a true hunger artist. I craved a really agonizing orgasm. And I had a profound thought: How does a feel-good drug make you want to harm yourself? A simple cat-scratch is a tease; I'm triggered to finish the job.

Die just a little bit.

---

[55] "High Enough" by the Damn Yankees.

Perhaps not enough to take you
ALL the way to the other side,
but enough to have your way
with the beauty of the dark side.
because a bleeding heart is a mending soul.
The problem is the Body – it can only
take so much emotional abuse before
it breaks, and crumbles under pressure
like a city of lost children or the sacking of Rome,
full of intrigue and lush betrayals by familiars,
your best friend turned lover turned love interest
turned significant other turned your Other,
feels like family more than family,
whom you'd trust with your very life –
with your very own knife –
is like being forced to put the blade
in your family member's hand and
making him executioner of you against both wills.
But someone has to do the dirty deed,
and who better than the person you know best?
No one should die alone, never fear a stranger.
It's a frightful world when your most trusted
confidante becomes your worst fear.
When your safety becomes predatory…
I don't understand why people are the worst
at being human, and humans are the worst
offenders of humanity!

"I hear your voice…sounds like an angel sighing…"[56] Asher convulsed on his own hit in the next room.

"I'm on air – oh god, I think I'm flying!" She had

---

[56] "Like a Prayer" by Madonna.

no idea that she was actually lying face down on the carpet in a wine stain. The broken bottleneck filled with ice cubes and long-stem wilted roses seemed to be talking to her.

"It's like a dream, no end and no beginning."

"Oh god, I think I'm falling!"

"My life! You electrify my life! Let's conspire to ignite all the souls that would die just to feel alive!"[57] Asher had run frantically into her room, grabbed her up like a corpse, stood shaking her limp frame with each syllable, her feet barely touching the floor, he had her so high.

She weakly reached out her arms to him, pawed at the yawning space between them. "Hold you…in my arms, I just wanted…to hold you," she gasped.

"If you promise not to – fade away, never fade a-way," he returned. "I will be chasing the starlight until the end of my life."

"I don't know…if…it's worth it anymore," she whispered as she soared so high she was entering black holes and revelations with their shades of gray matter called human matter that mapped out the middle ground between the avatar and the Io.

---

[57] "Starlight" from the album <u>Black Holes and Revelations</u> by Muse.

NATALIE MCCOLLUM

Chapter Twelve

Your Red Right Ankle
(*Angels Don't Leave Footprints*)

This is the story of your red right ankle
This is the story of the boys who loved you
Who love you now and loved you then
Some were sweet and some were cold and snuffed you
And some just laid around in bed
Some had crumbled you straight to your knees
Did it cruel did it tenderly
Some had crawled their way into your heart
To rend your ventricles apart
This is the story of the boys who loved you
This is the story of your red right ankle.[58]

There was suspicion that Asher has assaulted Auryn like keying a car. Why else were her ankles bleeding? Oozing, rather. A tiny intricate web of scratch lines had sprouted from the point of her ankle bones like a slowly evolving tattoo, but the "ink" appeared backlit

---

[58] "Red Right Ankle" by The Decemberists.

behind the pale veil of thin skin, the way blue veins show through, rather than embedded in the visceral canvas like synthetic body art. Marley had developed a somewhat motherly radar for Auryn, taking the wingless under her figurative one. But Asher said, "Angels CAN'T bleed; they're not mortal." That was his defense covering his track marks.

"But 'Remember that the angel cannot be separated from the witness. There is no substantial and concrete evidence save for what the witness saw and felt,' Malcolm Godwin cautions in *Angels: An Endangered Species*, page 15," Marley quoted back at him, turning his own practice back on him, to his hypocritical annoyance. "This is why Asher and Auryn can't get rid of each other," she confided later to Izzy. "They are somewhat attached at the hip; otherwise, she doesn't exist. And it's back to the psych ward for him. They *need* each other for their survival and very existence. So long as they are not free of each other, they are free from society. It's the perfect codependent relationship."

Let It Bleed

I cut myself on you—
    You told me, Let it bleed.
I wanted to get down to the grit of the wound,
    It felt like, Let it bleed.
I wore it like a red badge of courage—
    or was it a scarlet letter?
    By the books, Let it bleed.
Sky came down to mix with earth
    So that I cannot tell the water from the dirt
    Doesn't matter, Let it bleed.
Beatle wisdom rendered me,
    Let it be.

I did a remix of my creed:
    Let it bleed.
Washed my bare feet in thorny stains,
    A ragged bandage Let it bleed.
Put the blood and the bones, the scratches
    and the fibers in a holey bag,
        My own impurities soaked through
        and Let it bleed.
I stitched it up, then ripped you out—
    I Let it bleed.
Because of you, for you, in spite of you—
    I Let it bleed.
Passion made pain feel good at last
    That's why you got to Let it bleed.
This life—it's love and agony
    So Let It Bleed.

One time Asher asked Auryn a question. "Here in some stranger's room, late in the afternoon, what am I doing here at all?"[59] They were lying haphazardly on a pinstriped bedroll on the tenth floor tenement of their rattrap motel. Asher was smoking a bowl, gazing up at a Munch painting on the wall. It was *The Girl and the Heart*, 1899. Auryn was idly picking at the ends of her hair, trying to separate tangled strands. Fine threads of her hair were still attached to his heart – it bled – and hurt, not unlike the scene hanging ominously above their heads. A red-haired woman was pulling frantically at her roots, while a man lay sleeping in the background. Auryn's candy heart went out to the girl, who seemed bound in locks of hair and torment over a regrettable morning after.

"Tell me, as a semi-mortal woman, do you have any

---

[59] John Lennon, "I'm Losing You."

rape fantasies?"

Auryn had a lock of hair between her teeth (she had developed the annoying feminine habit of chewing her hair, but she didn't bite her nails, those razor-sharp things that were more like kitten's claws). She sat up, grabbed his bowl, took a hit, handed it back, then said, "Now, run that by me again?" Being on the street so much, she was picking up a lot of idiomatic.

"You kno-w-w," Asher drew out his words stoned, "*rape* fantasies. Apparently all women have them, according to a story by the acclaimed Margaret Atwood."

"What's it called?"

"'Rape Fantasies.'"

She hesitated on semantics. "Is that a sex fantasy, or a death fantasy?"

God, she was good. You couldn't get anything past her. "Let's find out," he said slyly, more so to see what her reaction would be. He craved a kinky partner.

She didn't move, so he went to the closet and pulled a pillowcase from the top shelf. It was stuffed to the seams like a full laundry bag, but Asher had no intention of airing his dirty laundry. He dumped out a pile of neckties in the middle of the bedroll. All kinds and colors snaked together – conservative stripes and solids to goofy character-themed designs. "Silk won't cut into the skin like rope," he explained. She merely flopped onto her stomach and chewed her hair. He took this for consent, so he gently bent her leg back at the knee and wrapped a scary clown tie around her thigh and ankle, tying them together in a neat knot. He did the same to the other leg, with hardly a sideways glance from his voluntary victim. Then he tied her wrists behind her back, handcuff style, and flipped her over on her back so she could look at him.

She looked like a kitten tangled in a ball of yarn, and totally bored. "Do you trust me?" he asked, heightening the power play.

"Vampires will never hurt you."

"Not if they're all tied up." He casually plucked a stray feather from the crown of her head; there was always some downy thing showing up randomly on her appearance, like she *still* hadn't groomed since the accident. He tickled her bare stomach with it. He realized for the first time she had no belly button. He peered closer, thinking maybe he had missed it. Just smooth, nearly translucent skin, with no evidence that she had ever spent time in a womb, connected to another human being. He let the feather fall.

Following his gaze, she asked a follow-up question: "Do you trust *me*?" He backed off a bit.

"What am I playing with? Fire? Will you melt if you fly too close to the sun, or if I throw a bucket of water on you? Do you even float? Or am I really *just that sick*?" He sank to his knees on the mattress, fingering the feather again.

"Well, I'm no Houdini," she admitted, struggling against the bondage for the first time. That brought a sad smile to his face. "I've got an idea; if you let me go, I can do something that might help you feel better."

As soon as her wrists and ankles were free, she jumped up and grabbed his field coat. She snapped a button off the front then plucked a few strands of hair from her scalp. Finally, she rummaged around the tiny studio until she found a pincushion in the drawer of the antique vanity table. Squinting her eyes, she licked the split ends of her hair and threaded it through the eye of the needle. To Asher's horror, she then placed the coat button over her stomach, trying to gauge accurate placement of a biological navel. "Wait!" Asher cried out as the needle was poised in the air, ready to penetrate. "Are you fucking out of your mind? It's merely a birth defect, a congenital anomaly; of course this isn't the first time you've been bound by another…?"

"You can sew it up but you still see the tear,"[60] she almost sang what he already knew. "And as you can see, I have no scar. I won't even bleed, Asher, don't worry, I'm practically akin to Raggedy Ann." She looked up mischievously. "And, isn't that every guy's fantasy? Limp like a ragdoll. No struggle." And with that, she pierced her papery thin skin through the buttonhole, over and under with the silky red twine, until she had a shiny brown belly button stitched on her abdomen. She tied the final knot and bit off the remaining hair, looking down at herself and admiring her handiwork. Her cut-off tank top showed it off nicely. Asher just sat helpless in the corner, totally defeated.

"Hey, now I could be a Belly Doll," Auryn joked, referencing Izzy and Marley's gothic belly dance troupe. She swung her hips around, sticking out her belly button as she masqueraded toward Asher. He smiled weakly again. He had to admit, she looked cute in her little bloomers, hopping around like that. He regained some interest, and got up from the sidelines to participate again.

"Well, if you can't bleed, maybe you wouldn't mind some metal," he said as he fished around in his rucksack. She had stopped dancing, curious to see what tricks he had in mind this time. He produced a

---

[60] U2, "Sweetest Thing."

shiny pair of handcuffs, real handcuffs like he'd swiped a souvenir from a vacation behind bars. He dangled them in front of her, the metal clinking as it swung on the chains.

"I trust you," she whispered faintly, her eyes wide.

He grabbed her ankles instead of her wrists, and clasped them on. "A bit different than silk ties, isn't it, my little voodoo doll?" he teased. She kicked at him playfully, but he jumped away and she ended up yanking on the right cuff harder without any resistance to break the motion until she got to the end of the chain. A simple law of physics caught her red handed. Or red ankled, rather. The cold metal edge cut into her ankle bone, and a delayed reaction to this knee-jerk reflex showed up drunkenly, like an impaired driver hitting the brakes too late. A thin red line made its way down the angle jutting out from her instep. It was so tiny, like a piece of thread, but then it multiplied, branching out from the original cut in all directions, mapping her foot as if there was indeed a circulation system hidden under that translucent wrapping paper.

Asher looked at her in astonishment. "I thought…" then he sniffed the air. It smelled faintly of alcohol, or something equally intoxicating. He looked down at her red right ankle. Then he got down on his knees and bent his head and licked her wounds. It was a rare position of subordination on his part, the sadist bowing to the masochist. She was bleeding something other than blood; something not water based, like human blood, but sharing more chemical properties with iodine or wine. He twisted his head to the side so he could gaze up at her. "Vampires will never hurt *you*," he repeated, "but I…I could get drunk off you." Like a ravenous wolf he licked her wounds dry.

She lay there and let him, but the tension crackling between them on an invisible live wire was almost more than she could bear. Something so sensual, so visceral, so alluring, so dangerous. She begged him to unlock the handcuffs; she was afraid of what she would do if she let this go on indefinitely. When she was free, she rubbed her injured ankle. It had purple stains and tiny red track marks. Asher, too, was overcome by the reality of everything. "So much for fantasies, of the sexual or morbid orientation," he said cynically, sitting down beside her on the floor.

"Now I wonder if there really is a difference." She let her words fall, staring straight ahead into space, and then slowly turned her head to look at him. *Whether it's a man or a manuscript – angel or demon, they may just be one and the same, and the difference may not make that much difference.* She finished her thought privately. They sat there for a long time, till shadows fell across the walls advancing dusk through the cracks in the drawn shades.

Finally, she got up and gathered up her things. "Where are you going?" The tinge of anxiety in his voice didn't go unnoticed.

"I think I need to go elsewhere," she answered vaguely.

"Why? I thought you wanted to be with me."

"I just need to be by myself for a while."

In her mind, it went like this: she shacked up at the YWCA after burning her bed and getting evicted for damages she couldn't pay – she sought refuge in a women's shelter after contemplating suicide, setting herself on fire *sans* insurance – *he is my bad habit, my pre-existing condition that renders me one of the millions of uninsured*[61] – doing heroin and nearly overdosing on

115

Asher's watch…she disappeared off the clock.

So there was talk of an "abusive relationship" among Auryn's wingéd people. It was criminal as a bullet through the brain, according to Halo 14; they shook their 14-karat gold encrusted heads at such disgrace that something mortal about her attached itself to something immortal about him, hanging in limbo on a loose nine-inch-nail misshapen by chaos of well-seeming forms – *love is an alcoholism to her, only it's a boy, not a beer.* This speculation was mostly attributed to Poe, with a little help from The Killers: "Somebody told me you had a boyfriend, looked like a girlfriend. Where were you last year?"

Asher kept remembering things, though he wasn't really sure if they happened. Perhaps they were dream memories. Except that, he hadn't slept in almost two weeks. *I've been sleepin' so strange at night, side effects they don't advertise.*[62] All the contacts with the spirit world he ever had in recent years were the hallucinations and delusions he suffered, driving him to do what no one would understand.

Artists are very nasty people. / We prefer to see what they make, not actually, what they do.

Except maybe, an ethereal being about as real as the ones he encountered when he was having an episode during the heights of creative output, scribbling furiously while dead fans screamed in his ringing ears, *write faster! write faster!* Like, an angel, said the Parenthetical Voice, *if such things existed beyond the blank page.* He was manic to find her.

---

[61] This book was written pre-Obamacare.
[62] "We Are Nowhere and It's Now" by Conor Oberst of Bright Eyes.

ASHES TO ANGELS

I was standing
You were there
Two worlds collided—

"They [in this novel, Asher's screaming 'fans' in his head] spoke of being pinned to the chimney as if by two great beating wings, and of the slight blond fuzz above her upper lip that felt like plumage"[63]—a symptom of cutaneous porphyria – the extra fine hair growth on the forehead.

I told you that
we could fly
'cause we all have wings—
but some of us don't know why![64]

Everybody was an out of body experience. He saw himself everywhere, standing on street corners, huddled in doorways watching the rain, lighting up in dark alleys. If all life was just perception, then when you ceased to perceive, how would you know you were dead? And, if you don't know when you're dead, then who's to say we aren't all walking around in some afterlife *right now?*

That there
That's not me
I'm not here
this isn't happening
In a little while
I'll be gone
The moment's already passed
   yeah, it's gone...[65]

---

[63] (Borrowed from) The Virgin Suicides, page 148.
[64] "Never Tear Us Apart" by INXS.
[65] Radiohead, "How to Disappear Completely."

This had been happening a lot lately, his mind becoming surreal. It seemed to fan out from his body, like a six-wingéd figment of this involuntary state, alternative half-consciousness, into an *other*world for a significant length of time. He would have to discuss this with his therapist. It must be a complication of his split condition, otherwise known as "alterations in relatedness" to The Lost Generation in their existential exodus to the post-modern plague: *Jesus Christ, it was like thirteenth century Angel Fever, the greatest cause of atheism in the world today, and what an unbelieving world finds unbelievable. The mania was too early seen unknown, and known too late!* "Two halves are equal / a cross between two evils." Half-Jack had been haunting him all through his twenties, and it wasn't an enviable lot.

ASHES TO ANGELS

Chapter Thirteen

The Anti-Saint Valentine's Day Massacre

In the National Violence Against Women Survey, approximately 25% of
I'm trying. to let you know just how much
women said they were raped and/or physically assaulted by a current or
you mean to me. and after. all the things we
former spouse, cohabitating partner, or date in their lifetimes.[66]
put each other through. Said the Demolition Lovers. of My Chemical Romance.

On Valentine's Day, Asher sent a package to the shelter, trying to retrieve Auryn like personal effects in the Lost-and-Found. That was the letter scrawled on the notebook paper tucked inside the V-day card. The V-day card said this:

---

[66] As printed in the "Violence Against Women and Girls" fact sheet of <u>The Vagina Monologues</u> program published for a college theater adaptation.

NATALIE MCCOLLUM

My Bloody Valentine,

I want you
to wear this
when I kill you.

♥

Ash

Inside the box were a dozen black roses and a kinky piece of lingerie. It was black, and lacy, and binding. The delicately folded tissue paper was deep purple. Almost the color of ultra violet rays or merlot wine or whatever an angel bleeds on the color spectrum.

Auryn looked up from the gift of dalliance and dainties, unsure of what to say to her uninvited gentleman caller. "Like anyone worthy," she finally breathed, "I am flattered by your fascination with me."[67]

Asher grinned discreetly when he caught her vapid form through the crack in the doorway spilling out bathroom light: "She wears my love like a see-through dress,"[68] he thought; this was so cruel. He left her after claiming, "I Kissed a Drunk Girl."[69] She pushed him back with both hands: "But THIS – is not allowed! You're uninvited." The room was dark; the little bathroom cubicle was shadowy with the vanishing effects of vampires. After a steamy shower, there was a lingering fog on the medicine cabinet mirror, creeping slanted toward the lower left corner, where there was still clarity enough to see the face in the mirror that was not her own reflection. There were

---

[67] "Uninvited" by Alanis Morissette.
[68] U2, "So Cruel"
[69] Something Corporate.

tiny flecks of rusty-brownish blood on the toilet seat and in the hand sink, but – *it's not her blood!* A voice dripped from the faucet, which seemed to be leaking someone's purple-tinted blood: "...[I]t's not wooden stakes that kill vampires. It's all the emotional baggage and letdowns they have to carry around for century after century."[70] She recoiled gracefully at how life supplied the reality to the fiction, but not without a flutter of her heart in lieu of deposed wings. Bloody Mary's arrival, prefaced by her voice out-of-body, hung on six words waiting for breath not her own.

"Bloody Mary."

"Bloody Mary."

"Bloody Mary." (3x)

Auryn looked in the cracked mirror and said it three times.

Broken inside: Auryn, in a fine frenzy, snatched up the half-drunk bottle of Vampire brand merlot and sent it flying across the little studio to the opposite wall behind the bed, where it hit the unframed looking-glass hanging in shards on a nail above the wrought-iron bedpost. Shaking and sobbing, she watched the long red curvy tendrils run down the stripped wall as from a flesh wound. The stain drizzled down the peeling yellow wallpaper with frayed edges like a pair of fungus-infected overgrown fingernails curling at the tips, now painted red with the smell of alcohol wafting from a drug-store nail polish. It spilled from the mouth of the torn paper to the roses strewn on the

---

[70] Haunted on vamps, page 142.

floor, tossed aside in a fit of rage when she first shattered the mirror with her fist. The moving stains synchronized with her saltless tears (characteristic of non-carbon-based life forms) and the rain on the window from which Adia watched. With palms pressed flat against the pane outside, Adia's blue lips moved to the beat of Auryn's every act:

"Well I couldn't tell you why she felt that way, she felt it every day. And I couldn't help her, I just watched her make the same mistakes again."

Maybe it was the poor lighting; maybe it was the way the shadows played with false impressions and transposed reality; either way, Auryn failed to notice the ghostlike figure whose peppermint-stick bones impressed upon the window like a fossil. The black roses turned their true color now, classic, clichéd, and darkly romantic. *"Like a bed of roses, there's a dozen reasons in this gun."*[71] Now entering a state of mental vertigo, flitting back and forth between her perceptions of Asher the predator and Asher the person, Auryn tore at fine threads of her hair[72] and spun around sporadically in convulsive pirouettes like demented ballerina. As a grand finale to this spastic choreography, she tripped up to the crooked cracked mirror, where upon arrival at this bewitched location, a false calm beset her when accosted by her split image. The reflection of her spirit troubled her. "The difference between how you look and how you see

---

[71] My Chemical Romance, "Demolition Lovers."

[72] See Munch's painting *Ashes*, 1896: "Fine threads of her hair are still attached to his heart – it bleeds – and hurts as an eternally open wound." Quoted in <u>Emunch: Words and Images of Edvard Munch</u> by Bente Torjusen.

ASHES TO ANGELS

yourself is enough to kill most people," a line from <u>Haunted</u> did just that. All that appeared was a fossilized skeletal imprint not unlike the negatives produced in a roll of film: the soul-less were unphotographable. "And maybe the reason vampires don't die is because they can never see themselves in photographs or mirrors."[73] Her Brain Trust was a library of synapses overdosed on fiction. Not quite a vampire, the closest thing to a mortal's claim on immortality was her wings, so they showed up instead, one in each half of the mirror. Her bare shoulders shook at the symmetry; the scar down her spine curled like a burnt tendril of paper. "You can sew it up but you still see the scar."[74] Desperate for a body image, she resorted to the ultimate taboo:

"Bloody Mary."
"Bloody Mary."
Pause.
"Bloody Mary."

"What's wrong, what's wrong, now," crooned Adia at the window, straining to see. "Too many too many problems. Don't know where she *be*longs, where she belongs."

Auryn's attempt to force mortality by necromancing her dead relative failed, of course, because as a supernatural she was safe from the otherwise certain death attached to this superstition. In the cat fight that ensued, it became evident to the naked human eye at the window that nobody's home:

"Her feelings she hides
Her dreams she can't find

---

[73] <u>Haunted</u> by Chuck Palahniuk, page 144.
[74] U2, "The Sweetest Thing."

She's losing her mind
She's falling behind
She can't find her place
She's losing her faith
She's falling from grace
She's all over the place!"[75]

"Mary, Queen of Scots!" Adia's eyes grew wide and then she slumped down under the gutter as the needle struck blue. She later assumed that whatever she had witnessed was just part of a heroin trip.

If you or someone you know has experienced violence in the United States, please call one of the following numbers:

National Domestic Violence Hotline: 800.799.7233
Rape, Abuse & Incest National Network: (800) 656-HOPE
National Victim Center: 800.394.2255[76]

---

[75] From the music video, "Nobody's Home" by Avril Lavigne.
[76] As printed in the "Violence Against Women and Girls" fact sheet in The Vagina Monologues program published for a college theater adaptation.

ASHES TO ANGELS

Chapter Fourteen

The Busted Lovers

It was about that time the paranoia set in. Shortly following the Ides of March. Tax season.

"The government is out to get us," Asher shook his head as he shuffled through his mail, stopping suspiciously at an official envelope containing documents. "Yep, they keep tabs on *every fucking citizen*. They have files, they have records, right down to your grocery spending. 'We'd like to know a little bit about you for our files / We'd like to help you learn to help yourself' – so goes their song and dance. It's true," he insisted, looking up at Auryn's impressionable face. "It's the national chains that leak; like Kroger? The Man is the government's informer. 'So here's to you, Mrs. Robinson, Jesus loves you more than you will know'...I'm going on a hunger strike." He slid the tax form out of its envelope and did a quick retinal scan of its contents. "Um, I'm thinking noooh," as he flippantly checked the "Deceased" box next to his name. Auryn, peering over his shoulder, grew wide-eyed.

"You're faking your own death?"

"It's better this way," Asher replied coolly, as if he had done this every year for the last ten. "I don't want the government knowing my whereabouts – they have too much info on people. It only gives them more power to abuse. I'm safer if they just believe I'm dead." With that he sealed the return envelope with his own spit and tossed it casually in the mailbox on the door. "Come, let's have a smoke."

They shuffled down the street in no particular direction, dodging glances while masquerading in the sunshine and dodging cars while jaywalking the intersections. They wound up randomly on the train tracks of an overpass spray-painted with graffiti art. The railroad bridge cut diagonally across the Parkway, creating asymmetrical street patterns full of one-ways and dead ends. The Lower East Side was the trashy end of town, the creative womb of the artists' hub, a breeding ground for poison ivy, and a litterbug to the womb ecology hotly contested by feminist eco-terrorists and angry vegetarians.

[Ani Difranco's song, "Both Hands" with its line of "graffiti on my body" plays in her head.]

"'Here comes that story again, all about that television show'"[77]…the lyric, invoked for the purpose of referencing the movie they had just been watching back at the Commune, was the only preface she gave to what she did next. Standing there on the bridge, she grabbed his hand and discreetly drew a razor blade across the palm, then her own, then quickly clapped their hands together and smeared his into hers, as she hung her head over the railing to hear the wind blow.

"Damnit, what the fuck are you doing to me!"

---

[77] Joan Osborne, "Let's Just Get Naked."

ASHES TO ANGELS

yelped Asher as he flinched in surprise. "What are you, some kind of natural born killer?" Auryn was now kissing his hand, licking his blood, trying to mix her DNA with his to fertilize her own mortality.

But his blood only left a stain on her hand, like graffiti on her body. She had nothing to give back, no blood to exchange with Ash. As a half-vampire, it seemed she could only take life from him, not give it. They couldn't even be blood-lovers. Full vampires were luckier. At least they were once human; though turned, they still retained more human characteristics – including wounds with the capacity to bleed – than angels, who had no previous carbon-based life form to resource. Thus, the "compound," being organic, was merely a suspension of incompatible elements – wedding his blood to her open wound was like mixing oil and water.

Drops of his blood and her tears fell over the railing as she leaned her temple on their clasped hands and comforted herself with a ballad that seemed to swell on an updraft carrying a chorus of children's voices from the murk somewhere under the bridge:

> *Down in the valley,*
> *valley so low*
> *Hang your head over,*
> *hear the wind blow.*
> *Hear the wind blow, love,*
> *hear the wind blow;*
> *Hang your head over,*
> *hear the wind blow....*[78]

Wandering Womb: Their unborn children of a lesser

---

[78] Christy by Catherine Marshall, page 168.

god[79] would just like to say—

The FBI estimates that only 37% of all rapes are reported to the police. U.S. Justice statistics are even lower, with only 26% of all rapes or attempted rapes being reported to law enforcement officials.[80]

> Daughter of a Poison Love
> Do not weep for Thorns
> Suicide isn't just Death
> It is Love too.
> ~Gráinne, a cross between two evils.

Two worlds collided. However, if the bloodlines could mix, if the wires crossed in foreplay, then these two hybrids – one named Gráinne and one named Kieran – would be the offspring of a human and a half-blood. *'Cause we all have wings – but some of us don't know why!*[81]

---

[79] The title of the play by Mark Medoff and 1986 movie comes from a line in Alfred, Lord Tennyson's Idylls of the King.
[80] "Violence Against Women and Girls" again.
[81] "Never Tear Us Apart" by INXS.

ASHES TO ANGELS

Chapter Fifteen

The Prison Diaries
<u>What They Did</u>.

"Busting up a Starbucks…We slept in Sundays"

"Tomorrow we can drive around this town, let the cops chase us around…Tell me, Do you think it would be all right, if I could just crash here tonight? See I'm not fit for driving, anyway I got no place else to go…You know, it might not be that bad, You were the best I ever had – hey Jealousy." Faking his own death on a tax form seemed like the perfect disappearing act. But The Man and his white-coated henchmen were too keen even for the most cunning mad genius. Especially when that mad genius already had a psychiatric history on the books. Any "normal" criminal would have done time for fraud, but this particular case was found "not guilty by reason of insanity" because – who writes himself off dead on a tax form? The Feds scratched their heads for weeks. Unbeknownst to Auryn, he sat in jail for exactly 24 hours – *and at the gate of the Embassy, our hands met through the bars, how I longed to hear you say* – until the cops determined he was a suicide risk – *no, they cannot catch me now!* – (this was the court's exasperated interpretation of a single check mark in the "Deceased" box on Form 1040EZ) and they shipped him off to incarceration of a different nature: the state ward. *We will escape somehow.* At least, this is how Auryn heard it months later when he showed up asking if he could crash in her hostel room one night drunk on Gin Blossoms.

She let him in through the bathroom window.

"What the fuck are you doing here?! Where have you been?! What's happened to you?!" She eyed his hospital garb suspiciously. He looked like an ex-con busted out of prison. The thin cotton pajama pants hung loosely at his waist, drawstring untied, and the mint-green shirt formed a lopsided v at the neck, revealing briar scratches on his shoulder.

"What do you mean, 'What's happened to you'? Like you weren't there. I mean, thanks for the grand angel dust bust, har-har, but you didn't have to go tripping off once I hit ground." He dusted himself off. He had managed to salvage his own sneakers, probably the only remaining article of clothing on him that wasn't hospital-issue.

"What! I didn't bail you out. I've been here, the whole time, looking for my wings. Poe still has them. I couldn't fly you over yesterday without my wings, now, could I?" It was a weird role reversal to play the part of logic. Not that he was the star of that role, either.

"I swear it, baby! An angel on angel dust came up to my window on the seventh floor, you see, flew in and sprinkled faerie dust on me, fresh good stuff, like she'd just scored an eighth off Peter Pan, and took it straight to my cell and rescued me from that loony slammer. Did you know they tried to poison me in

ASHES TO ANGELS

there? Tried to put it in my food. Like I don't know what lithium does to the kidneys. If I lose a kidney, would you donate me one of your kidneys? Well, would you? I mean, I'd give you my last cigarette if you'd love me for it; would you give me your last kidney if I told you I loved you?"

Auryn's thoughts were flying so fast, she could barely focus on his own choppy stream of conscious. Kidney, last kidney, what are you *talking* about? "I'm not sure a human-immortal transplant would work; I don't think our organs are an exact match...." All she could think about was this wingéd rescuer he claimed had assisted him AMA. Either he was deluded by his own hallucination or...*Poe??* Surely not; why would she help the Other Side? Helping Auryn indirectly by helping Asher didn't fit. Reuniting her sister with her delinquent lover seemed contrary to the demon's own interests. Motive, motive, what was the motive? *Every human motive is selfish.* Poe could fake it for the papers but she was no human. *A fate worse.* Auryn nervously obsessed over this strange development while Asher rambled on about the latest outrages and injustices dished out to the inmates of the institution. She looked him over thoroughly. He certainly looked like he'd taken a good fall. But from the seventh story? As a mortal housed in the fragile human body, he should have broken his neck. She shook her head; nothing made sense in this upside down world. Perhaps she had fallen the wrong direction. The number of ways to fall from the sky was as limitless as the sky itself. Perhaps she was the one upside down.

NATALIE MCCOLLUM

Chapter Sixteen

"St. Teresa Came to Me in Dreams"

What They Saw.

Auryn crosses *The Scream* from de Stijl, the Munch Museum in Oslo, Norway, where Edvard Munch's painting was stolen. It turned up at The Sideshow at The Murk, a big old abandoned opera house used for art shows now. The studio apartments above it were bands' storage space covered in graffiti like "Emo kids do it better." Recovered by police, by undisclosed means, on 31 August 2006, *The Scream* along with *Madonna,* female nude in charcoal, survived "The woman who gives herself away – and obtains a madonna's painful beauty—"

"Excuse me, miss, but – well, you were standing so still, I thought you were a mannequin." A hunched old man had hobbled up to her while she was staring at a wooden post upon which Asher, the featured artist, had written lines and lines of continuous poetry all around the structure, all the way up to the ceiling support. She slowly tore her attention from the spiraling poetry. At her unfocused gaze, he explained further, "I mean you didn't look real, from a distance, that is. These old eyes, not to be trusted. Optical illusions, that's about all they're good for." He chuckled unsteadily. Strange compliment.

He was a Friar Lawrence, of sorts. They met him at the art show. He was admiring some sixteenth-century Dutch-inspired morbid religious work – acrylic on canvas. You know the icon that's all bloody with thorns and the Jesus Freak looking all anorexic and hanging pathetically off a tree like a limp fish. The visual that's supposed to inspire guilt and self-mutilation. Cults dig that stuff. The local priest offered to hide the lovers-on-the-run in his country abode, for a little rehabilitation of their rotted souls, at least until the media coverage died down a bit and people pretty much forgot the tax scandal and gravitated back to dull normality. Their strange benefactor's name was Father "Romeo bon Jovi," according to the slip of paper Asher read like a ransom note to Auryn. He looked at her for gut reaction. "So, what do you think? Sounds a bit too charitable to be trusted, but the man seems harmless." He went to grab the ringing phone in the next room.

Auryn felt her scissored wings hang in the balance.

Asher came back in. The phone cord trailed him like a dungeon chain, twisted around his wrist like a manacle. "The priest is on the phone, your mother disowned you," he stated darkly. "I'd go with the Jesus Freak and boo this staged Lilith Affair." The receiver dangled off its hook. The line lost its connection. The dial tone droned on, each telltale beat framed by its own dead giveaway, like a tape-recorded conversation between victim and criminal bleeding evidence in lieu of a forced confession.

NATALIE MCCOLLUM

* * *

Mister Father Romeo bon Jovi's summer house was actually a quaint country villa shrouded in the overhang of a lost city from another history book, another fairy tale, another blank page. Its stale mysticism hung like heavy fog in every nook and gable and archway, defying the intruder to disturb its hundred-year slumber. The entire structure felt like an exhumed coffin.

Father Romeo bon Jovi claimed to be an artist, of sorts, "more a part-time dabbler," he smiled crookedly, and he was absolutely struck catatonic by Auryn's angelic quality. "You would be the perfect model for a painting of an angel I've been wanting to do," he crooned thickly. Auryn could practically feel the maple syrup running out of his tap, all viscous and sticky. "Tell me, have you ever sat for an artist, my dear?"

He even offered to pay her for the sitting.

"Do it," Asher nudged, "we need the money." Auryn didn't really need the prompt; sharing genes with a randy demon meant she also shared a little flare for exhibition. She was curious to discover her potential, but she felt oddly uncomfortable with this so-called priest. As the Sixth Angel, her sixth sense could read people like a vampire can smell blood under the skin.

"The Scream" hung in agony above the actual bodies, the highest art forms, now committing performance art on a rickety bed frame for a stage.

> *Burning, burning, time keeps turning*
> *and the only way to take it back*
> *not even poets have the knack*

ASHES TO ANGELS

According to medieval magick, I prick
my finger and the world sleeps
a hundred years, suppressing a hundred fears
of what it's too late to cure.

"Is that painting on the wall AUTHENTIC?! What's it doing here?" she gasped in between her own screams of agonized ecstasy.

Asher looked up from his pleasure, distractedly, but he got a rise out of the implication of what he saw. He whistled at the sheer mockery of it. "The *Priest* stole *The Scream*? Our Munch thief is Father Romeo bon Jovi?"

Suddenly he leapt out of bed. "So, the Catholic church owns everything, does it? Well see how the tables turn. Looks like I can pay my taxes now, a modest exchange: one whole thievery corporation." He was pulling on his old gray acid-wash jeans.

"What are you going to do?" Auryn couldn't guess his next move.

"Do you realize a tip-off means pay day? Here is our latest source of income just walked in our door. Or we walked through his, rather." He grabbed his wallet, cigarettes, and keys off the ornate dresser. "Stay here and make sure he does the same. I'm off to inform the police we have their guy. We're gonna be rich, babe! Just wait and see."

"What if he asks where you are?"

"Say I went into the woods to meditate and...pray, yes, throw that in there, to *pray* to ahhh, Buddha."

"That's a different religion."

Asher shrugged. "Buddha, Mohammed, Saint so-and-so, Prophet what's-his-face. Same difference. Just a bunch of dead guys. He'll know what you mean." He was climbing out the bathroom window. "Shhhh," he put his finger to his lips. There was a wild gleam behind his eyes, emanating from somewhere way back, behind the pupil and iris and retina, even. A light invisible to the naked (human) eye, always there on the color spectrum, at once all colors and the absence of color. It was the color of the soul. Something so integral, there was no finding it. Like her wings. And then he dropped to the ground and his frenzied little face disappeared.

Auryn sat in bed a minute, wondering what she should do. Should she go find the fraud? Perhaps she could engage him in the studio, where he needed to finish the painting. Better to pull a *femme fatale* on him, before he made a Madonna out of her.

ASHES TO ANGELS

Chapter Seventeen

"I Kissed a Drunk Girl"[82]

Mister Father Romeo bon Jovi's shrine was a good place to get drunk. It had *a lot* of wine.

> *Dear World,*
> *(love letter/suicide note continued,*
> *thwarted though my attempt may be.*
> *Call it poetry.)*
> *I cried myself to sleep last night —*
> *It's just another day in hell.*
> *I can't seem to escape this reality,*
> *It clings to me like fiction.*

But it was perfectly acceptable to drink alone.

"Have you come here for forgiveness? Have you come to raise the dead?"[83]

Suddenly, she stopped short, her hand still in the open door of the wine cabinet. She slowly turned around to face her snarky intruder.

"Have you come here to play Jesus — to the lepers

---

[82] Something Corporate
[83] "One" lyrics by U2.

in your head?!"

She covered her ears, spun around in a fine frenzy, "Noooooo!! I am not guided by voices, I have no lepers in my head!"

Father bon Jovi had her note in his hand. It bookmarked a certain place in a paperback novel, from which he threw words back in her face. "Suicide, as a mortal sin, is a matter of intent," he said, looking up from reading. "Adia, Veronika – it's very difficult to know what was in those girls' hearts. What they were really trying to do."[84] He stepped closer, into the light. "However, for practical considerations, I'd advise against committing the ultimate dark act. You don't want to become your sister. You'll end up right back where you – she – started, and this time you've got no wings to pawn." She put her hand to her mouth and screamed. The bottle of wine came crashing to the floor. *The Scream* hung in agony above her own. "Funny, what you make of the afterlife: you'd sell your own soul to bust up immortality and crash the worldly party – it's like you've died and gone to heaven, without the awkward 'dying' part," he smirked.

This sinister clown, more akin to a court jester than a priest, moved closer, breathing on her neck as he dropped his final line: "You've come halfway to hell by the time you reach this planet, and you're half vixen by DNA. Welcome to the world. C'mon, waif. Quit the human race before it quits you."

"Joker! Sick bastard!" She lunged at him to claw his neck with her razor-sharp kitten nails but he

---

[84] In the words of his fictional counterpart, Father Moody of <u>The Virgin Suicides</u> pages 37-38, by Jeffrey Eugenides. Adia and Veronika added to the text.

ASHES TO ANGELS

overpowered her and caught her by the wrist instead.

She gasped out from behind the hand that clapped over her mouth, "Now you've gone and done it, hope you're happy! (In the county penitentiary.) It serves you right, for kissing little girls."[85]

Drunk Auryn then proceeded to leave a frantic raving message on Asher's phone:

"Instead of committing suicide,
I slept with you."[86]
But there really wasn't much choosing to do.
It was not one or the other;
I downed my shots of you together.
A mixed drink called fire-over-ice,
An opportunity to cut and slice.
My wrists held down I could not fake;
And afterward you say I am just –
your drunken mistake.

Two years ago you wrote about me:
Forgot to censor x-rated feelings
I wasn't supposed to see.
I called you on it,
when our future was at stake;
You sloughed it off like a hangover,
"It was just a drunken mistake."

But the night I knew you the first time
I thought you had changed your mind;
I gave it to you because I thought
My second chance was on the line.

---

[85] "Missed Me" by the Dresden Dolls

[86] Original version by MJ White: "instead of killing myself I slept with you." Her line of poetry is quoted here with permission.

She said,
"I don't wanna LOSE your love tonight…"
He said,
"I just wanna *USE* your love tonight!"

But your addictions too early seen unknown,
And known too late!
That's all I ever am to you,
your slutty angel
And *perfect drunken mistake.*

    Sobbing, she pawed her way over the bed sheets tangled up in clothes shop-lifted from around the world, and dragged herself across scattered poems on loose pages littering the bed. She dropped to the floorboards and scuffed on her knees to the barren corner 'neath the window. Curled up under the dewy windowpane, she lunged for the phone on the barstool in said corner and dialed Asher by the light of a single bleak star:
[Ringing]
[Ringing]
He picked up mid-shriek.
[Pause]
"Hullo?"
"Asher?" she whispered weakly, with tears dripping from her voice not her eyes.
"What."
"Can you," [sob]
"What is it, Auryn?"
"I miss – need – want…you," she choked haltingly.
"Honey, why you calling me so late?"
She choked on words, and so choked up none.
"Honey, why you crying, is everything okay? It's

ASHES TO ANGELS

kinda hard to talk right now—" he glanced furtively at the bedroom door ajar— "My girl's in the next room—"

"What? Where are you? I thought you went to tip off the cops."

"I ran into Raven. It's nothing. Go on."

She told him about the priest. What he had said. The Big Reveal. "Half underwater / I'm half my mother's daughter / a fraction's left up to dispute."[87]

He drew in a sharp breath. "So this pervy poser is mixed up with an international ring of art thieves? I wonder what other black market schemes he's masterminded? Prostitution? Blood money? Armageddon? Perhaps the next nuclear catastrophe is simply burning a hole in this dealer's pocket, waiting to be bought and sold under the table."

She nodded into the phone. "The whole collection – half-off the price they're asking, in the halfway house of ill repute."[88]

Then he sobered. "Wait – don't hang up." She was traumatized.

"Half accidental
half pain
full instrumental
It's half biology
and half corrective surgery gone wrong."[89]

He delayed her drunken dial with a song to soften the blow:

"Hold on, little girl,
Show me what he's done to you:
Stand up, little girl,
The game of love can't be that bad

---

[87] "Half Jack" by the Dresden Dolls
[88] See above.
[89] See above.

When it's through, it's through…"[90]

He pictured Raven and he fancied Auryn—

"Sometimes I wish she was you."

"Ash? I miss you."

"And yes, I dreamt of you too."

"I guess we never really moved on."

"Can you—"

"Can you come get me?"

He sighed, and his hand gripping the receiver went limp as his inhibitions. "Girl, you make it hard to be faithful with the lips of an angel…"[91]

"I need someone tonight," she cried at last. *And I can only hope that his feelings get in the way.*

"I'm on my way."

> *Build up your confidence, so you can be on top for once!*
> *Wake up! Who cares about little boys that talk too much.*
> *When it's through, it's through.*[92]

Confession, 2 of 3--

Auryn speaks:

12 o'clock, noon. I just step out of the shower, towel wrapped around me, steam rising from the claw-footed porcelain bathtub where I tried to wash away my virgin hangover like the rest of the wine I poured down the drain last night I was too drunk to finish on my first intoxication; it ran like blood from wounds that didn't bleed. Some of it still clings like rain

---

[90] Mr. Big, "To Be with You"
[91] "Lips of an Angel" by Hinder.
[92] Mr. Big, "To Be with You"

droplets to the remaining scattered fake-dyed petals in a station of the metro: The apparition of these faces in the crowd; Petals on a wet, black bough. I don't know, it must have been the roses…

I become increasingly aware of a soft rapping on the door. They aren't using the brass knocker. I stand there frozen, wondering how long "they" have been calling. I wonder if I should delay gratification even more while I paw through my closet for something, *anything*, decent to present myself to this unannounced caller, but at the last minute I am so curiously terrified of what I will find when I open the door, that I cinch my towel tighter and fling open the door like I will soon do with my scanty garb. I expect the postman looking for an affair, or a bored neighbor who's strayed in a fit of wanderlust, but I spook at the blackened-out memory that all comes back to me of precisely what led me to this wretched state the morning after my first time with alcohol…he stands there and doesn't even have a chance to say it best when he says nothing at all, before I slam the door in his face with a rush of adrenaline that makes me stronger than my means. I stand there behind the closed door, shaking under my skin that has become the wet towel. I am both appalled at his audacity to actually *respond* to the drunk-n-dial – *can't he tell a sober sentence from an incoherent slur?* – and his sense of credulity that sacks my own, like the sacking of Rome. It strikes me in that moment behind closed doors that he has finally bought into the whole Kafka propaganda to the effect that, *When the Angel of the Lord comes to you, do not tell him how you feel. His feelings are so far superior to anything you could ever know. But show him some simple **thing**, and he will stand amazed.* At this revelation, I slowly crack open the door at the summons of his second knock, even more fearful of what awaits me this time, but unable to stage even passive resistance in my state of wild shock.

Tap, tap.

[Clears throat.] "Who is it?"

"Ash."

"How do I know you're not some impersonator rapist or stalker?"

"You fucking just saw me!"

"That sounds kinda stalkerish."

"Excuse me, miss, but way back when, I do believe it was YOU who fell on your ass out of the blue as a sorry excuse for a pick-up line!"

"Oh, please, that's the oldest one in the stalker book!"

Pause. Thoughtful consideration. Then, "There's a book?"

"Sure. The Book of Stalkers. I'll let you borrow it."

[Scuffing noise outside.]

"Well, whatever the case may be, I'll have you know one thing: The people who will kill you are the ones who KNOW you. You will *never* be murdered by a stranger."

I was getting restless as the blind interview went on either side of the door, a parlay of formalities making a mockery of animal mating ritual. As the talk show hostess, I decided to turn this blind date into something a little more interesting.

"You want me? Fucking come on and break the door down,"[93] I tease him in with a catcall prelude to my curtain call. The striptease is about to get busted.

---

[93] Radiohead, "Talk Show Host"

ASHES TO ANGELS

I let the door swing the rest of the way open on its own, a morbid long drawn-out creak extending from its hinges like the breaking of bones the breaking of bread before wine. As if the first time, I re-engage the shock and I drop the towel, the whole length of it, completely unaware of my complete naked skin contrasting his complete clothed body, all the way up from his black scuffed work boots, his fatigue pants, and faded green field jacket with the frayed cuffs.

"What's this?"

"A poem."

"On an orange?"

"For breakfast. I wrote it for you."

"It's noon."

"Just read."

Through the smeared scrawl on the rough rind, one line I can clearly distinguish sticks out to me: *You are beautiful when you breathe.*[94]

"Eh?" Raised eyebrow.

"What do you think?"

"That's kind of creepy."

"You wrote it first, my Muse." This accompanied by a sickly sugary grin.

I do not even feel the towel around my ankles, do not even register the fact that he has never seen me so vulnerable, yet so aggressive as a pelted animal not-quite-dead as I lunge toward him and kiss him furiously though still furious at him. I don't know what I am doing any more than naked Eve and Adam, my mom's first lover in the estranged entrapments of an arranged marriage that she rejected, rebelled against,

---

[94] "Based on a true story." Line lifted verbatim from report of an actual orange with love poem presented to original poet's love interest, as quoted by ex-boyfriend of said poet.

and defaulted on in favor of an incubus, the love story told as a horror story and horror story told as a love story that spawned me and Poe, – *our father who art in hell.*

[*I heard the dude blamed the chick and the chick blamed the snake, and I heard they were naked when they got busted—.*][95]

As for Asher, his eyes slick me over once, from the shoulders in a downward spiral then rise like steam from the towel curdled at my feet. He doesn't protest, which is poetry to me. He can feel my rage in that kiss, that soft longed-for kiss that lifts us above the torn-out page of a stolen magazine, a shop-lifter's romance in which this passion is a plagiarism, and he is gently pushing me down the long hallway, it takes us 5 ½ minutes to get all the way down, until we reach the door frame to my yet darkened bedroom where we cannot see out the window without our shadows getting in the way. Like the Demian sending his little bitches down into level 6 of hell, the Sixth Angel banish'd to the City of Dis, he only has to nudge my white shadow's shoulder blade his nails grazing it like flint striking flesh to get me covered up wrapped up inside the darkness of a protruding thorny heart, wherefore he descends after me in a sleight of supernatural I never saw coming on to me, putting off his mortality like clothes and *we both go down together.*

A Defence of Poetics[96]--
Asher speaks:

---

[95] The Hold Steady.
[96] A title of an essay by Percy Bysshe Shelley.

ASHES TO ANGELS

She was beautiful and veiny. As I watched the towel slip from her shoulders in genuine shock and loss of self-awareness, I saw an intricate spider web of mute vascular blue play show-and-tell with the light refracting and contracting and doing other strange things underneath her near translucent skin. The network of delicate thread-bare veins sprawled outward from the center of her chest, like it was growing off the precarious crevice that formed the dent where her two rib cages bridged her heart, and from there the spiny green-blue then reproduced itself in a repeating geometric pattern betraying the infinity of Pi to a cracked code, reduced to a simple brittle crack habit splayed in de-oxygenated vessels over her pale breasts all the way up to her neck and around her back. She was the x-ray of a vampire with all 216 pressure points and erogenous zones mapped out to insufferable numeric perfection.

                    Significant Layer

                    my uncensored place,
                    idle as the wilds

              i know a place where i go
              when i want to be your POW
              --missing in action with you

                  it's hand-
                            me-
                                down
                      love laid bare:

              my fatigued field jacket

NATALIE MCCOLLUM

frayed at the cuffs
where you grabbed me
    by the sleeve
ragged at the hem
where i crawled
    over rocks and dirt
        to get to you

stained on the collar
by the blood i sweat for you
when this soldier's coat
is all i have left of you.

my place is being wrapped up
    inside of your fibers
in muted green of the field
    and brush
you shed your skin for me
when i was too cold in my own
like the animal inside *the boy*

you fit me too well;
where body becomes 2
i cannot tell.

so i wear it every day,
in ripstop war and peace,
a vintage relic of you

'cause i know one of these days
i'll get drafted by eternity too
and then maybe the material
i can't take with me
will already be stuck on

ASHES TO ANGELS

a part of my soul

as you.

[signed,]

Asher
061404

I don't know who really started it. There was a lot that happened in that 5 ½ minute séance to seduce which leads us to the overwhelming question of who came on to who. In the exchange of souls coursing down that shaft, a lot changed with the changing pulleys of the ballroom elevator rigged up by System of a Down, hiking us up and jarring us down, and as much as could have gone blissfully wrong went all perversely right.

So before I knew it, we were making out on her poetry. See, she carries around her life in a scarlet corduroy messenger bag. I didn't realize she had my poetry journal in there too – the Late Great one, that crumpled-up bastard of a self-fulfilling prophecy – and she that little blood-sucking thief. But she had no qualms about getting felt up, I guess the corrupt feeds off the corrupt. Or art feeds off art. But maybe they are really just the same thing, if there is no difference making it hard to tell. But all she told me was, upon inquiry to foreplay, that she was drunk enough to know she wanted to do this, but not so drunk that I should feel guilty for taking advantage. Which is to say, the very inverse of what she just said. *Perfect. I've got you just where I want you.* I flipped the lines for her, and the little acrobat sent me flying with the dynamo of a trapeze artist, like a tiny ballerina I could crush in my groping hand she was very flexible and supple in her soft yet firm young flesh. I bit into it raw, asserting myself lord of the dance, and thus began the Romance of Young Tigers[97], unofficial soundtrack to a horror movie filmed on location, in which you cannot tell the dancer from the dance.

*   *   *

Auryn woke up screaming Asher's name, woke up screaming aloud a prayer from her secret god, the great Horned One, in foresight of hornier things to come, but it was only a false alarm, a misread pregnancy test because she hadn't gotten knocked up, or even banged. The only evidence of the big bang theory was the blood-stained, tear-soaked, black make-up smeared pillow, upon which they had both fallen in ecstasy and exhaustion, having nonetheless gotten off on each other. She knew she would never have it like this again, the only time she ever had an orgasm was the first time, when he fingered her in places so shocking it sent electric currents like a beating pulsing hot-wired butterfly sacrificed at the stake of a matchstick to the devil. It was still buzzing through her, in double-jointed spasms like a live wire dormant but not quite dead so that if you happened to prick and stimulate the tendersore erogenous zone, it flared up like a blown fuse and then fizzled out until the next bump-and-grind. He, meanwhile, was on the high road to proving just *why* it is said that poets, as a collective species, are *just that good* – that is, in bed.

[*Rockstardom does not make the relationship – but it can*

---

[97] This is a real band.

ASHES TO ANGELS

definitely break it.]

"Fuck off, raving fan # what's-your-face! I'm not looking for a *relationship*, just a romp in the sack."

At this, Auryn stirred with the sway of last summer's wind chimes still ringing in the dark severity and severe beauty of winter haunting the dead silence of former irreplaceable times. Asher glanced over at her – she looked hot and horrible. And he still looked horny. The beast was obviously still hungry; it had only gotten a taste test, a mere preview of the goods. There would have to be a sequel: if he could get her to take off her *im*mortality, there was nothing – and nowhere – he couldn't get her to take off. *From caffeine to mortality*, he mused with an abusive nostalgia. *Take 672 South to that green light Blink 182…bypass the hospital this time, go in for the kill: break in through the alley back of the fire escape. Hotel room 515.*

[*Get a room!? Get a life!!*]

Asher lunged at some unseen aggressor, clawing at the air until he realized there was blood on his fingers. He looked over at Auryn for explanation and then they both looked down – down the twisted mess and threadbare mass of legs and clothes and sheets until they saw that her ankles were bleeding red alcohol. At first he was pissed – "I thought angels don't *bleed* if you cut 'em" he groaned, throwing his unbelief back in her face like using the enemy's weapons of mass destruction, the very same that your army of one was out to destroy for the good of atheist-kind – but at the bitter smell of vinegar he dragged her out of bed, down the ash-strewn hallway where wingéd people lay fallen into earth's ashtrays after a night spent fraternizing with mortals. Neither Ash nor Auryn saw the tiny fairy folk. They were tripping over each other's high-top shoelaces to get to the kitchen, where Asher, in a rare act of humility and sacrificial pride, knelt at the kitchen sink in a hobby ring ritual setting up his razor wire shrine to wash the razed bones with dirty paper towels begotten of a beautiful fucked-up man. It was 2 am.

[White space]

Wakes up. Smashes a half-full wine bottle she throws against the bedroom wall, watching the red run down in terrible tendrils and tenacious tentacles. Grabs the old acoustic. Sits on the bed and starts strumming. Gets up off the bedside and smashes her fist into the mirror – "It's my life!" Thrust. Puts her hand through glass. Impact. Releases it, and pulls back. "Don't you forget!" Gets dressed: out of her daisy dukes and skully knee-socks and into her black stuff, wide metallic grommet belt and Chuck Taylors. Follows Asher down the stuffy, peeling, watermarked dark tenement hallway downtown, the watermarks on the outsides of the buildings that survived the Great Brooklyn Flood of 1913. That's A.D. to you, homey sapie….The Specific Building: The Murk on 3rd, the grand abandonment – old opera house? WORK PLAY SHOP LIVE. Its white flags still wave in self-defeating self-surrender. Outside across the street. She's everywhere. Haunting him, hunting him down. In the apartment windows above the street. Getting out of a cab. On a billboard. Just around the corner. She's everywhere, and nowhere to be found. Always just in the shadow of his footsteps. But when he turns around, no one's there. "Can you, Ash, look out the window, without your shadow, Auryn, getting in the way?"

She turns on her heel. *I didn't think so.*

ASHES TO ANGELS

NATALIE MCCOLLUM

Chapter Eighteen

A Beautiful Man with a Guitar

It was 10 years on (*or so it seemed, but I don't know, it must have been the mushrooms*), you resurfaced in a motorcar (I only saw one hand waving in the backseat window): you a delirious angel, trapped under a frozen pond, your eyes glazed over the sheet of glass, one blue palm pressed against your own mirrored image a plea for rescue not waving but drowning.[98]

"In sleep you sang to me, in dreams you came; that voice which calls to me and speaks my name…" *Auryn saw herself wandering in from some other function that she had fled, a costume ball or somesuch, and heard this voice from another room, echoing, ringing, haunting, luring, drawing her in. Like one in a trance, she followed it. Peeked around the corner and stayed there, mysteriously capturing the attention of the singer and hooking his gaze at a distance, holding it until he dropped his eyes and owning it whenever he dared lift them again…to the figure along the wall. She was a dark, solitary figurine hugging the wall as she alternately shuffled and stomped down the hallway – she dropped a dollar in his open guitar case*

---

[98] "Not Waving but Drowning," a poem by Stevie Smith.

ASHES TO ANGELS

at her feet before moving on.

> wake from your dreams
> the drying of your tears
> today we escape
> we escape[99]

"Auryn," he murmured. Asher stuck his head in the doorway, left ajar. The flat was empty, hollow, silent. Not even the ghosts of the ghosts of the dead dared rustle a curtain or steal a breath, lest Time pick up where it left off. She stirred, her red right ankle moved tentatively under the sheet. When finally her head lifted to gaze unrecognizing at the tall thin shadowy figure hovering momentarily in the doorway, this time he spoke to her in riddles and he spoke to her in rhyme:

> pack and get dressed
> before your father hears us
> before all hell breaks loose

Her eyes fluttered shut at the lyrical lilt of his voice reciting the words to a pop cult song. She drifted off again on the wave of their minstrelsy languor, and when once more she stirred, he was propped at the foot of her bed with his acoustic guitar, idly yet subliminally strumming exit music for a film. She watched as his fingers flitted over the strings with a silver pick like angel wings.

"Mmm, but my body aches to breathe your breath," she was either stalling for time or just being uncooperative. Asher, strung out on the adrenaline of

---

[99] Radiohead. "Exit Music (for a Film)"

effecting the planned getaway in royal fugitive fashion, was not to be persuaded to abort the plan for an improv trip down into the mother earth's black hole to litter womb ecology with angel dust. Not now. There would be time for that later. But he must be strategic, and tactful. In the presence of an angel, a word could either make or break their break-away. He recalled Kafka, whose rules and wisdom choked him: "When the angel of the lord comes to you, do not tell him how you feel. His feelings are so far superior to anything you could ever know. But show him an image, some simple *thing*, and he will stand amazed."

"There will be time, there will be time," he reassured, "To prepare a face to meet the faces that you meet; There will be time to murder and create, And time for all the works and days of hands that lift and drop a question on your plate; Time for you and time for me, And time yet for a hundred indecisions, And for a hundred visions and revisions, Before the taking of toast and tea." At this her eyes flashed. At the prime of life in her element, she played the game of call-and-response with her own degree of wit to prove that Asher had met his match:

> Do I dare
> Disturb the universe?
> In a minute there is time
> For decisions and revisions which a minute will reverse.

> For I have known them all already, known them all:

Have known the evenings, mornings, afternoons,
I have measured out my life with coffee spoons;

ASHES TO ANGELS

I know the [V]oices dying with a dying fall
Beneath the music from a farther room.
   So how should I presume?

   The playful charm danced in Asher's eyes. He couldn't resist a word game, a duel to the death with his own demolition lover. Tickled at her jest, he tickled her.

> And I have known the arms already, known them all—
> Arms that are braceleted and white and bare
> (But in the lamplight, downed with light brown hair!)
> Is it perfume from a dress
> That makes me so digress?

   He slid along the side of the bed next to her and tousled her hair. She smoothed her arms, reveling in the attention and tender affection like a drunken lullaby, the love child raped by a drunkard's prayer. "Might I have a word with Eliot," she mused, "I'd edit his line because in the lamplight, I'm lined with light white down!" She looked up at him for recognition. It was true that her skin sparkled with faerie dust, the leftover sawdust vestiges of her vestigial wings, the metaphorical emphasis depending on whether you were talking to a Jewish carpenter or a Darwinian. But their rambles in the sun-soaked countryside had done much to improve the health and vitality of her complexion, a vast difference from the state in which he'd found her a tattooed tramp, a dirty daughter from the labor camp, whom he'd laid down in the grass of a clearing. She'd wept the tears of resistance, but she'd been willing.

"Mmm, I'd wager you're lined with a lot more than just the downy stuff," he whispered in a rare moment of genuine loving affection. His wandering hand caressed the silky pale skin across the top of her chest, just under the delicately chiseled collar bone where the skin was thinnest and all her blue-green veins showed the way to her heart like a treasure map of sprawling lines and neverending mazes in which the seeker, once trapped, would never find his way out. His gentle fingers found their way further downward, sneaking illicitly under the top of the sheet that hovered just above her breasts where their pale soft rounded curve barely peeked out. His hand brushed over them, stroking the pleasing shape and getting a rise out of the way the tiny nipples pricked up and hardened into a solid firm protrusion when he played with them. She looked earnestly into his face the whole time, watching earnestly for the affirmation she so craved.

"Do you, do you like them?" she asked, barely audible below a whisper, afraid that by asking the question, the answer would self-destruct.

He smiled, almost shyly, she thought with surprise. "Mmm, they're nice," he murmured, still lost as she was in the sway of the moment. "They're really, really nice," he slurred, mesmerized. She could feel him want her, *really want her*, and it scared her suddenly, because she didn't know what she'd do if she actually got what she wanted. He lifted the edge of the cover a bit, with all the grace of a gentleman, just to peek, to look down in the prying darkness of what lay below. Then, with perfect chivalry, after he'd stolen the eye candy he'd wanted, he tucked the summer quilt back up against her fragile chest, like putting away a treasure back in the protection of its locked chest. He patted the spot then shuffled up to go. She felt a wave of desperation as he rose off the bedside, his body breaking contact with her skin. She raised her hands up at him, clawed at the ever-widening space between them as he moved off. There were so many things she wanted to say to him in this moment, a million fragmented thoughts and desires swarming the distance between heart and mind, and she was trying desperately to choose one, *just one*, that would suffice and speak for them all. But she couldn't seem to get a handle on anything, because she didn't want to scare him off with the intensity and depth of her passion flowering just underneath her breast bones and plunging its roots like twisted thorny vines down the length of her torso and midsection all the way to the tips of her toes like an electrifying orgasmic live-wire wracking her every muscle torn life and limb. Her very soul felt as if it were being drawn and quartered in some medieval executioner's spectacle, and her diary of a naked soul on display for the freak-show revelers. At last, she gave up to the hopeless despair of the situation, and sunk six feet under the grave reality of the fated blow to poetry for the body. She consoled herself inwardly, *but you said it best when you said nothing at all, I guess.*

So he mouthed the words like a mime breaking an ethical vow of silence,

> breathe keep breathing
> don't lose your nerve
> breathe keep breathing
> i can't do this alone

A faint hint of a smile played at the corners of her mouth. "Your words keep me alive!" Like a mischievous wood nymph she kicked at the covers and rolled over on her bare stomach like the mattress was her lily pad and she, Morgaine of the Fairies, the enchantress herself. For a split infinity like split atoms dividing into two unequal halves, Asher thought her sun-soaked reddish haze of hair, with its uneven razed wispy ends, as she tossed the tangled mass over her shoulder, could have been those long-lost fairy wings, tinged at the tips of the feathers dipped in blood instead of ink from the tattoo needle. She caught his mesmerized stare, and giggled her baby-doll delight at the transfixing effect of her womanly wiles. He shook it off with a final warning:

> you can laugh
> your spineless [wingless] laugh
> we hope that your rules and wisdom
> choke you[100]

With that, he tossed her threadbare carpetbag onto the foot of the bed. "Your clothes are in there. I want you dressed and ready to go as soon as I call the cab." He stood there motionless, solid, like an iron curtain.

She sat up but drew the covers up as she did. "Do you think I'm going to *let* you watch me dress? This show isn't free, my man. According to my empty little coin purse here," she swung the cord around her neck tantalizingly, "you haven't paid to get in. No tip, no strip." He would have argued the point, if not for the urgency of the time-sensitive delivery awaiting its destination. He clenched his fists, spun on his heel, growling under his breath, *Would you give me no choice in*

---

[100] Radiohead, "Exit Music (for a Film)," Ok Computer

ASHES TO ANGELS

this, I know you can't resist trying to re-open a sore.[101]

"So leave me be, I don't want to argue, I just get confused and I come all undone. If I agree, well it's just to appease you, 'cause I don't remember what we're fighting for," she called after him defiantly as he stomped out of the swung doorway, hands shoved deep in his torn jeans pockets searching for a loose joint.

"Ten minutes – by the time I'm high you better be coming down," the blunt was already in his mouth, the match in contact as he descended the ladder from the loft.

He did a double take when she emerged from the loft, lingering in the white-washed wooden door frame with her bag in hand, oversized movie star shades like a tease on the bridge of her nose. He rose from his perch on the rustic picket fence, and gave a low bow. "My lady."

"Let us go then, you and I, When the evening is spread out against the sky," she flirted, tauntingly as she swayed her hips a-rhythmically to the beat of the rhyme, a poetry for the body sexing up the soul. She stepped daintily down the stone walk in her knee-high European leather boots, with all the sophistication of the celebrity that she was. "Let us go, through certain half-deserted streets,

> The muttering retreats
> Of restless nights in one-night
> cheap hotels
> And sawdust restaurants with
> oyster-shells:
> Streets that follow like a tedious
> argument

---

[101] Sarah McLachlan, "Time," <u>Surfacing</u>

NATALIE MCCOLLUM

Of insidious intent
To lead you to an
overwhelming question..."

"S'io credesse che mia risposta fosse
A persona che mai tornasse al mondo,
Questa fiamma staria senza piu scosse.
Ma perciocche giammai di questo fondo
Non torno vivo alcun, s'i'odo il vero,
Senza tema d'infamia ti rispondo."[102]

He knew not where that language came from, or that he had known it. He spoke the words as if the Muses themselves laughed and chanted to an interpretive dance in his veins, a mating call and response to the Fantasia in his blood.

---

[102] "If I thought I replied to one who might go back to the world, this flame should never move. But since — if what I hear be true — no one has ever returned from this gulf alive, I answer without fear of infamy." "The Love Song of J. Alfred Prufrock," by T.S. Eliot.

ASHES TO ANGELS

Chapter Nineteen

Slumming

"This is the story of [my] gypsy uncle, [I] never knew 'cause he was dead," Asher sang to her on the drive through the countryside back into the city. "And how his face was carved and ripped with wrinkles in the picture in my head."[103]

"And remember how you found the key to his hide-out in the Pyrenees?" Auryn joined in, to Asher's surprise. No power in the verse could stop her. "But you wanted to keep his secret safe, so you threw the key away."

At his puzzled look, she replied, "I met you before the fall of Rome."

Not to be outdone, he chanted back, "And I begged you to let me take you home."[104]

They didn't get very far.

It was raining when they woke up alone in Grand Central Station. Rush hour was past. All the business commuters swept away like ash from the cigarettes

---

[103] "Your Red Right Ankle" by The Decemberists. Also Auryn's line.
[104] "It's All Been Done" by the Bare Naked Ladies.

littering the tracks. Asher shook Auryn's shoulder with a jittery hand. She stirred, and slowly opened her purple-blue eyes. Things came into focus in crimped psychedelic waves. They found themselves huddled under a tarp on a bench near the rails. That subway musician must have felt sorry for them. Or it was just good karma: Auryn had dropped a dollar bill, albeit stolen from the Starbucks tip jar, Asher extracted from his torn ratty jeans into the street performer's open guitar case. Like a madman laughing at the rain, a little out of touch, a little bit insane, it was a Robin Hood spoof on his part, stealing from the poor to give to the poorer.

Asher lifted Auryn up and brushed her off, making sloppy apology under his breath for their shabby state of affairs. His eyes darted around for the nearest exit. "Come, fair lady," he took her hand roughly, "the world awaits." The prince of thieves spirited away his maiden like stolen yet undamaged goods.

On the bus mall, en route to their rat-trap hotel, Auryn laced her arm through his, sniffing the mothballs like angel dust embedded in the frayed felt peacoat. Looking up at him with stars in her eyes, she rambled in darkly euphoric lyric, "If I should lose my fame and fortune, and I'm homeless on the street, and I'm sleeping in Grand Central Station, it's okay – if you're sleeping with me."[105]

He glanced down at her, folded on his arm, her feet barely touching the street, and patted her tousled auburn head fondly. "Okay, kiddo. You're a good pet." They tripped over to the steps of the Art Institute with the big jade lions on either side of its

---

[105] Whitney Houston, "My Love Is Your Love"

fantastical triple-tiered staircase, and sat down at the top landing, petting and fondling each other like wasted lovers under the pear tree. Things like *The Scream*, the Munch painting floating past them on a pair of angel wings rift of their owner. Things like, "Hail to the Thief" playing on Radiohead while said existential ghoul bailed on the dead poets' society below said airlift. The art thievery was so surreal in its execution that it looked more like a Salvador Dali composition than a Munch. Like the one with the limp wrinkled clocks, time was vulnerable, put in a compromising position by *The Persistence of Memory*. A wrinkle in time, from the bed sheets to the ashtray, "unfathomable to mere mortals is the lore of fiends," as Hawthorne would have it.

As psychopaths would have it, "This might sound weird, but how do you feel about shacking up in a graveyard?" They had run **out of** money for another night in the motel.

"Graveyard neutral." So, under the light of a full moon, they made out on someone's grave. A bottle of merlot split between them helped with removing inhibitions and superstitions necessary to commit this sacrilegious act. Then Asher, after all the strenuous kissing and groping, got hungry and ate some cookies out of a box left on the dead's mound. "Thin mint, my favorite." Auryn told him a little girl named Angel had left them there on All Soul's Day to feed the ghost of her alcoholic grandfather. "No worries," he closed the box half full.

She pushed him on the chest so that he fell backward from his knees to his ass. "You are *so* haunted!"

"Not with my pet vampire slayer," he countered with a slight quiver in his usually self-assured voice.

He said this with his arms reached out for her to help him up. Instead, she folded her arms across her chest and stood back.

"Nuh-uh," she shook her tousled auburn curls, matted with dead flower petals on a wet black bough from the roll in the dirt. "I *am* the vampire, potentially the slain, not the slayer, remember? 'Two halves are equal, a cross between two evils' – half angel, half demon. You've seen her, my evil twin."

"You mentioned a certain slutty sister, but I can't recall as having done a retinal scan of this eye candy, seeing as we *never* made it to the club."

"*Strip* club, and I'd prefer not to watch you gape and gawk at my arch-nemesis," Auryn quickly corrected, brushing herself off. "And with all due respect, mister, you HAVE seen her," she fished around in her pocket a moment, "does this look familiar?" And she produced the fake photo I.D. he had pushed on her at the piano bar, the club they actually did make it in and out of, but just barely.

He peered at the photo as if seeing it for the first time. "I, I thought that *was* you," he tripped over his own explanation. "Seriously, I found in on you at the accident scene – it was the only thing that gained you admission to the hospital. You'd still be a ward of the state if not for that lucky find. Seriously, unidentified persons who can't remember what happened or where they came from – they lock people up for that. Amnesiacs." Now it was his turn to fold his arms across his chest, defensively.

Auryn threw up her hands. "Asher, it's what I've been trying to tell you, two halves are equal. I'm a cross between two evils. Half vampire, half angel. I can't bleed, I don't have a fighting chance, not a

ASHES TO ANGELS

prayer. How is something that can't bleed supposed to be photographable? As a non-carbon based life form, I can't even carry out photosynthesis – I can't even relate to the plant world, let alone the animal kingdom."

Asher had no idea what to say to that. It was sheer madness, the ravings of a lunatic, surely. "Flora, fauna," he waved off her science fiction, "I'll just call you 'Buffy.'"

Now she was clenching her fists in vexation at his refusal to take her seriously. "'What's in a name? A rose by any other name would smell as sweet,'[106] and a briar by any other name would hurt as badly to the touch. Using the nomenclature of a pop-cult vampire slayer on me won't bestow the mortality I so crave."

"I wish you'd unclench your fists," he said in a flat tone. He shoved his hands in his pockets. "C'mon, pet, let's go home.

"What the home?! What the pet?! What's not to believe? I'm not real! I can't 'Belikeu'[107]; we are worlds apart. I'm not a girl, I'm not even human!"

She was shaking in her socks by now, so badly that the black and white stripes were sliding down her noodley legs and pooling in wrinkled layers at the tops of her combat boots. Asher saw this and grabbed her by the shoulders. "Listen to me! You're fine! You're just delusional, like me; here, take these—" he dug in his jacket pocket and produced a small pill bottle— "anti-psychotics. Thorazine will help with the paranoid delusions. They work, then you'll stop freaking yourself out." He pried open her palm and

---

[106] Juliet.

[107] See The Playlist: "Belikeu" from the album Satellites for Animals by KittyMonkey.

dumped a handful. "You poor schizophrenic girl."

His display of catharsis blew a fuse inside her. "You're crazy! You think I'm just a deluded psychopath who thinks she's an angel? You think I'm just like you, then who's to say whose version of reality is correct? You can't even distinguish fact from your own damn fiction. Don't believe what you see? Watch this!" She threw the purple pills in his face and took off running toward the fence.

"Auryn, no!" Asher raised a hand in alarm when he saw her start to scale the chain link, heading directly for the barbed wire at the top. Before he could stop her, she had one leg over the wire, catching the inside of her thigh on the barbs in the exact same place, anatomically speaking, where she had jabbed Poe with the scissors after cutting off her wings and effecting her own defenestration. Asher ran after her, but she had scrambled over the other side to evade his rescue. By the time he got there, she was hanging by the leg caught in the wire. A big ugly laceration ran down her inner thigh, but no blood dripped from the jagged seam. She hung there upside down, limp as a rag doll, arms crossed, a lopsided silly grin torturing her face, totally immune to laceration gravity.

"Now do you believe me? I'm stuffed with fluff and my candy heart is crack. The air I breathe is angel dust."

He had stopped short, his hands hung motionless at his sides. "PCP? *Pulvis et umbra sumus.*"

She shook her head. "Nah. *You* are but dust and shadow. I'm just a bad acid trip."

He jumped on the chain links and proceeded to disentangle her leg from the wire while she continued mouthing off. "Hey atheist, you know what angels are? Drug addicts. Doped up on religion and sex and TV. Shooting up heroin. The best orgasm you ever had. Trainspotting. High on meth, with a little help from their friends. A figment of a fried mind. Sunny-side up. Sex on ex. The ecstasy of the busted lovers. Poetry written on LSD...." He yanked her off the fence. She was weakening with her words. He set her on her feet. She was standing on shaky ground. Her knees buckled with the rush of gravity.

"Easy there, gravity," he steadied her, but she waved him off.

"I am *not* gravity's girl. Just because I don't have wings doesn't mean flying is out of the question."

"Nothing really exists, so I suppose anything is possible." He had started to move off toward the gate from which they had forced entry. She kept up her mad litany like exit music for a film, becoming less coherent with each musical step in the major scale: whole step, whole step, half step; whole step, whole step, whole step, half.

"Angels are simply the product of a painful ecstasy. Ask Saint Teresa of Avila. Spirituality is simply a union of the psyche and the earth. Ask Joan of Arc: Can you take me higher? 'Her desire knows no pain...she hardly knows whether she is in the body or out of it.'"[108]

She trailed him at a distance all the way back to the subway.

---

[108] <u>Angels: An Endangered Species</u> by Malcolm Godwin, page 246.

NATALIE MCCOLLUM

Chapter Twenty

Canal St.: The Balcony Scene

…and from my 10th floor tenement where once our bodies lay – ***you jumped.*** *He's sitting outside my studio, since he's got none, now,* she thought, peeking from behind the heavy red curtain. He was in the backseat of an idling cab, chain-smoking. *In a parked car in a crowded street, you see your love made complete.*[109] He saw her, blew out the smoke from his nostrils French style. It blurred his vision, like love is blindness. "Tell me," he called up, "tell me, do you think it'd be all right, if I could just crash here tonight? See, I'm no shape for driving, anyway I got no place else to go. You know, it might not be that bad, you were the best I ever had – Hey, Jealousy."[110]

She leaned out over the windowsill, balcony style, and called back in response: "Bad Move."
--he said.
turn. look.
It could be him, unless you're tripping.

---

[109] U2, "Love Is Blindness."
[110] The Gin Blossoms.

ASHES TO ANGELS

It could be the one you gave your last cigarette to.
The one whose bed you last shared.
The one you considered killing yourself for.
And now he can worm his way back
in a hoodie with hugs and drugs and maybe
throw in an L-word. For insurance.
Dangerous, four-letter word.
Poison on the lips, siren in the ear.
The sad bastards
murder their darlings
on guitar strings.
You can leave him groveling
on the other side of the chain links.
Tell yourself he's a special kind of creep.
The way he appeared out of the dark
womb-space of a Halloween night.
In an alley.
Between cars.
Drunk and desperate.
Yet here *you* are, cradling that text
message like it could save your life.
Maybe it could.
Don't look back.
if you hope to live with that delusion.

This is what she was thinking when, as if reading her thoughts, he tried again, asking, if she wouldn't take him in, then:

where do all the poets go?

I left the hospital AMA
Crutch in arm
hobbled like the angel of death
with broken wings—
(he had it coming)—
to the trashy curb
Hailed a cab stalled

171

in the gutter on Broadway
to take me to the stars
or Saturn's rings
or wherever cocky 20-somethings
go when they've been shot down
from delusions of invincibility
and messing with mortality
See, I was on my way out, or up,
I told the hippie behind the wheel
All I've got to my name
is a starving checkbook,
expired insurance card,
and my charred journal with
10 cent lines to live on
handwritten in a red too hot and wet
to pass for merely ink,
recorded in the year
of somebody's lord 19—(unknown).
Burned all those rejection slips.
in a cauldron of New Age
implications back of the alley.
fell heart-first from the fire escape
there in Dickensian fashion
at the sit-in we wrote protest poetry
waiting out December's hangover
with no Christmas. It's criminal.
Too long ago, don't remember.
I'm just asking for a little grace.
So tell me, tell me,
where do all the poets go
like when Spoken Word
recites a postmodern death wish?
and what if the blinking light
I see in your pix doesn't
direct me by the wrist?
I saw you two years ago
in San Francisco waiting

ASHES TO ANGELS

for the water to receive you
but I have reason to suspect
you are still there checking out
that girl nicknamed suicide
So if I get out of my body first
I'll save a place for you,
among my cult of dead poets,
(and I'll watch for you.)

Auryn melted as he described his circumstances to her. *That* was how you talk to an angel. She remembered, the first time he held her, she felt the earth itself stir and move through his wrist, hand, up her arm to settle in her dark heart. At that something terrible and tragic happened between them, and the aftershock was still being felt with the scale of an earthquake's reverberations on her planetary life. Of apocalyptic import. It had something to do with the end of the world. What if she *caused* the end of the world? Prematurely. It wasn't set to happen until either the Mayan calendar ended on 12-20 of 2012 OR Nostradamus's mathematics proved the theorem in 2048. But what if a small voice, writing at gunpoint taking love like a bullet through the brain, triggered it…What if Spoken Word / was the shot heard / round the world?

What if
What if you alone
caused the end of the world?
You fell so hard
So hard and so far
You pulled the whole world
The whole world down with you

Book of the Muse, Long December, 20--.

Couldn't he see she idolized the ground he walked on? Couldn't he even *see* her? She left him a signed note: SEE ME. Love, Synchronicity.

After the scandal and Hollywood horror with the overly affectionate priest, Auryn was living indefinitely on the tenth floor of a motel on Canal Street, where you could hang your head over, hear the wind blow. She didn't have the money or credit, as an angel, to rent an apartment. "We don't need a lot of money, we'll be sleeping on the beach, keeping oceans within reach,"[111] he crooned up to her slit in the drapery. Veiled in the orb of light from the half-moon lamp occupying its own spherical womb-space on a vandalized bar stool next to her bed, Auryn moved as a shade across the wooden floorboards to the large lone window nearby, where the electric avatar's incarnate alter ego flooded the void between the temporal and the eternal, making up the difference between the material and the cosmic. But Auryn, suspended somewhere between the mortal and the divine, with lethal loyalties to both and unable to decide which had the stronger pull on this Ionian middle ground halfway between heaven's hell and Aquarian earth, felt the eternal "seeping" through the physical, just as the great Celtic mystic of the twentieth century, Lord MacLeod of Fuinary, had described this "thin place," when once she asked his own displaced shade what the Other Side was like down there, and if communing with the Un-Dead was possible in reverse: no power in the verse of the human condition could stop *them*, but what of the

---

[111]   Over the Rhine, "Etcetera Whatever" from The Home Recordings on <u>Good Dog, Bad Dog</u>.

ASHES TO ANGELS

Satanic verses begetting the *angelic condition?* He'd given her a book of *Celtic Prayers from Iona* compiled by some mortal Auryn didn't know or care about. Now as Auryn approached her constelled Rose Compass to beyond the beyond, she found she could not read the stars, the constellations were all out of order like disembodied limbs reassembled in the most kinky fashion, as if the tampering con artist had attempted to re-make a soul out of a soul-less vessel, and failed miserably. The constellation Lyra, that harpy, lay among the wreckage of strings and wires in the battered woman's shelter of her own ravaged womb, that negative space where such things as angel wings and guitar strings get caught in each other's recycled atoms hard-wired like barbed wire. Maybe it was because Lyra was her mother's avatar, a goddess-mother to Lilith of sorts, that Auryn, upon viewing this cosmic war-wreck, felt six shots fired across the synapses, struck a chord, hit a nerve on a high note that twinged like the plucking of a finely tuned six-string running the hip-span across her belly. But what the case may be, she couldn't look out the window without her shadow getting in the way. The shadow of her wings, spreading their beautiful darkness over the glass, nailed to the frame with thumbtacks that left no fingerprints by the user, who had not the ability to bleed nor be photographed on black carbon-copy negatives and silent film reels. This thwarted her mug shots, but "the cops said it wouldn't show up on my record," Auryn insisted of her planned inadvertent suicide attempt, in which she would try to convince her foilers that it was accidentally-on-purpose, with a pre-meditated poem: "I did not *mean to commit suicide /* I did not *mean to do it* by your side" – a lyric from "Bloodletting" which would, by extension of its co-authoring, incriminate Asher. When he'd found her suicide note, scrawled on a bloody paper towel soaked into the wine-stain her footprints tracked in after she got mugged by "a beautiful fucked-up man setting up his razor-wire shrine" to her red right ankle on the carpet one night, he foot-noted her: "Auryn, (n.) -- A little neurotic, potentially schizophrenic, but *there is something so hot* about a girl who would **jump.** My dating history consists of "safe" girls; maybe I shouldn't play it safe anymore. Maybe I'm ready for a girl with a little history [Freudian slip: *hystery*] herself...*There's just something about Auryn*..."

Coming down from her depressive high, Auryn shivered and felt a deist desperation: she gazed with the Sight not of one who has eyes but who is so wise, her words and wisdom choke her. She choked up, letting the cathartic release of pity and fear flood her system and purge the pipelines running the length of her torso the vascular system of the emotions gone hypo-glycemic though jacked up on ten packs of sugar in the caffeine spurting through her veins with all the narcotic desperation of a crack addict looking for her next fix. She slapped her wrists across the glass, banged her fists on the window, barely able to elicit The Scream illicit, caught in the water that went for the throat, rubbed salt in the wound that can only be healed by the sword that inflicted it. Where was that sword? "Asher..." she wailed and trailed off, "*Where are you? Where is the other side* of the world? That's all you are to me: you're the Other Side of the world, and I can't get there, *with or without wings*." The world was calling for angels, she knew, and she had cut off her wings. Last call. 2 a.m. The flapping and the screwing. She heard the uncanny sounds again, coming from the rafters. She beat again. She beat in sync with the alternating call and response of a tightening and a loosening. Beating her tiny white knuckles a million times a minute like a hummingbird, until at last the glass gave – and all at once she had cracked the window. She hadn't felt the pain. She hadn't known she had actually made impact until, "Oh look, now look what I've done! Oh the mess, the hassle, I've said too much, and now I've gone and done it, I've *really* done it now!" The whole window now displayed a complex spider web pattern of cracks and chips and dents all radiating out from a central fault line in a spiral maze replica of the natural world's classic repeat-offender: geometry. The proofs were in the past tense. She felt one single long tear sting its way down the curve of her neck, all the way to her collar bone and then the crack between her chestplates, where her breastbone dented and cradled the salt-less drop in that dent and where she could feel her heart but not her soul. As she reflexively licked her lips, she tasted her tears as they were, salt-less, a forbidden fruit of knowledge rotting on the Celtic Tree of Life and Limb from which hung her body shadowless, her shadow wingless, her wings soul-less, and her soul wireless. Torn limb-from-limb, the Daughter of this Poison Love, the little red orb of seed and flesh, poison apple of fairy tale turned nightmare, she thought, *Too much sugar. Causes violent dreams. Must get accidental death and dismemberment insurance.* Grasping the little red coin purse around her neck, she gave it a pull and *yanked. What does anything mean any more when nudity as far as your naked soul doesn't even hold up as insurance? POD.* On further consideration: *I should have known this was over as soon as it started.* The silk cord which continued down the open neckline where her vocal cords trailed off snapped with a flick of the wrist and tore off with the weight of her own words. It was like pulling hair. Clutching the cut strings in her fist, she tore off like a reckless romantic so far past the end of her line, it had knotted and out of the stump sprouted the dichotomous seedling of a pair of wings. A freak of nature, an adrenaline rush while the sky is falling under the atmospheric pressure of laceration gravity, a meta*physical*morphosis, a *morphling*.

> *Auryn speaks:*
> I was a little bird
> with one wing.
> I chopped it
> off myself.
>
> *Asher speaks*:
> You have a broken wing.
> Just cut it off!
> For god's sake,
> *Just cut the damn*
> *wretched thing off!*

So. She did.
No. You jumped.
It was Christmas Eve. There was broken glass. There was blood on her hands.

She did not know this. She did not care. She still could not feel pain, bleed as she might. She could not say to her soul, "Bleed like me," if her body could not give the desired response when the disembodied soul stepped out of its *self* to check for vital signs. She had none. Any signs of life were false alarms, and as such, her charge through the streets on Dark Thursday, this darkest of nights, seemed a false start, but she ran anyway, a ghost of a girl blurred through tears and fog rising from potholes and melting snow, downtown across the icy isolated streets bejeweled in black, flitting in and out of abandoned alleys and under fire escapes and over small fires tended by the homeless on this damn cold night. If this were a scene in a movie, or if you the casual observer could hear the music playing in her head, the theme song in the background would be "Map of the Problematique" by Muse. Her last-ditch split ended her in a ditch, canal side to a small reservoir beneath the railroad overpass. She ran there because it was the place where things came together at the crossover to split infinity – the train track bridge, where many a mortal has contemplated the measure of a man on the rails and found the scales balancing too far to the wrong side to keep him from losing a balance of his own choosing, falling delicately between worlds. Here at the stream her stream of conscious split as well. One half stuck and spun in its tracks like a record player off its needle, the other half tripped and fell ahead in a paroxysm of euphoria like a heroin addict stuck on hers. Nerves numb with overuse, a veritable voodoo doll all stuck with pins, was the disproportion that these virgin pain receptors in an angel newly outfitted with the ability and corresponding anatomy to bleed. Auryn, when she fell down in the ditch canal side and scuffed her knees, did not know she was in fact bleeding, the scene of the crime and the point of entry being those innocent patches of soft white raggedy ann skin cells showing their maiden corruptibility where her plaid knickers fell just short of the kneecap and her black-laced combat boots gave it up to the sheer stockings that failed miserably more so in reaching beyond the shins. Her slouchy stockings left high and dry but not out of sight a double-jointed vulnerability delicate as a sheet of thin ice exposed as a blank page betraying the red mark in the center the morning after.

But it was still the nightmare before.

And she had promises to keep. Miles to go, six feet under, before going under the anesthetic effects of sleep.

She stopped short when she heard it. The voice was at once imperative and transitive as the entrancing Phantom of the Opera himself. Auryn caught her breath, "In sleep you sang to me, in dreams you came. That voice which calls to me, and speaks my name." The female voice was lethal hooking her by the rock lyrics glazed into the sickly sweet venomous voice, like poetry on a sugar high, the crack habit by congenital defect of the poet's Muse. In front of Auryn, where she had stopped at the mesmerizing mermaid call, was a ladder. A fire escape, hanging off the side of the overpass like a trellis. Like a Siren's lethal love song, the voice of the demon was inviting, nay, imploring her to climb. She started scaling the ladder like a girl-Romeo mounting the trellis of the balcony.

"If a body kiss a body," chanted the avatar of the demon, perched precariously nimble as a tightrope walker on the top-most railing of Canal St. bridge. The Soho District's distinguishing landmark served as the divide between the ghetto and its commune residents, and the carnival look of the artists' hub. It consisted of the concrete bridge intersecting the brick road which passed under the tunnel painted in a clownish color wheel of pop-surreal Salvador Dali-inspired novelties, most prominently a controversial adaptation of return to Oz via the Polar Express. Someone had spray-painted over the Rhine on one side of the overpass and in so doing beheaded the dubious Tin Man conductor.

The hooker meanwhile regarded her catch with the shrewd eye of a businesswoman. "So...we meet again." She spoke straight-up to her arch-nemesis with all the seduction of a lesbian Siren. But the hook was in Auryn's *dis*orientation, not the lack of a prefix. Her roots were dead as a language invented in Jabberwocky. She felt a rising confusion and a rush of adrenaline that made her body temperature soar and turned her on to 106 degrees Fahrenheit when she glimpsed the wings glittering just beyond the rise and fall of the demon girl's shoulders, humping their mate's backside in a hunchback threesome. The demon fairly rippled with pleasure. They *were* the intended bait, but too early seen unknown and known too late! The perfect bait for a de-winged angel, for poor Auryn. That Shakespearian timing was the brilliance of it. The demon trickster would congratulate herself later. But presently, the subject was sobbing, and this threw the demon off rather than getting her off. She had not anticipated such a tough customer. She decided to abort the plan, switch tactics. The girl had been left high and dry and vulnerable as a fish out of H_2O – the first time. In her circus ring brain, Poe activated emergency controls, swallowed a time-release pill.

Meanwhile Auryn was standing on the rails at the rail, jabbering something about how "I met you in Montauk," and when Poe jabbed her in the rib upon "riding the guard rails with that girl nicknamed Suicide," suddenly they weren't strangers anymore. It **was** awkward. Sisterly antagonism manifested as the familiars of both witchy women. But the Pisces, the fish out of water who grew legs, as usual had to get the last word in on the Spoken Word being fired at her in saltwater by a fire sign. *Water always wins over fire.* So Auryn was crying helplessly, shaking in terror and entranced defeat, but listening to the demon sister, listening to the Terror through the wall, flaunting it, faking it, offering back Auryn's wings **IF** she took them on faith, on "credit," on a flight of fancy and JUMPED *before* her wings. The idea was to jump off the Canal St. bridge to receive her wings AND her mortality. As Poe quipped, "Mortality Test – the only way to prove it is to DO IT." Promptly affixing a disclaimer to the jingle, at Auryn's stare: "It's like a paternity test – once you prove it, it's put to rest. But, also like virginity – once you lose it, it's irreversible. Worse than an STD, too, because if it hangs around, it'll hang you too."

The explanation was mock pageantry, but Auryn got it. Once she "earned" her mortality in reverse of the classic pop angel "earning" her wings, she got back her down payment, her collateral, her *wings*. It was a mockery of the literature, a perversion of the child's rhyme and reason, "every time a bell rings, an angel gets her wings," because the angel who has earned her mortality is the one *for whom the bell tolls.*

Poe moved closer to beam her infra-reds directly into Auryn's ultra-violet eyes. Eclipsed, Auryn looked away. Still sobbing, she was actually considering the deal. Yet again. She winced at the awareness of her one very human trait – her consumerist vulnerability. The demon, like a dog able to sniff out fear, sensed this and played the good hand of cards she'd just been dealt. Auryn folded.

"You know the deal," she moved in on her target, "it's all been done before. Though, from the looks of

ASHES TO ANGELS

you, little sis, I'd bet the game of love hasn't been good to you. So I'll cut you some slack," she shifted the heavy studded props on her back. "Here we are again. You and me, at the edge of eternity. Last time, you sold out for a poet, a sell-out himself, if you ask me. So get him back. And *get him* back. With these. Men fall for them like flies. Trust me," she tugged at her plunging neckline a bit to reveal a few dollar bills peeking out of her bejeweled brassiere, "I KNOW."

A spastic chill of fright and delight rippled through Auryn.

"So – do we have a deal this time? Are they sold – or are you?"

Auryn's eyes darted to the cold blue steel of the guard rails with the dark void hanging in the balance beyond. It seemed the world stood still, waiting on a cue, awaiting her response on this not-so-silent night, waiting to see if she chose fight or flight, waiting to see an angel *jump*. And fall. In love. Rare, never-before-seen footage. Something came over Auryn. The words came from somewhere else:

"I have bought…[sob]…the mansion of love…[choke]…but not yet possessed it…[cough]…and although I am sold…[hiccup]…not yet enjoyed—"[112]

Poe the demon waited.

She stroked Auryn's damp hair.

She kissed her sister's temple.

Indeed, love *is* a temple, love the higher law.[113]

"Then have my lips the sin that they have took,"[114] Auryn took the words straight from Juliet's lips.

---

[112] Act 3 Scene 2 lines 26-28 (Juliet – Capulet's Orchard).
[113] U2, "One."
[114] Act 1 Scene 5 line 108 (Juliet – Capulet's House).

"Sin from my lips?"[115] Poe encouraged, and Auryn finished, "O trespass sweetly urged," her voice broke and she broke out in a bloody cold sweat, "**GIVE ME MY SIN AGAIN!**"

At the release of liability, the demon took over, as authorized in the binding verbal contract. She grasped Auryn's upper arm and directed her to the side of the railroad tracks, at the edge of the painted balcony. "Lesson One," she presented in a firm voice, "Romeo Must Die."

Auryn was still sobbing, but there was no going back. Poe's gentle grip on her arm became vise-like, digging her red-hot manicured nails in.

"Now, this is what you're going to do. This is ALL you have to do. You're going to step up to the rail." [Auryn sobbing.] "Climb up on the guard rail." [Auryn sobbing.] "Stand on the ledge. Now, here's the trick. The trick is to keep breathing. Hold steady." [Positioning her.] "Hold your arms out to your sides. Like you're flying. You'll feel it in a moment. Now, here's the part. This is the part where you just step off the bridge – just like that. And you tell yourself, 'It's all okay.' And you jump."

The words as Poe said them were so simple, so soft and kind. Barely there. *It's all okay. And…you…jump.*

So. She did. And she was betrayed by a bloody kiss.

The angel fell, ironically paralleling her first fall out of the sky when she fell for the guy. But there were no wings to catch her, to break her fall rather than her neck. Poe sat high above on the railing, legs crossed, cackling like a raven and giggling grotesquely

---

[115] Act 1 Scene 5 line 109 (Romeo – Capulet's House).

ASHES TO ANGELS

at the sheer *idiocy* of love. "Did you really think *for a moment*, I'd give up these? Not on your life, babe. Damn, where's a poet when you need one?"

She spoke too soon. Sometime after the jump, Asher, swaggering his way out of the bars at closing time, was struck with sobriety at sight of Auryn's flight. He watched her jump and regained his composure just as she lost hers. It was the first time he had actually seen Auryn's sister AND her wings. It was the first time he had seen her fly. Asher now shook his fist and screamed at the demon atop the bridge, "Karma Police! Arrest this girl, her Hitler hairdo is making me feel ill, and we—" he looked down helplessly at Auryn, now in his arms— "we have crashed her party."

Poe screamed back, "Arrest this man, he talks in maths, he buzzes like a fridge, he's like a detuned radio—"

He gritted his teeth, "This is what you get when you mess with us—" Then, "I DEFY YOU, STARS!"[116] He stood there shaking, holding a fallen angel in his arms for at least half the night but left with her sometime after all the bars closed. Word-mad, word-struck, word-drunk, he had stood there paralyzed, shocked out of his swoon, and watched Auryn jump. He never thought she'd do it. He was seeing it without seeing it, in that disbelieving state of surreality like witnessing the bombing of twin towers. It felt like swimming; the world underwater, happening in slow motion, which, he thought ironically, must be exactly what it feels like to fall. Slightly out of focus, not quite real. The furthest thing from actuality. It was oddly dislocating. No wonder Auryn constantly confused fact and fiction: she never knew which end was up.

---

[116] Act 5 Scene 1 line 24 (Mantua. A street.)

He must save her, then. "I'll get the ankles, you get the wrists." His superhero complex kicked in for the supernatural, collapsed in a bonehouse not ten feet away. "I felt so symbolic,"[117] he would later say, in defense of his decision to leave the scene of a crime – with the victim, not the "body" – in tow. "She's not *dead*." Half-carrying half-dragging her, he stumbled home with all the Christmas drunks.

---

[117] Counting Crows – "Mr. Jones"

ASHES TO ANGELS

Chapter Twenty-one

The Whoroscope:
Angel Reads Her Zodiac

"Rome did not fall in one day."[118]
(but)
"I met you before the fall of Rome."[119]

"When she jumped, she probably thought she'd fly." The attending physician looked up from his charts at Asher, standing at the head of Auryn's bed. It was that exact statement that had gotten her moved up from the ER to the psychiatric ward on the seventh floor of the hospital. Here she was again, a busted angel incarcerated on Christmas Day, six months after her first flight – or lack thereof – had landed her a relationship in the emergency room. She was still unconscious, but somehow had managed to break only her arms – they were suspended in slings that, in the absence of the real thing, looked like makeshift canvas wings. The ER doctors were amazed that she had missed breaking her neck. She should be paralyzed, if

---

[118] Graffiti on a red brick wall. (*Petals on a wet black bough.*) Wayne Avenue, downtown Dayton, Ohio.
[119] "It's All Been Done," by the Bare Naked Ladies.

not dead. The attending had assessed her condition and it had been determined, upon consultation with the psychiatric intern and the information they could gather from Asher, speaking on her behalf while she lay somewhere in her black hole, that she voluntarily jumped off the bridge. Asher wanted to incriminate Poe, because he saw her there gloating over the crumpled heap of Auryn, but he had not actually witnessed her involvement in the accident, and so he could not be certain that Poe had actually pushed her. Given the wily ways of Poe, her job was probably ridiculously easy: she had likely provided merely the emotional nudge to mastermind her own scheme, playing the victim's strings with all the deft subtlety of a vicarious puppeteer.

Asher hated hospitals; the hovering medical personnel made him nervous, paranoid even. He'd spent time enough behind the locked door of the seventh floor to know. He also knew, in the course of standard operating procedure, the matter of Auryn's origin would come up. It was easy the first time: some girl he'd found in a car wreck. He didn't have any more knowledge than they did. But clearly the bystander effect wouldn't pass this time. So he made something up.

She is half human because her sister was a suicide who, according to legend, became a demon-vamp in the afterlife of suicides. But Auryn was merely an attempt (an unsuccessful suicide, not a completer), so she's a half-suicide which, theoretically, equals a half-vampire. Therefore, if she is half-vampire, and if all vamps were previously human, then she's got human DNA, or rather an unpure mix of human-vampire DNA, second only to uncut heroin. This is how she has the potential to be mortal and the potential to be with *a mortal.*

ASHES TO ANGELS

Raven was on the right track with her story forecasting the origin of Auryn: she is a reincarnation of a former love, just the spirit of that love in a body that was already tied to the train tracks once. Auryn and her demon twin sister mimic the Chinese concept of the dual soul: Poe is the lower soul (P'o), and Auryn, as an angel, is the higher soul (Hun). "Two halves are equal, a cross between two evils…" he sang softly to himself.

If only he could know how right he was.

Chapter Twenty-two

"Sorry I Missed Church; I Was Busy Practicing Witchcraft and Becoming a Lesbian."

Invocation to Pan

O Great God Pan,
Beast and man,
Shepherd of goats and Lord of the Land,
I call you to attend my rites
On this most magical of nights.
God of the wine,
God of the vine,
God the fields and god of the kine,
Attend my circle with your love
And send your blessings from above.
Help me to heal;
Help me to feel;
Help me bring forth love and weal.
Pan of the forests, Pan of the glade,
Be with me as my magic is made![120]

---

[120] Extracted from The Standing Stones Book of Shadows, by Scott Cunningham. Wicca: A Guide for the Solitary Practitioner, Llewellyn, 2004. p. 147

ASHES TO ANGELS

August 1st, 1981. If she could re-write the bible, why not rock'n roll too? They were the same thing anyway.

"Heaven ain't close in a place like this, somebody told me,"[121] Asher drawled as he took a lazy drag off his cigarette. He nodded toward Auryn, sitting on the floor, looking at a record album by The Killers.

"Do you believe in rock 'n roll, can music save your mortal soul?"[122] she asked, looking up at him sprawled on the ward's ratty couch cushions. His temper flared up with a flick of the Bic for his next cigarette. He threw an EMF album jacket at her.

"You burden me with your questions, you have me tell no lies. You're always asking what it's all about, don't listen to my replies. You say to me I don't talk enough, but when I do I'm a fool. These times I've spent, I've realized I'm gonna shoot through and leave you." Asher's diatribe was getting manic, as he ran his sentences together like lyrics.

"The things you say! Your purple prose just gives you away. The things you say! You're unbelievable!" Auryn shot back. She took a swig of wine from the communal bottle Marley handed her in a brown paper bag. They were getting away with all sorts of illicit things in the psychiatric ward during Sunday visiting hours. She composed herself. She licked her purple lips. Then she winged it: "You burden me with your problems, by telling me more about mine. I'm always so concerned with the way you say you're always at stop to think of us, being one, is more than I've ever known. But *this time*, *I* realize *I'm* gonna shoot through

---

[121] "Unbelievable" by EMF. Lyrics quoted in conversation.
[122] Don McLean, "American Pie."

and leave *you*!" Purple lips made poison love.

"The things, you say, your purple prose just gives you away," Asher mocked, "the things, you say – you're *un*believable!"

"Oh, what the fuck," Marley broke in. "What the fuck."

"Good point," Asher turned to the impartial third party.

"What the fuck."

(Good point.)

"What the fuck."

"Whoa, bad." Auryn elbowed her way back in the debate.

Asher turned on her again. "Seemingly lastless, don't mean you can ask us, pushing down the relative, bringing out your higher self."

"Think of the fine times, pushing down the better few," Auryn protested. "Instead of bringing out just want, the world and never think of your attitude."

Asher regarded her carefully. "Brace yourself, with the grace of ease. I know this world, ain't what it seems."

"It's unbelievable," Auryn sighed.

And everyone here hated everyone else and everyone here was wondering what it's like to be with somebody else and everyone here was caught up in the passion or the PAIN![123]

Everyone here looked around the circle at everyone else. Today, Sunday Bloody Sunday, most of the commune had come for visiting hours. Group field trip to the loony bin. Marley sat directly across from Izzy. She was glad that Adia wasn't there because she

---

[123] See Matchbox 20's "Back 2 Good" lyrics.

was starting to suspect that Izzy had a thing for Adia. Adia had sent a card, but Luca knew the real reason behind her absence. She felt a little paranoid that once she walked in there she wouldn't come out. Her appearance screamed meth addict, and she wasn't about to give herself up in enemy territory. Those nurses would have her committed before she could even lock herself in the bathroom. Everyone suspected these motives, but no one said anything. Especially not Luca. He wore a dark oversized hooded sweatshirt himself, on the assumption that, given the environment, the look of a mugger was less suspect than evidence of addiction. It must have been the ideal day of the week for this motley crew to visit, because none of the staff said anything. The Sunday staff was bored. The regular doctors and therapists went home on the weekends, so the weekend staff was less informed and, if the patients played it right, practically clueless. They only saw these freaks once or twice a week, and the weekend schedule was notoriously full of loopholes and easy getaways. Things were slow, observation was less acute, and half the aides fell asleep on their watch. The patients got away with murder. Sex in the mop closet. Cheeking meds, or in some cases, raiding the medicine cabinet for cough syrup highs. Beer smuggled in a paper coffee to-go cup. However, in spite of all these murders, not one was a suicide. As long as no one died on their watch, the substitute prison guards figured they did their job.

The Poets: a ragtag band of bohemians residing in the Lower East Side and Village, who found each other and lived together. Asher – occupation??...(failed artist) and Auryn the sometime resident with Ash; Izzy the belly doll; Marley her lesbian lover. Izzy, who wore a neon blue bobbed wig, and Marley, who wore a neon purple wig of the same fashion, were often mistaken for twins, and they got a very perverse kick out of that common misperception. Both were self-proclaimed "goth girl" belly dancers in a punk cabaret troop called the Belly Dolls. They had black and white striped knee socks under their black sateen tap shorts. Their favorite number sounded like: death rattle of my stillborn child. Poe the Avatar – still running around in the snipped wings of an angel in devil's shoes – not a resident of Mantua Commune, but it came to represent Auryn's sanctuary from her arch-nemesis – "you should get one!" Adia & Luca both seemed terminally ill, melancholic, hopeless lovers, heroin addicts with the gaunt, ghostly look of anorexic patients, the modern face of such scholarship as *Fasting Saints to Anorexic Girls: The History of Self-Starvation* including "Possession and Witchcraft," "Miraculous Maidens," "Hunger Artists and Living Skeletons," and "Morbid Miracle or Miraculous Morbidity?"[124] See also Malcolm Godwin's *Angels: An Endangered Species*, describing the theory that angels are the medieval products of hysterical anorexics: "Her desire knows no pain...she hardly knows whether she is in the body or out of it" (246). Luca gave the eyewitness account of the Jesus Freak rapist to the AP news after shooting up, so how reliable of a narrator was he? It could have all been hallucinations the product of a drug-induced psychosis. Angels are simply drug addicts. Or the product of a painful ecstasy, like Saint Teresa of Avila, who was so pierced by the spirit (an angel stabbing her

---

[124] By Walter Vandereycken and Ron van Deth, New York UP, 1994.

through the heart with a long golden spear), that it presumably caused agony and ecstasy similar to orgasm. But it *was* a self-fulfilling prophecy for both A. & A. The rest of the Mantua Commune included Dorian and Jo Pitts the dealers; Raven, the Moon-Dark Angel of Death slash Reverse Cupid of sorts (or simply a vengeful ex on the manhunt), and Damien, the tattoo artist and Asher's best friend.

"We all begin with good intent when love is raw and young, we believe that we could change ourselves, the past can be undone"[125] –

> "If there is no love in your heart – so sorry
> Then there is no hope for you – true, true
> Tomorrow people, where is your past?
> Tomorrow people, how long will you last?"[126]

Visiting hours were long expired by the time the delinquent weekend staff finally thought to shoo the poets out. Marley, always the realist, commented over her shoulder to Asher as soon as they were out of Auryn's earshot, on the other side of the locked door – the staff practically slammed it in their faces – "Basically, what we have here is a dreamer. Somebody out of touch with reality. When she jumped, she probably thought she'd fly." Marley took liberties of the creative, medical, psychiatric, and likely a host of others, not the least of which being the plagiaristic sort, when she assessed Auryn's bizarre behavior by referencing a fictional evaluation in *The Virgin Suicides* as if it were the DSM IV itself. Auryn broke both her arms in the accident, and "when she finally tumbled

---

[125] Sarah McLachlan, "Fallen"
[126] Ziggy Marley.

out [of the taxi cab] she lifted both slings like canvas wings…." Marley was struck by the resemblance to the image of Cecilia on page 16 of this book.

"And the next morning I woke up in a motel in Las Vegas and I had *seven* new piercings!" Auryn told Asher on the unit's only pay phone. The patients had to take turns after meals, which meant the weakest caller usually got slighted. Someone would inevitably go over their time limit, having phone sex, so the last in line would have to wait yet another day to tell her family that she was getting a *brain transplant*. Einstein's. Until the effects of the morphine wore off, Auryn didn't realize she'd been lucid dreaming about the wing-snipping, going back to the slot machines, the game of chance, the deal in hell's casino, and selling her soul to her demon sister. Asher just nodded and smiled into the phone.

"We're busting you outta there, babe," he said. "Marley and Izzy and me. Everyone wants you back. The big house show is coming up; you don't wanna miss the hip, happenin' event of all time. 672 Mantua is the place to be."

"They're letting me go?" Auryn perked up, grasping the receiver tightly as if trying to get a hold on reality.

"It's a little thing called 'AMA'. I'll talk you through it. Done it lots of times myself. They can't hold you against your will without the courts involved. Just do your best to act normal, in the meantime, to convince them you're all better and no longer a danger to yourself."

Auryn still felt uncertain. "How do I act *normal*?" She didn't trust her instincts since they weren't altogether human.

"Just resist all your natural impulses." Auryn was

too flustered with the seemingly open-ended interpretation of "normal," "human" behavior to realize how unflattering that was.

Chapter Twenty-three

Burning the Commune:
"Escape from Mantua"

*Stagger onward, rejoice,
And honor the fate you are,
traveling and tormented,
dialectic and bizarre.*

*W.H. Auden[127]
*(post-it note tacked
on the bulletin board.)*

At the house show Ash strummed a guitar painted with Van Gogh's Starry Night, his poem-songs half sung at the old Sycamore Grove movie set, where Auryn stepped on a shard of broken mirror in the grass leftover from the summoning of Bloody Mary. The witch, however, refused to grant the usual consequences of death or injury (Auryn would have liked convenient access to a bloodletting, but in her case, of course, the curse was withholding mortality, rather than banking on it).

---

[127] Misprint of lines from Auden's poem "Atlantis."

ASHES TO ANGELS

The House Show at #672. Exhibit #3: "In case of emergency, break juju." c. 2008. On Halloween there was a roaring art show at the Commune complete with bands and visual art exhibits on two floors. However, the neighbors complained and called the cops "and the band played on" though the ship was sinking by the time a careless cigarette dropped by some catatonic loitering in the staircase started a fire accidentally-on-purpose. Said catatonic claimed it was his own contribution – "performance art" like smashing a box of silver ball ornaments on the floor after the music. "We didn't start the fire," a kid named Id told police, "It was always burning since the world's been turning."

Ring around the Thorns,
Pocketful of pins,
Matchsticks, matchsticks,
We all sing sin![128]

672 turned into more of a rock concert, with rickety scaffolding for a stage copied off Baz Luhrmann's Sycamore Grove Theater movie set. A few local bands and solo acoustic sets provided the musical theme to this Woodstock of sorts. Bands were regarded as collective gods, the way the audience practically knelt before the singer's pedestal at the microphone. Then, when the crowd joined the final song like a Greek chorus narrating an ancient theater production, "the flames climbed high into the night to light the sacrificial rite,"[129] and Auryn saw Poe laughing with

---

[128] Friend rock: The last line is the title of a musical composition by Romance of Young Tigers, a band hailing from Dayton, Ohio.

[129] Don McLean, "American Pie."

delight the day the music died. Angel-headed hipsters rocked out, "How can we dance when our earth is turning? How do we sleep while our beds are burning?"[130] Flailing limbs. Talking heads. "The time has come, to say it's fair, to pay the rent now, to pay our share! The time has come, our bags are packed, it belongs to them, let's give it back!" Some punk rocker's t-shirt graphic became their chant around the bonfire: "Come to the Dark Side – we have cookies!" Indeed they did, at the adjournment of the third dimension *here at the end of the world in reverse.*

"Will we burn in heaven like we do down here?"[131] Asher's question to Auryn was more of a snide comment. *To reverse the reverse is* not *to re*vert.

"'All goes onward and outward, nothing collapses, / and to die is different from what anyone supposed, and luckier.'"[132] She stoically chanted fame to the obscure. Small fires still burned sporadically amid the rubble and ruins, flare-ups of broken originality, re-created authenticity self-contained in the little hot spots gracing the wreckage and wake. As they stood around in a ragged ring, skinny and sooty like chimney sweeps, Ash looked over at Auryn. She hugged herself as she watched burning atoms disintegrate to ash. Both hands had colorful third degree burns like graffiti on her body. It occurred to him the vampire test had failed. She was but dust and shadow, not ash. In a rare show of sympathy,

"Are you human?" he whispered tentatively, as if he was uncomfortable with either answer.

---

[130] "Beds Are Burning" by Midnight Oil.
[131] "Witness" from the album <u>Surfacing</u> by Sarah McLachlan.
[132] Walt Whitman.

She considered this. "My sign is vital; my hands are cold."

"How does it feel?"

"It hurts."

She looked over at him, gauging her believability as human being by his reaction. Her eyes were deep, endless, haunted in their sunken sockets. "The pain, the sunshine…it's terrible and wonderful all at once. It feels…amazing!" The exclamation was more a cry of tortured ecstasy than a sigh of relief. She was struggling with it. "How does an immortal deal with mortal feelings?" She looked up at him searchingly, as if she could really extract the answer from the abstract depths of his eyes if only she willed it hard enough.

He shook his head. "Beats me." A wry smile cracked his lips. "Even we humans aren't very good at it. Half of us have to be doped up just so we don't self-destruct in the creative process."

Her eyes followed the flames swallowing their former hide-out. "I've never had to come to terms with my existence. I always just *was*. No beginning and no end. But to think one would have a *choice* in the matter…." She looked back at him. "No power in the 'verse could stop me."

"No choice in the beginning; big choice at the end," he corrected cryptically.

Suddenly they heard the wail of sirens as fire trucks raced around the corner, coming to an abrupt halt in front of the cindering loft. The crowd started to scatter when public attention showed up. No one wanted to be framed the arsonist. Except for the poor catatonic, who now beheld his glorious performance art without the slightest thought to its crime. Some guardian angel had had the last-minute sense to drag him out before the pyromania got going. Now he slumped under a tree, searching his pockets for another cigarette, while everyone else ran in all haphazard directions. The sacrificial scapegoat everyone was more than willing to vote their spokesperson. Cat disappointed the police, though. They were hoping for a really high-profile arrest, but for once the lead didn't bleed. "I have no insurance," Cat moaned, "so I can't really do anything. Can't set myself on fire; can barely walk down the damn street without tempting fate. I might break a leg if I don't tip-toe around on eggshells. Life is too dangerous for living. It's bound and determined to get you, by its very nature. So why'd'ya think I'd set myself on fire without insurance to save me?" The cops shook their heads in contempt. Just another loony accident. At best he'd be incarcerated in the state hospital, rather than the slammer full of normal, socially acceptable inmates.

Asher grabbed Auryn's blistering hand. She cringed a little at the touch; however, her hand was indeed cool where it should have been inflamed. "Let's go," he urged, keeping a sharp eye on Cat, giving his backwards statement to the police. News crews were starting to arrive on the scene.

"Where?" The logic was setting in with the scar tissue. Now they had sabotaged their space, they were essentially homeless. All in the name of art.

"Anywhere but here," he pulled her along as she struggled to keep up with his brisk pace. "Destination not important. The trick is to keep moving."

"The trick is to keep breathing," she coughed as the smoky air followed them. Never mind the burns; let men burn stars; the real danger was smoke inhalation.

Asher, with his seasoned smoker lungs, didn't seem

as bothered by the polluted air, ironically, despite his mortal status so much more vulnerable than hers.

They were already a few streets over from the loft, but as Auryn looked back she could still see a few unruly flames whipping just out of reach of the water hoses' spray. Teasers. Suddenly she choked, her breath caught in her throat; Asher turned impatiently to the reason for the delay. "C'mon," he tugged on her hand again. "Don't look back; too many of us can't get past our past because we do stupid human stuff like that."

"I thought—" she coughed again. "I thought I saw—" Suddenly Asher crouched down.

"You ever had a piggyback ride?" he tried to distract her and make up for lost time. "Get on." To his relief, she complied, and jumped on his back, wrapping her arms around his neck. "And supposedly *you're* the one who can fly. Shouldn't this be the other way around?" he muttered as he adjusted his pace to the relatively minor load. "Easy there," he flinched as she dug her nails into his neck. He relaxed a little as the distance between them and the "crime" scene grew. She realized he was headed toward her old hostel. She hoped the landlady wouldn't give them any trouble. She hadn't been too thrilled the last time Asher had shacked up on the fly.

"One bed per person," she insisted after she'd discovered Auryn's unauthorized double occupancy. "That's how the rates go."

He let her slide off his back a few blocks from the brownstone. "You still have a room there, right?" A risky amount of assumption lay behind his afterthought. "And a key?"

She sighed as she dug around her hobo bag. "Asher, when are you going to tire of being a fugitive?

You're always on the run from something. I never claimed membership in the Guardian Angel Order. Yet, even without a pair of wings, I'm always saving you."

He scoffed at her. "That's *your* story, not mine: *you're* the runaway, *you're* the one who fell helpless at my feet, and by some predetermined force of fate, I'm supposed to save *you* from wherever the hell you came from!" His frustration was apparent now. She was a little shocked that she hadn't picked up on this resentment which seemed to have taken root when she and the earth made contact. Like a vine it had grown and twisted until it broke the surface of his subconscious. Something the cop had said at the intersection came back to her: "She's *your* responsibility now." She had heard every word, every comma, in her coma. Was Ash merely fulfilling a social obligation, administering a salve to his conscience? Was she the poison in his ivy? Surely she was more to him than just an innocent child, a kid sister, a daughter of a poison love…

He broke her thoughts with diplomacy, for once. "Look, we both need a place to stay; if you want, I'll pay my fair share. How can we sleep when our beds are burning?" he pleaded with her. "The time has come, to say it's fair, to pay the rent, to pay our share. The time has come, our bags are packed, it belongs to them, let's give it back." In spite of his lyricism, he was talking sensibly now. There was just one thing.

"You get your own bed," she demanded, not just because the landlady would have a fit that she was getting ripped off with a two-for-one. Auryn looked down, a shade of red blossoming in her snowy cheeks. "I'm not…ready." She looked up timidly into his intense gaze, afraid of what she'd find there. Oh, his eyes, his eyes! If only they had not that eternal sway. They're a penetration of sorts.

A knowing smile spread slowly across his lips. He put his arm around her slight shoulders and escorted her to the hostel's wicker gate. "Let's get bunk beds. I always wanted one when I was a kid, but it didn't really make sense for an only child."

She relaxed her shoulders under his touch, osmotic relief transfusing her nervous system that such vulnerability hadn't earned her a rejection slip. "You can be on top," she offered, "I'm afraid with my jumping and falling history, I'm a liability without my wings."

He smiled again, more to himself this time. "Good looking out."

NATALIE MCCOLLUM

Chapter Twenty-four

Alms for the Poets

They returned to the scene after the fire and found his name removed from his doorknocker and mailbox, he couldn't unlock the door in spite of all the keys he tried like a slumlord, with his large brassy medieval-style key for a chain. Locks changed, furniture gone, place cleared out, so he broke in (to his own apartment!).

Broke into the old apartment (this is where we used to live)[133]

<u>What They Found</u>

Broken glass, broke and hungry
Broken hearts and broken bones
(This is where we used to live)

This note was tacked on the door:
Disconnection Notice:
We may disconnect your service without advance

---

[133] "The Old Apartment" by the Bare Naked Ladies.

ASHES TO ANGELS

notice if:
DANGER TO LIFE OR PROPERTY EXISTS. READ: SUSPECTED SUICIDE INDICATIONS OF AN ATTEMPT LEFT BY THE AFFECTED PERSON(S):

X no response to phone messages
X bills left unpaid
X utilities disconnected a month ago
X whereabouts unknown.

Such is the nature of Asher's state of affairs.

She said:
Why did you paint the walls?
He said:
Why did you change the locks?

"Why did you clean the floor?" Auryn asked in reply.

"Why did *you* plaster over the hole I punched in the door?!" Asher shot back with a roar.

Auryn shrugged. "This *is* where we used to live."

Asher raved on. "Why did you keep the mousetrap? Why did you keep the dishrack? These things used to be mine. I guess they still are, I want them back."

"Forty-two stairs from the street," mused Auryn, "crooked landing, crooked landlord. Narrow laneway filled with crooks."

"Why did they pave the lawn?" Asher was annoyed to distraction. "Why did they change the locks? Why did I have to break it, I only came here to talk," he finally admitted in defeat.

Auryn tried to keep up the morale. "How is the

neighbor downstairs? How is her temper this year?" She giggled, "I turned up your TV and stomped on the floor just for fun."

Asher sighed. "I know we don't live here anymore. We bought an old house on the Danforth." His delusional eyes finally strayed to Auryn as she leaned nimbly out the window to hang her head over, hear the wind blow. "She loves me and her body keeps me warm," he crooned to himself. "I'm happy here," a little too convincingly. "But—" he shuffled over to join Auryn at the window, "this is where we used to live."

Auryn looked up and shook her head. "Broke into the old apartment," she mock scolded.

"Tore the phone out of the wall," Asher continued, listing the vandalisms.

"Only memories, fading memories, blending into dull tableaux," Auryn chorused sentimentally.

Then Asher, in a turn of emotion, "I want them back. I want them back."

He said:

> Ulysses grant me the strength to scour the wastelands of my birthday deathbed (and smelling like a rose all the while). I walk this lonely road – the long and winding road that leads to your door. You heard me knocking but I couldn't get in. Tried to break on through to the dark side of the moon and the only thing I had to fear was no soma and nobody to help JC complete his mission. Caiaphas and Jack K can share a cell, and I'll stand guard if you'll show me how you do that trick but keep the beans in the can. And don't forget, the best part of waking up is milk and lemonade,

around the corner Fudge and Soup go together like angels and schizos, but I still haven't found what I'm looking for. I think the poet said live simply so that others may simply live fast, die young, and leave a tip for little Suzy (she's on the up but on the outs with INXS). I'm buyin' what you're sellin', but it's cold out and you're not wearin' a sweater (and I'm low on gas). Don't stop until you get it get it, because when you've got nothin' to live for you've got nothin' to lose. Negative b plus or minus the square root of b squared minus four a.c. you
when I c U.[134]

She said:
Oh, Asher. You poor beautiful fucked up man.

They came into some money after turning in the priest thief. *Alms, alms, alms for the poets.* Asher's tip led to an arrest. He never had to give his name. They lived in the invisible spotlight of anonymous heroes for a while. It was strangely depressing. Paranoia set in like acrylic paint. Always looking over the shoulder in case one of his hit men might have fallen through the cracks, come back for revenge. This wasn't how celebrity was supposed to look. How did a good deed manage to make him feel like a smooth criminal?

"Auryn, are you okay, are you okay, are you okay, Auryn?"

Our Lady of Sorrows, You gave me a charred letter and a black rose for a ransom note and bail. On the steps of the capitol, and at the gate of the embassy, our

---

[134] "Mike Boblitt responds to Natalie McCollum's 'Ashes to Angels,' 9/15/05, Eng 693

hands met through the bars, how I longed to hear you say: NO THEY CANNOT CATCH ME NOW! *We will escape somehow* – *somehow.*[135]

"Don't let them see your back." Asher was more bark than bite as he draped a sheer tunic over her exposed shoulders.

"[Cross'd] the Patron Saint of Switchblade fights. You said. We're not celebrities. We spark and fade. They die by threes." She protested only a little as she shrugged into the little angel wings graphic t-shirt that cleverly distracted from the long scissor scar like a badly stitched seam down her spine, with a wispy screen print on the back. *Count the stars in multiples of threes.*

"Look, I don't mind you coming here and wasting all my time, 'cause when you're standing oh-so near, I kinda lose my mind,"[136] Asher said as he stroked the hidden scar, feeling every vertebra along the way. She flinched, as if it were fresh and still hurt. "It's not the perfume that you wear, it's not the ribbons in your hair," he playfully fingered the auburn ringlets tied in multi-colored streamers. She squirmed away from him and bounced into the bedroom, up on the billowy comforter and burrowed under the folds like a rabbit in a hole. He followed her in, hands shoved nonchalantly in his pockets, continuing their game of cat-and-mouse. "I don't mind you coming here and talking in your sleep—"

"I do not!" she conveniently woke up and poked her head out from her little goose-down nest.

"You walk, too."

---

[135] The Decemberists
[136] The Cars, "Just What I Need."

ASHES TO ANGELS

"Walk – or fly?" she prodded with a sly note on her voice.

"I guess you're just what I needed," he finished the song, evading her interrogation as to her own nocturnal behavior. "I needed someone to need." He hugged her in a bundle of blanket like a long forgotten teddy bear from childhood. It was a rare act of tenderness for someone who tried so hard to play the heartless bastard. It was his vulnerable side she clung to. Humans these days, what had gone wrong? It was the only real human characteristic they still retained. Why were humans the worst at being themselves? That was the part she feared. Never mind mortality; death, as Lennon had once said, was merely getting out of one car and into another. But life – that was downright scary. Imagine having a choice: why tempt fate? Suicide made more and more sense, the longer she ran around with these children of the poison love. Bite the bullet, and bite the apple, for god's sake, for everyone's sake.

"You wanna…take a trip?" he sloughed off the moment with an abrupt new idea.

"On what?"

He shook his head, grinning knowingly. She had definitely spent too much time with him and the gang. Those two words comprised straight-up evidence of her nearly complete corruption. "Naw, I mean a train ride. A geographical trip, not a chemical one."

"Oh, has your chemical romance come to a tragic end?" she teased.

"Tragically, yes. For the time being. There hasn't been any good herb around for a while. Dorian's working on it. He claims there may be mushrooms soon. What I'd like is some really good acid. You know, a mind-fuck. In the meantime—" he leaned close to nuzzle her nose, resuming his swoon with moony eyes and sugary lips— "I guess my sweet tooth will keep me from going sour."

"Or south."

Damn, she had a little mouth on her. But he revenged his declined advances. "It's settled, then! We'll go south. South of Soho – to France! We'll go dig the scene, the art, the life. I'll find work; you'll find your wings. We'll be the greatest two people who ever lived! We'll live fast and die young. And while the seagulls are crying, we'll fall but our souls will be flying!" He finished off this impossible monologue with a grand flourish of his arm, swooping her up in the same motion. He set her on her feet, visions of sugarplums and other such grandiose luminosities swimming, rather than dancing, in his delirious head. As soon as her feet touched ground, they both set about packing, scurrying around in a fine frenzy throwing whatever articles of clothing and personal effects happened to be littering their peripheral vision into rucksacks and carpetbags. In ten minutes they were flying down the stairs of the loft, tossing their bags on the doorstep while Asher called a cab. Adia and Luca were huddled together on the steps, sharing a smoke after their latest shot of their latest addiction. Adia looked terrible; her bones stuck out everywhere in overlapping angles and geometric inconsistencies. She had red track marks on her feet. Her dirty hoodie shrouded similar incriminations on her arms and neck. Luca wasn't much better, but at least he still had some meat on his vegan body. He nodded to Asher as the runaways swept down the steps of the brownstone.

"Where you two off in such haste?"

"Entrance to trains!" cried Asher, barely able to

contain himself.

"Runaway train never going back." Auryn's version didn't do much to clarify.

"Godspeed You! Black Emperor," Luca replied absently.

"Adia—" Auryn stopped suddenly in her own dirty tracks. "I do believe I've failed you." She looked at her friend forlornly.

"No, honey, it's all good," Adia shook her fragile skull as if it were too heavy for her neck. She seemed not to know what she was saying. "You go find what you're looking for, go claim your life. Me, I got all I want right here, and I'll be sitting right here on this doorstep till the last night of the world." She smiled sadly.

Auryn went and hugged her friend. "I will come back for you, and we will have a grand old time. Like sisters. You are like the sister I never—" Just then the cab pulled up and honked. Asher was swinging the bags into the trunk.

"Let's go, m'lady!" He was pulling her hand. But Auryn was still caught in the middle of her unfinished sentence. What was the end to that sentence? How was it she felt more akin to a mortal than her own half-sister? And a drug addict, no less. These children of a lesser god made angels look like acid trips. Perhaps that's all she really was. A bad habit, a tragic flaw. Asher's heroine, and heroin. Would he save her, or shoot her? Perhaps he was saving the best for last, and she would be his last trip.

And then she was in the backseat of the cab, looking back by looking forward in the rearview mirror, and it was ten years on and she resurfaced in a motorcar, not waving but drowning.[137] The oceans in the sky followed her, and she was swallowed in the pool of her own body.

---

[137] The poem by Stevie Smith.

ASHES TO ANGELS

Chapter Twenty-five

Id
(The Twelfth Voice)

Id & P'o. Poe's alter ego was a shape-shifter named Id. He represented exactly what the Freudian term means. Id was seduced by Auryn's hooker sister, who was *still* running around in the wings snipped from an angel in devil's shoes! "Like any hot-blooded woman, I have simply wanted an object to crave,"[138] pleaded Poe.

"I can resist all things but temptation," Id tried out a little Oscar Wilde on her.

"Unfathomable to mere mortals is the lore of fiends," said Poe with a toss of her shiny black mop top, plagiarizing Hawthorne, p. 240. But then, later, Pavese in 1940, "We always love madly someone who treats us with indifference."

Poe the suicide-turned-vampire: "Her parents named her Hallelujah, the kids they called her Holly, she's been stranded at these parties [where she met Id], they start kinda wobbly but they get druggie and they get ugly and they get bloody. Hallelujah came to in the

---

[138] "Uninvited" by Alanis Morissette.

Confession booth and fasted with infection and smiled on an abscessed tooth. Crashing through the vestibule, she climbed up on the X and found she liked the view. Holly said to the priest, 'Father [Romeo bon Jovi], can I tell your congregation how a "res-erection" *really feels?*'[139]

[*You're a real sweet girl who's made some not-so-sweet friends.*]

Poe and her Id clenching fists, grasping hands: *This is it.* DON'T *let me* break up with you this time, ever again. Even if I beg and plead and *say* I'm gonna sleep with another man, *that* just means it's working. Don't let me jump ship on you again – don't leave me hanging on this ledge you talked me out of a very precarious decision. I'm just gonna go with it and not think: don't let me think about it. I think too much, that's what gets me in trouble.
The temptress.
"So you were separated from your id," Id surmised. "Why, I've never heard of such a thing." He idly dropped a grape in his mouth. Clearly he had. Id was always saying the exact opposite of what he meant.
"I think these fool feathers have something to do with it," Poe growled, shaking her shoulders like a wet dog. "Not *only* are they not human, they have absolutely no animal instinct, either. If they weren't bringing in all the money at Alley Cat, I'd saw 'em off myself. For once, I actually see the logic in Auryn's fanciful little whims." She picked at a feather, curled its long quill around a black lacquered fingernail.

---

[139] Separation Sunday album by The Hold Steady, Tracks 10 and 11 from a burned CD.

ASHES TO ANGELS

Id smiled demurely. "Well, Madam, I suppose you'll have to indulge in a little raw animal pleasure to get your id back," he drawled suggestively. His double entendre wasn't necessary, and that's exactly why he said it. He lived by the law of opposites; gratifying carnal urges on demand was outright defiance of social etiquette, and so he did it, simply because of that.

However, he wasn't sold on the theory that opposites attract when it came to said urges. Relationships could not be reduced to the same elementary principles of atomic behaviors, with their positive and negative electron couples; no, these two demon lovers were perfectly matched silhouettes of each other. Unfortunately, ids were a lot more difficult to sew back on than shadows. Peter Pan had it relatively easy.

"So, what *are* you going to do with that fluff?" Id held a lighter to the feather Poe had been playing with and watched it disintegrate along the spine to ash. Poe flicked the charred quill like a chicken bone she had just finished gnawing the meat off of.

"When I'm done playing 'Angel' at the club," she mused, "I suppose I'll pawn them for something better. Something better worth my time and money. Gotta keep the gentlemen on their toes. They get bored with same old costume every night. A constantly evolving persona is essential to defending my title as the leading crowd-pleaser on the catwalk."

"You don't like it here very much, do you?" Id was disarmingly candid sometimes.

"Anima!"

He ignored the pop psychology. "You'd rather go back to hell."

She finally faced the fork in her gut. He was slowly, agonizingly making spaghetti of her intestines with the turn of the screw.

"It's no paradise here. Paradise Lost, more like it. If I'da known committing reverse suicide from the bowels of the underworld would merely land me in a place not much better than Limbo, I'da thought twice about hitchhiking with little Miss Suicide-isn't-just-Death-it-is-Love-too."

"Love *is* the cheapest of all religions," sighed Id, ripping off Pavese's journal again. *The ripper.*

ASHES TO ANGELS

Chapter Twenty-six

"She's Been Calling Me Again"

Asher called to the punk approaching from East 5th, "Dude, you strut your rasta wear and your suicide poem and a cross from a faith that died before Jesus came!"[140] It was Damien, his best friend and celebrity tattoo artist by profession.

Damien wore knee-high black combat boots and tight black knickers with a metallic-studded belt. A chain-link fob hung from his right pocket, and he wore a cinched vest like a corset to match his shoestrings laced taut as guitar strings. When the laces on his vest loosed their death grip and came undone, the masochist's chest revealed a huge cross with fire and roses spread across its breadth. Tattoos covered both his arms in lieu of sleeves. Topping it all off was a bleach-blond razor-straight mohawk spanning the length of his otherwise shaved pale scalp, front to back. His left eyebrow was pierced; he had a nose ring, a labret, and ear lobes plugged with size zero gauges. The whole spectacle was so epic, it made you

---

[140] "Building a Mystery" by Sarah McLachlan.

want to choke.

On Separation Sunday[141], Asher and Damien fight over a girl:

> Your little hoodrat friend makes me sick

(Damien nodded to Auryn across the way, still huddled on the curb with their bags where the taxi had left them.)

> but after I get sick I just get sad
> 'cause it burns being broke,
> hurts to be heart-broken,
> and always being both must be a drag.
>
> SHE'S BEEN CALLING ME AGAIN!

"What? Impossible!" Asher flicked the butt of his cigarette, scattering ashes against the wind, so they flew back in his face.

Damien protested, "And she's been calling me again!"

> Your little hoodrat friend's been calling me again
> And I can't stand all the things that she sticks into her skin
> Like sharpened ball point pens and steel guitar strings
> She says it hurts but it's worth it
> Tiny little text etched into her neck

---

[141] Conversation lyrics by The Hold Steady, from the album Separation Sunday.

ASHES TO ANGELS

It said Jesus lived and died for all your sins
She's got blue-black ink and it's scratched into her lower back
Says, "Damn right I'll rise again—"

Yeah, Damn right you'll rise again! Angry vegetarians staging a PETA demonstration across the street protested the same. Damien pumped his fist into the air with a flourish to end his rock opera solo. He couldn't make *Rent* either, but on the street, everyone's a rockstar when everything feels like the movies and you bleed just to know you're alive. Especially when you wake up the morning after in a motel in Las Vegas with seven new piercings. *Never drink with strangers, unless you want to end up in a foreign country.* "Damien! That's NOT what you told me last night!" He could hear the shrieky little voice now. He turned from his thoughts back to Asher.

"Look, if you don't love her, if you're not into her, if you're not even attracted to her, then why the hell do you run around with her? Why encourage her? You can't seem to leave her any more than you can your own shadow. What the fuck, man?"

"Because there's something so attractive about *getting* her."

Damien stepped back, shook his head, threw up his ringed fingers in surrender. "Then fuck her and be done with it. I wash my hands of it. No virgin blood on my conscience. *You* play Dr. Kevorkian."

Asher, entranced, put his fingertips together as if conspiring with the Bard. "From ancient grudge break to new mutiny, where civil blood makes civil hands unclean!"[142]

---

[142] <u>Romeo and Juliet</u>, Act 1, Prologue, lines 3-4, Chorus.

NATALIE MCCOLLUM

ASHES TO ANGELS

Chapter Twenty-seven

Bleeding Lessons

The Cutter.
Wrist-slitting poetry.

The night that Auryn cut her wrists she was high.

"The boys, the boys: 'round here, they make me want to carve their names in my arms and bleed out from *every name* so that whoever finds my body can read not only who went down ON me, but who's going down WITH me, six feet!" It might have been the best thing she ever wrote. It was so, *inspired*.

Ash:	"My arms, Hold you in my arms, I just wanted to hold you in my arms."[143]
Auryn:	"Fade into you...strange you never knew."[144]
Poe:	"When we bleed, we bleed the

---

[143] "Starlight" by Muse.//
[144] "Fade into You" by Mazzy Star.

same."[145]

Lesson 1

A Special Place for Suicides

Asher leaned in toward her like a vampire making out with his victim. Hickeys were for pussies; a mortal knock-off of the real thing. Only the cruelest lovers survived the bite and bang. "Which would have to involve someone who's half-vampire anyway, otherwise she'd either die or turn full-blood…." He peered closely at her. She had to admit, she was impressed with his vampire scholarship, but she averted her eyes. Under duress of his gaze, the con finally 'fessed:

"Yes, she was a cutter. Poe killed herself. And ended up in a custom-made hell, which for her, was just another version of the world she tried to ditch, only a little worse." (*Every hour, every waking moment, I'm choosing my confessions.* [146])

3 of 3: Confession

There is no answer:
What I cannot eat
is eating away at me.
Must I render myself
in bequest of the dead?
It is more alive to be
cut and vulnerable, but

---

[145] "Map of the Problematique" by Muse.
[146] "Losing My Religion" by R.E.M.

ASHES TO ANGELS

My addictions shot me
down to my knees by the
first nick of the wrist
Delicate tokens of my shame
Will I starve if I live
on stolen breath, this
a beggar's prayer?
It is in violation of
the premeditated that
I only feel beautiful
in my hunger, for want
of bread and roses,
I linger between them
and darkness, so the wine
runs through my blood—
If you find me in the
carpet stain tonight
do not weep for thorns:
Suicide isn't just death
It is love too.

"She didn't become a vampire because they didn't bury her anywhere near a crossroad; they wouldn't even cremate her because they were so paranoid about her being a suicide, she already had that strike against her rising bodily with the dead at the end of the world; so she's just a demon. But I—" Auryn stumbled here, forcing herself to meet Asher's intense gaze as it drew her story like blood— "I landed at one."

Lesson 2

The Mythology of *The Catcher in the Rye*

The last thing Lee Harvey Oswald read before shooting JFK was this book. He raved about it, as do other psychopaths. Serial killers tend to identify with

Holden Caulfield; apparently a correlation between psychotic patients and the Holden complex has been upheld by the government's tracking of sales demographics of Salinger's book.

> Q: Do more crazy people tend to connect with *Catcher* than so-called normal people?
>
> A: "I'm not homicidal, but I *am* attracted to Suicide like falling in love with a vampire," Auryn commented. "Suicide with a capital 'S' because anything that gets me passage to your world is my Holy Grail."

"Then I am your vampire lord Kieran, and you, my angel, are Gráinne, my most unholy grail." Asher could feel himself falling, falling in love with Auryn's wings. They were Forever 26.

> she stood there under the gutter
> beside her depressive other half,
> by degrees growing manic.
> two versions of neurotica
> embalmed in their shared baggage,
> busting up a starbucks.
> it was humid. it was hysterical.
> they watched the rain, they watched each other.
> pressed up against the glass, she felt molecules
> graze her like a serrated knife like the tension
> between them grazing the edges of each other
> with every shift in weight and shift in gaze,
> till the shift of fate had her removing her plastic
> frames to wonder why she found herself framed
> in the rain with someone she once feared
> and why friends and lovers make the best enemies

and why all this was so forbidden
and all the more alluring for it?
he took drags off a hand-rolled cigarette
and spoke of open-ended things.

they may be crazy,
they may be a double dose of anti-psychotic pills,
they may be tripping on heartache the bitterest acid,
they may be hallucinations of each other,
they may be a pair of schizophrenic statistics at age 26,
but they don't care –
in the absence of roses,
it must have been the mushrooms.

later, they will ask each other again and again,
"we've been together so long –
i hope it wasn't just the drugs –
what happened to the energy we had?"[147]
and she will continue to write poems
about things that don't seem to exist
until she writes poems about them.

"My life is brilliant, my love is pure." Asher picked up his six-string and started strumming a popular song, leaving open the shabby guitar case for tips from subway passengers. "I saw an angel, of that I'm sure. She smiled at me on the subway, she was with another man—" he stopped short. "Oh, wait – maybe that man was *me*, and that angel was…you." He gazed directly into her eyes, his blue-green going faster than the speed of light into her purple-grays. It was like two rainbows colliding. A meteor shower in which kryptonite, for once, was not toxic. She caught her breath. It was the first time, albeit figuratively, that he had acknowledged her possible angel-hood. She

---

[147] "Let's Just Get Naked" by Joan Osborne.

quivered like a slender feather in the wind. He caught her by the wrists as the corners of her merlot mouth slightly turned. "There *must be* an angel with a smile on her face, when she thought up that I should be with you!"[148] he rushed the ending as he twirled her with equal haste into his arms, both of them soaking up the lyrical irony. She could see from his face that he was fucking high. She gave a tragic sigh. He caught her fast in a hold steady. "What?"

"I *am* that angel," she insisted, "'cause I don't know who I am without you, all I know is I should."[149]

He stepped back, still holding her wrists, scrutinizing her. It was the first time she had faltered on her true identity. Even though she had insisted, she always insisted, on her angelic status, she had simultaneously in the same breath doubted it. She had just staked her entire identity, existence even, on him and his presence in her life. The realization unnerved him. It was like deciding if someone should live or die. It was like playing god.

He didn't say anything for a long time. *How do you talk to an angel?* he wondered. They both just stood there, staring at one another, two worlds come face to face underground and suddenly there was no boundary line. It was like being given legs after a lifetime as an amputee. Neither had quite enough faith to actually put weight on them. All they could do was half-assed support each other like two cripples sharing the same crutch.

Her thoughts meanwhile went to Raven, mouthing

---

[148] James Blunt, "You're Beautiful" from the album Back to Bedlam.

[149] Missy Higgins, "Where I Stood."

these same words on moving day at Mantua. She had dared stand where Raven once stood, in Asher's erratic life, and here she was invoking Raven's song. *Good poets borrow, great poets steal.* As usual, Eliot's school of thought provided a defense of poetics. But it disarmed her, to think that she had become Raven, standing in Raven's place, saying Raven's song. It was hard enough to delineate her own Self from those she loved, like a fluid sketch that refused to stay in the lines, let alone distinguish her outline from those of other people. She didn't need to be confusing her identity with Raven, or anyone, not even Asher, much as she wanted him.

Lost in thought, and apparently translation, she realized Asher had been speaking to her. "…but I won't lose no sleep tonight, 'cause I've got a plan."[150] He was sadly smiling again, taking her playfully by the hand, leading her on. "C'mon, honey, let's go back to Bed-lam."

---

[150] James Blunt, "You're Beautiful" from the album <u>Back to Bedlam</u>.

NATALIE MCCOLLUM

Chapter Twenty-eight

If Wishes Were Whores

Then paparazzi would fly. The concept of the ubiquitous camera: *The Blair Witch Project* introduced the documentary style of telling story on film. After a free screening at the art theater Orpheus in East Village the night prior, Auryn decided she wanted to go see the photography and film exhibit at the MoMA, her second choice since the Louvre was a no-go. Perhaps when she became a model, she would make it to France.

"You were standing so still, I thought you were a mannequin," another eccentric old man hobbled up to Auryn in the art museum and spooked her with the strangely familiar compliment.

"Um, thanks?" Auryn had been admiring some rather curious artwork. Its ambivalence agitated her to distraction. She hardly considered the implications of the old man's comment until much later, when she realized she had been compared to a human replica, not the *real thing*. But for now, she was trying to decide if the photo was challenging the fine line between art and pornography, or – a pair of wings folded in on themselves in all-too-familiar layers of feathers and fluff....She wanted so badly to believe that this artist was Judy Chicago's protégé, but the name on the placket was a dead giveaway: spelling her name like the Chinese lower soul was a poor choice of alias. Auryn felt violated; here "P'o" had stripped her of her wings only to plagiarize them. Showcasing them as her own rather than giving attribution to their true source seemed beyond the terms of their original "deal." *The whole collection, half off the price they're asking, in the halfway house of ill repute.* Her indignation growing the longer she lingered, it was here Auryn made a resolution: she would get her wings back. It would take cunning and subtle deception to outsmart a foxy vixen like her twin, but, after all, *two halves are equal, a cross between two evils*...and who knows how better to work your own weaknesses than your own kin? "You will never be killed by a stranger," Asher had once told her in the same breath as *vampires will never hurt you. Because I am one,* she thought now, gazing directly into the x-ray photo of her soul. *If not flesh-and-blood, then its mirror image.*

NATALIE MCCOLLUM

Chapter Twenty-nine

Video Killed the ~~Radio~~ Porn Star

Adia got the part.

Adia would have a spotlight monologue in the upcoming production of *The Vagina Monologues* as part of the Ladyfest coming to the Village art district.

Auryn had to settle for an interview on a little piece she wrote and published in a local zine: "Synchronicity," a feminist memoir of sorts. It went something like this:

"Synchronicity"

Auryn woke up screaming Asher's name.

Though she couldn't scream when she wanted to — she was so crushed under his chest it stilled her vocal chords and not even an apologetic whisper or plea to him could find unobstructed passage. The bruises showing up days later…

By the first flick of the wrist, the world heard Poetry scream when it snapped. *I am Auryn; my name is Poetry. I can recite every poem ever written, because I AM every poem ever written!*

ASHES TO ANGELS

She pulled out the only evidence of human activity in that place from the cupboard, a tattered envelope housing the journal letter she wrote him that she did not send, though still found herself wondering, at off-moments, if he ever got it. The date was 22 july 2005:

"I sacrificed my body knowing too well there was an extremely permanent chance that this was just to borrow my body to feed his carnal male hunger. Good poets borrow, great poets steal. Who rapes angels these days? Only poets. They exchange words like body fluids, because they share a common language. You were an 80% chance just using me, 10% chance genuinely choosing me, and the rest is hard to say. I risked it on the 10%, to try to win you 100%. Bet my body all or nothing. Then sold out – the ½ virgin is only the first ½ of the double suicide. But the forfeit was rather necessary. His part was now ready to come. I now have a rough, minimalist idea of what rape feels like. There was especially one particular moment when I actually remember a conscious awareness running through my head almost in words, or something like them, of how he was doing more to me and to a greater, rougher, more violent and uncontrollable degree than I wanted or thought he would, and I was powerless to do anything about it – both physically, he had me pinned down so hard – my own shadow pinned to the heel of Pan himself – it hurt my legs, I thought my calf muscles would get Charlie horse and he would wake up from his alternative state of sub-being, a mixed drug of intoxication and frustration, adrenaline and arousal, to my screaming under his bones, the echoes of my voice suffocated under his throbbing beating chest, his heart right under my ear beating on me and beating me up, and breaking the sound barrier of his bones. Digging his nails into my torso, he etched me with marks impenetrable as tattoo ink that would show up and disappear off and on for years afterward like ghost writing down the bones. And when he put me on top, I was not waving but drowning in a Lilith affair."

She fingered her rosary as she saw the devil's child appear like a phantom before her... "in sleep he sang to me / in dreams he came / that voice which calls to me / and speaks my name."[151] His hand-me-down wife, Lilith, Adam's first mate second-rate reject, was trying to pawn off her ring in exchange for the rosary. An ad the girl cut and pasted like her own name, lifted from the cover of some rockstar's CD she accidentally shoplifted along with the classifieds section, the one and the same next to demon sister's "WANTED: Calling All Angels," proposing the outrage that one might condescend to PAY for her own death in order to attain something otherwise not free for all Failed Seekers….This anonymous ad said, "Adam tried to force her to lie beneath him in the approved patriarchal style of the 'missionary posture.' Now male Jews and Christians are not alone in their insistence of sexually 'being on top.' Moslems even state 'Accursed be the man that maketh woman heaven and himself earth.' Catholic authorities went so far as to say that any other position is sinful.

"Lilith didn't appear to share this male thesis..." *and neither do I.*

The letter trailed off after the ad until it came to again in a final bitter comment salved over in the tone of regret: "Sorry if these comments are more than you care to know. I don't care to censor myself for you

---

[151] Christine's song to <u>The Phantom of the Opera</u>.

ASHES TO ANGELS

anymore."

That was actually on a splotchy blue sticky note. The real part resumed with the part that was more journal than letter: "We were so meant for each other, that it was. not. meant. to be." 25 july 2005.

So. It was necessary. For art's sake. To write herstory. Like a "forced suicide," the rape of a slutty angel of music – a "pseudo" rape, vampire rape, consented rape by reason of the insanity implicated in being raped by someone you *want* to have sex with. What else is it called when you are raped by your best friend? She had worried about the huge challenge and feat of skill and pure craft and child prodigy it would take to write that scene, the climax of her tattoo, how to write the love scene like a rape, even though it's not a rape because she wants it, the rape. It had just been written for her. She acted it out herself. On location. She was her. Or rather, maybe really, the her was she. She was herstory. "The greatest story never told," as told by the bumper sticker on the car wrecked in a DUI violation. She, the soul survivor, testified in court later that month, on 26 july 2005, just three hours before being sentenced his "Drunken Mistake":

"Instead of committing suicide,
I slept with you."
But there really wasn't much choosing to do.
It was not one or the other;
I downed my shots of you together.
A mixed drink called fire-over-ice,
An opportunity to cut and slice.
My wrists held down I could not fake;
And afterward you say I am just –
your drunken mistake.

Two years ago you wrote to me:

Forgot to censor x-rated feelings
I wasn't supposed to see.
I called you on it,
when our future was at stake;
You sloughed it off like a hangover,
"It was just a drunken mistake."

But the night I knew you the first time
I thought you had changed your mind;
I gave it to you because I thought
My second chance was on the line.
She said,
"I don't wanna LOSE your love tonight…"
He said,
"I just wanna *USE* your love tonight!"

But your addictions too early seen unknown,
And known too late!
That's all I ever am to you,
your slutty angel
And *perfect drunken mistake.*

But she may as well have been drunk too. When it came to him, she was just as vulnerable; she had no control. All she had at her disposal was a self-destructive lethal addiction to him, her lover-abuser by the books: *We have this very antagonistic affection in which we do unforgivable things to each other, avoid each other like the plague, and then come crawling back on our soiled bloody hands and knees in moments of dire need, looking for redemption in the other.* She had read Pavese's diaries attempting to explain "why we love violently someone who treats us with the most indifference." That most human of all human mysteries was what she had always sensed about herself, especially post-ED (yes, POST, laxatives

ASHES TO ANGELS

and all, jacked up on coffee and 10 packs of sugar + 1 pack of cigarettes, half smoked on a budget half broke as a heart with osteoporosis impaled on cracked hips and coffee cups) – that her passion is what would ultimately kill her.

The world heard
P o e t r y
Scream when she
S n a p p e d

~By Auryn.

"Talk Show Host: Angel Interviewed on TV!" ran the headline in her head. She didn't expect to see a television crew, with their ubiquitous cameras voyeurizing her contribution to the festival. It triggered the exhibitionist curled up tightly in a deep and dark space within her, far away from her silvery flowy wings. Perhaps this was even better than acting after all; Adia's performance in a dark and drafty theater wouldn't show up on the six o'clock news. For Ladyfest, Auryn discussed artist Judy Chicago's vagina paintings and the correlating symmetry to her own wings, in her defense: "This is the story of [my] red right ankle, and how it came to meet [my] leg. And how the muscle bone and sinews tangled, and how the skin was softly shed. And how it whispered, 'Oh, adhere to me, for we are bound by symmetry and whatever differences our lives have been, we together make a limb.'"[152]

The talk show host just stared at her when Auryn finished her story. She forgot her script. And her

---

[152] "Red Right Ankle" by the Decemberists.

discretion. All she managed, quite unprofessionally, was, "My dear, have you been raped?" before calling the security guards to escort her obviously traumatized guest off the air.

Chapter Zero: The Torn-Out Page.
How to Become a Writer:
Red Ink.

Killer story idea (based on an autobiographically inspired situation):

   A writer is trying desperately to finish her first (and last) novel, almost a race against time, because she **cannot** die until it's written to its full potential. That's her self-imposed mortal pact. But her people, the outside world caught in her dying fantasy, are desperately trying to prevent her from ever finishing because they know once she finishes the novel, and sells the copyright to a filmmaker, she plans to commit suicide and sell her soul accordingly. The stakes are high -- It all comes down to a choice between literary greatness and human life. The mortal question: Do we sacrifice one life to make literary history for the good of a near-extinct race that is otherwise on its way out, or fall short of human potential *yet again* to save a life resigned to mediocrity? If indeed Nostradamus and Sir Isaac Newton's calculations are correct, do we go out with a bang in year A.D. 2048, or do we put a gun to our head and let men do the banging? Love is a four-letter word. It means that The Trinity was merely a Trifecta of writing, sex, and suicide. Where's the atheism in that.

ASHES TO ANGELS

Sincerely, Your Daughter of a Poison Love.
Here ends the Late Great Poetry Journal.

There was a warped sense of time. All the numbers on the clock faces reversed so that wingéd people told time counterclockwise and the hands pointed backwards in opposition to their original directions.

(MTV debuts on August 1, 1981 with this song): "In my mind and in my car, we can't rewind, we've gone too far." Adia didn't need (or want) a television appearance; she had her own camera. IF YOU DON'T CALL ME RIGHT NOW, I AM GOING TO CUT MYSELF. Adia pushed "SEND." She hated making threats to get what she wanted, and she had resisted leveling this particular one because she didn't want him to think she was psycho... because, clearly, she wasn't.

Luca was on the phone with her, pleading with his girl, bargaining for her life on stage one, a life lived in stage two that was already sold to saints and psychics when the princess pleads for the warrior's life. *I have bought the mansion of love,* Adia told him, *but not yet possessed it, and though I am sold not yet enjoyed,* as she was committing, unbeknownst to him, on the phone: "You want me? Fucking come on and break the door right down!"[153] Then, "I'm sorry, I'm sorry, so sorry," she sobbed, almost lyrically, almost mocking, with each slit of the wrist, graceful as drawing a bow across violin strings, a ballet of poetry, a love scene staged on a deathbed. "I did not *mean to commit suicide.* I did not *mean to do it* by your side," sang the mockingbird in a tone of poison sweet enough to kill a nightingale.

Deleted scene: An anonymous girl video-taping her own suicide in the nude. The music video is graphic,

---

[153] "Talk Show Host" by Radiohead.

violent, and XXX-rated because she slits her wrists and her hips in the bath and leaves the video tape for others to watch as her suicide note. The poets, those gangsters of love, picked it up because they thought it was bondage…porn gone fatally wrong. She was a completer at last with a carpet-bagger's suitcase, travel stickers from Verona, NYC, Atlantic City, *Atlantis*, Paris, London, Florence, Rome, Café Pamplona, East Berlin, Las Vegas, Narnia, Woodstock, Soho, Middle Hell's City of *Dis* (6th level for the Sixth Angel), Transylvania/Romania, Avalon, Camelot (modern Glastonbury, England). She shows up on the doorstep of the Other Side like an orphan huddled on the porch under the eaves, this runaway porn star of the steamy dark alleys on Xmas Eve, a carpet-bagger on the back porch of the world, playing the bagman's gambit, a sooty chimney sweep's (Raven's, the wingéd death-bearer) stocking cap, and long black stockings, and finally scales the trellis, alights the fire escape in Dickensian fashion ["In sleep he sang to me / in dreams he came / that voice which calls to me / and speaks my name"] caught between a phantom and a vampire in this rock-opera phantasy at the abandoned opera house, The Murk.

ASHES TO ANGELS

Chapter Thirty

In Defense of Strippers:
An Inquiry into the Nature of Band-Aids.

Over the Rhine's broken record got stuck on its track, playing over and over – "You're 80% angel, 10% demon, and the rest is hard to explain." The lyric started it all when the angel fell over the Rhine. Poe's origin had been deduced, like a game of logic, proving Auryn, the making of a ½ angel, ½ vampire. "Two halves are equal, a cross between two evils – It's not an enviable lot."[154] The stripper's stage name was Angel, and she wore a pair of costume wings on the catwalk, which just mesmerized the drunks and voyeurs. She danced to the song of "Half Jack":

> *half underwater*
> *i'm half my mother's daughter*
> *a fraction's left up to dispute*
> *the whole collection*
> *half-off the price they're asking*
> *in the halfway house of ill repute*

---

[154] "Half Jack" by the Dresden Dolls.

NATALIE MCCOLLUM

half accidental
half pain
full instrumental

it's half biology
and half corrective surgery gone wrong
but if you listen
you'll learn to hear the difference
between the half's and the half nots

and when I let him in
I feel the stiches getting sicker [sic]
I try to wash him out
but like they say

the blood is thicker

Her whole act came off like a *Saturday Night Live* parody of Auryn.

The war of roses, the war between the haves and the have-nots, when the spoils of war raise the stakes to the height of wings. Poe, if she couldn't have them, if she couldn't swallow both her pride and angel dust, was relegated to the have-nots. But if two halves are equal, just a simple cross between two evils, then by extension of that cross-section, Auryn *must be* her equal and opposite evil, that's the *real* angelic condition they don't tell you about: that Carnal Angel, being a cross halfway between god and girl, is actually a fate worse than human. Talk about a skewed merging of recombinant DNA, inhuman and inhum*ane*. They could also talk about the P'o versus the Hun: In Chinese spiritualism, the soul has two halves – the Hun is the higher self, the spirit who aspires to good and noble causes. The P'o, meanwhile, is the lower part of the dual existence, the animalistic side of desire, like the Id of the Freudian psyche. Poe was the Id of the soul. "Carnal angel" was really just a synonym lost in translation of "demon." So to ensure that the fraction left up to dispute would be neither left to dispute nor rightly reputed, the crafty soul-seller devised a plan, a new deal with the gang of Screamers: the Dealer sent her thieves to the Police, silently stalking her wings, dragging them into her war. The Avatar accused *Auryn* of stealing *Auryn's* wings! She pressed charges which, when filed in the police report, read more like the (half)wanted was a load of art thieves, and Auryn had begotten the wreck'ed wings half off the price they were asking, on account of their second-hand condition, second-rate only to and none other than, The Used.

The twisted logic of the if-then statement went something like this: If Poe was a former human who committed suicide, then she became a vampire vixen; if Auryn was related to her, then she was half vampire; and finally, if Auryn was half vampire, then she was half human as well, because all vampires (since Dracula, at least, who spawned the species) were once human. *The terror and the beauty of being human.* "I'm halfway there!" Auryn reasoned with the double helix.

"It's *half* biology," Poe, playing the devil's advocate, would have countered; Auryn might have only half the human DNA on account of her vampire heritage, but that very strand also meant that she could claim all the benefits of vampirism: according to legend, vampires could only have erotic contact with humans…and Asher was *so pathetically human.*

243

NATALIE MCCOLLUM

ASHES TO ANGELS

Part Three:

Shakespeare, Tattooed.

NATALIE MCCOLLUM

ASHES TO ANGELS

Chapter Thirty-one

Auryn Pleads for Her Wings

The tattoo parlour on St. Mark's Place was called Graffiti by the Bodysnatchers: In desperation for her sold-out wings (which Poe refused to give back – she's making too much money off them, and anyway "We made a deal"), Auryn decided to get a tattoo of a pair of silvery wings across her whole upper back, encircling the scissor scar along her spine and ending with razor-thin tendrils curling down the sides of her bottom. Supposed to look like the picture of the model in the Victoria's Secret catalogue (Angels Collection), the wings came out looking like a very bad art job crudely scratched in with needles used for shooting up by heroin users, and the color was not purely white or silver, but faded into dirty blossom and after all the scabs came off, a dark olive muddy brown punctured with streaks of reddish purple from the porphyria scars underneath the skin. "It's very *organic*," Damien insisted, "like nymph's wings. Perhaps in your case, nymph*et*," invoking the Nabokovian term not because she was an underage Lolita, but in reference to her tiny size. And that was saying a lot, as grown-up woodland fairies weren't known for their visibility anyway. "Like any uncharted territory, I must seem greatly intriguing."[155] Auryn couldn't resist a little lyrical flirtation, no matter how hopelessly devoted she was to Asher. Here she was, stripped to her waist, lying on a massage table while her number-one crush's best friend worked his hands and needles over her. One didn't have to be completely and utterly human to fall prey to *that*.

He smiled warmly in response. "Happiness is only a gash away."[156]

At Shriner's hospital in the burn unit where burn victims lay unrecognizable, the Sixth Angel responded to the sign: "PLEASE DONATE BLOOD."[157] It couldn't be all that hard; Asher had done it once, when he was desperate for money and looking for something to sell, an arm or a leg maybe, what was the going rate for kidneys these days? Body organs were in high demand; there was also the possibility of plasma (a much more painful procedure with a selective screening process) and subjects of psychological studies. Surely her half vampire heritage would allow her the role reversal of a modest transfusion to some would-be victim, had she the full-blooded capacity.

---

[155] "Uninvited" by Alanis Morissette.

[156] The Dresden Dolls.

[157] This call to action appears in Saul Williams' book-length poem, ,said the shotgun to the head.

ASHES TO ANGELS

But sitting there at the blood bank, watching as other donors' plastic bags filled with the rich red juice of life, her arm hooked up to the tube and the tree, the needle penetrating an apparent blue-green vein, she felt like a virgin with nothing to offer. The needle chased the vein for a hook-up, but the vein rejected its advances. The nurse looked puzzled as she drew the syringe. "Hmm, I don't why it's not drawing anything. Not a single drop. You ever done this before, honey?" She changed syringes and tried again, extracting not even water. "Guess you're not cut out for this, body's saying no, and we can't argue with Mother Nature, now, can we?" She rambled nervously, wondering if she should report this case to the Nurse Practitioner as cause for medical concern. "Heh, maybe you're the one in need of a donor, dear, rather than the other way around," she tried to joke, but Auryn jerked the needle out of her arm and ran out of the ward before any more incriminating evidence (or lack thereof) could confirm her status as a medical freak.

The nurse was on to something, though. Being only half vampire, her angel half definitely suppressed those blood-thirsty instincts, but *what if* she were to ingest some blood – human blood – to force that mortality into her dry veins? Intravenous efforts had heretofore failed; perhaps the oral method was the overlooked obvious route.

So I need to bite Asher. The thought caught in her throat, never making it out to the air, where the spoken word would surely confirm its horror. She inwardly cringed at herself; *how very un-human of me.* All this time she had been doing everything she could think of to be like Asher, make herself more human, and what it had come down to was, she had to do a most un-human thing to achieve it. O bitter, bitter, irony. Come to think of it, everything since her arrival in this human world bit with irony. And now she must bite it back.

She remembered the time on the painted bridge when she had cut his hand and hers and tried to make them blood-lovers. Now her evil genius had detected a loophole, a forced entry, whereby they could still make blood-love, if by somewhat vampirish means. *Somewhat.* She could hear Poe's smug sarcasm. When did she become her sister? She was merely trying to cross boundaries with humble, frail human forms and she ended up closer to the dark side, the underworld. She considered that for a moment. In her voluntary fall, had she leapt too far?

Vampirized, like her wings. In her head, Asher would go for a little bite-and-bang.

First things first.

The Scream strangled itself in her throat, standing there as she was at the cupboard, holding a pair of scissors in her left hand because all she had was spoons, millions and millions of silver spoons, when all she needed, as she told Izzy that one time in the café, was a knife. The sleight-of-hand job could be done at home, both hands, 'cause hell, she *was* the tattoo itself. A living breathing walking tattoo. She had its story branded into her back with ink that could be blood, and the difference was hard to tell. She stood with her razed wingless back to the absent audience, examining the empty cupboard, flinging open doors exposing the scattered crumbs among the spoons of various sizes and moldings and metals glinting dull and unaffected at her like a tarnished mirror reflecting back a tarnished soul, but no face. Everyone in the vampire community knew what that meant: no face, no soul. And conversely, according to reverse logic, no soul, no face

ASHES TO ANGELS

– vampires can't be photographed, the Undead are a very un-photogenic lot! *It's not an enviable lot.*[158] Continuing, then, with the twisted logic: No soul, no body. No body, no blood. No blood, no life. No life, no sex. No sex, no love. No love, no death. No death, no blood. No blood, no life. It was vicious cycle to human-hood, full of booby traps and quicksand and every unthinkable technicality a riddling wordplay could snag your life on. She rewrote it all the variant ways, millions of times like rearranging the Fibonacci sequence or the 216 digits of Pi decoded, sacked of its infamy and infinity, until finally plucking the last petal off a "loves me, loves me not" black rose. It looked like this[159]:

Version I: Her story

Version II: History

~~No face, no soul.~~
~~No soul, no body.~~
~~No body, no sex.~~
~~No sex, no blood.~~
~~No blood, no death.~~
~~No death, no love.~~
~~No love, no life.~~
~~No life, no body.~~
No body, no face.
No face, no soul.

No soul, no body.
No body, no blood.
No blood, no life.
No life, no sex.
No sex, no love.
No love, no death.
No death, no blood.
No blood, no life.

The List formed its own double helix re-winding

---

[158] The Dresden Dolls.

[159] "You can flit back and forth between these perceptions and experience a sort of mental vertigo. And if you do this, you are treading on the ground of craziness – a place where false impressions have all the hallmarks of reality." Susanna Kaysen, <u>Girl, Interrupted</u>, page 141.

and twisting in on itself, the agent of its own demise and the demise of its own agent. The first version was a microcosm of the pair – a part-to-whole synecdoche circling back on itself in the womb-space of creativity. The second version came up two lines too short, like a mutated strand lacking the chromosomes, preferably X&Y. How was one side to cross-over to the forbidden other if there was nothing to cross out? Two halves are supposed to be equal, a cross between two evils; it's not an enviable lot if there's nothing to seduce and induce the poet's envy.

She still held the pair of scissors in her left hand, the very ones that had done the dirty deed. A tiny piece of down still clung to one leg, while dried blood from the demon's leg stained the other. Sure, a pair of scissors could snip off a pair of wings, but they'd make for a nasty tattoo job. Unlike Peter Pan, she couldn't just sew them back on like a shadow; they were so much heavier than what the equivalent of a soul should be, so a makeshift pair of wings tattooed across her whole upper back would have to suffice. It just wasn't till three months later that she realized the whole of what had only been in and out of her awareness in fragmented shards, a mixed drink of bloody marys said three times before a broken mirror that had been pieced back together by the misinformed body piercer, Damien, come to check up on his handiwork and found his best friend's lover lying torn and naked and half-conscious on the floor – her heart still skipped a beat at this – she saw it clearly now without any cracks: her life since the boy, especially since long December, especially since this week, especially since this day, had been writing out her story and history. It was to be the greatest story never told, except on a bumper sticker.

ASHES TO ANGELS

It was not that her character had become her; rather, she had become her character! This person she created thinking it was fiction's problem, and her bloody problems had cross-migrated, as if sharing needles and ink pens had infected her own reality with fiction's pathogens and protagonists. Maybe it wasn't really a pen she had picked up to write in the first place: in wearing her own poetry, by tattooing her self onto herself, she had mixed media and written it down with needles, stitched herself open and shut with ballpoints. The point was, as she stood there at the cupboard with cracked coffee cups, and millions more spoons, she had measured out her life with coffee spoons borrowed from a Love Song stolen from Prufrock and had manifested grainy problems that found their full existence in what and who she was. The proportion of truth she found adulterating fiction was feeding off a real life, thriving on the trashing of a human soul.

Such is the tale she wrote on the back of her diploma and discharge orders (which might have just been different words for the same thing.)

~~*But not quite the end:~~

~~(ASH!!!! - I was writing this at the Emporium, kind of as a spin-off of everything I am channeling into the whole bone-house of the novel, and Damien passed by me and asked if I wrote Chapter Two as my second story for the portfolio. I said no, but that would have been an idea. I wished I had thought of doing that: instead of journaling these free-writes, writing the second chapter. But – I THINK I JUST DID.)~~

NATALIE MCCOLLUM

Chapter Thirty-two

The Playlist

He began, slowly, by feverish degrees registering on his face like a sundial, to explain himself to her: "This is the ghost-writer's song: it just appears and starts playing, but there's no track number on the digital read-out. On the previously scratched record stuck on Track X, say, since I don't know the number, now it's playing the full discography plus a song un*list*ed on the album—" = *portentous of the fall-out,* her mind took notes-to-self. *From Ash's notebook, Ok computer, music is coming out of nowhere...*It drifted on the coat-tales of haunting notes broadcasting between frequencies that clearly only she could hear – without a muse, his mind was mute. But – *When we last left the room, the Media Player wasn't logged on...get your Muse on, dude. In sleep you sang to me, in dreams you came: That voice which calls to me, and speaks my name.*

ASHES TO ANGELS

Ash's fever was rising now, and a feverish ash was rising too. He chain-smoked nervously, lighting new cigarettes off the dying ends of the previous. All stakes were raised, poised for a free-fall, every fan for himself, and now they were simply sacrificing idols and offerings to the bonfire on the altar of their addictions, that erected shrine in the Insane Asylum for Addicted Lovers: "The Fans (the voices in my headphones are *actually* screaming fans calling for a rockstar with no record label) + my altered reality and uniquely skewed sensory input ('alterations in relatedness' the medical community puts it so delicately)," he sneered, "means I hear LIVE and studio recorded songs (album version) in my head's background," *which is white noise slash negative space*, Auryn finished for him, privately. *It's as if they're actually playing on a record he hears from stereo speakers rigged in his head*, she decoded his thoughts and unspoken secrets. *A phantasm, what an orgasm sounds like translated into music*, the angel in devil's shoes reflexively translated into medical terminology; the psycho-wirings with all the technical grace of the techno-cosmic sound system.

Her brain's computer screen, hard-wired into the Brain Trust file folder, now had a print-out, decoded from the binary dead language of sibilant 0's and 1's, the Satanic Verse so averse to the iambic pentameter rhythms whose arrhythmia followed the rise and fall of the poet's breath, every heart palpitation conceding a fault line in the eruption of human respiration, that hairline crack placed so strategically in the glass ball, that the interruption of history was enough to break glass. The measure of a man was counted out in iambic pentameter, that which most closely matches human breathing rhythms and the cycle of respiration as the poet speaks. *His aura is a NEVERENDING rock opera, a progressively unfolding grandiose symphony in organic orgasmic crescendo and post-climactic decrescendo layered upon layer of embedded phantasmagoric music videos a molten rock'n roll freak show a hellish hallelujah chorus of vampires and gothic angels and punk faeries and other such nymphets of the symphony they christened* Lolita *at their reverse baptism on All Souls Day.*

Meanwhile, Ash was still speaking, she realized in shock therapy with the electrodes shooting up words upwards through her temples, an intravenous radiation exposure-injection of the cancer-causing Silent Treatment, a cacophonous carcinogen in its own right. Injection-rejection. Attempt failed. Reflection-ejection. Plan aborted, access denied. But THIS is what finally brought her down, when he said, "And this band called **Auryn** is sometimes singing the satanic verses..."

[Insert mix tape, "Songs for Asher & Auryn," here]

"Because of the way modern myth is created through references to pop culture and not-so-pop culture, I am adding to the myth by including a list of songs I've thought of when reading 'Ashes to Angels.'" He looked at her expectantly. He had melded history and herstory and named it. "Some may fit for you, some may not, some you may already have in mind. This is how myths go, each person adding a little bit of self to the story as it's told."[160]

---

[160] Playlist and commentary created by Brian Leingang. The author reproduces it here with gratitude for this contribution to the myth. *2017 update: commentary reflects early 2000's pop culture/state of mind.

ASHES TO ANGELS

The Playlist (with commentary)

1. Black Sheep

Choo Choo La Rouge
I'll Be Out All Night

2. The Kind of Noise You Can't Turn Down

This is a local band in Boston, but have been played as background music in shows on the WB (such as Dawson's Creek). They're a well-respected trio.

3. She Is a Bomb
4. Worst Mistakes
5. People Say

Papas Fritas
Buildings & Grounds
A Boston band that's made it pretty big on the Indie scene.

6. I Believe in Fate

7. I'll Be Gone
8. Else

KittyMonkey
Satellites for Animals

9. Wednesday

This is my former landlord's band from when I lived in Boston. They got great reviews, but were never signed because the market wasn't right. I'm continually amazed by this album, how my landlord, who is the

10. Authentic
11. Seamless

12. Glue
13. SugarRush

14. Belikeu

happiest person I've ever met, could write such songs. He and the lead singer broke up, then down the band broke. I find "Harder Place" to be one of the saddest songs I know, with a small twist of redemption at the end.

15. Harder Place
16. Pouch
17. Porcupine
18. All That Matters

19. Just Another

Pete Yorn
musicforthemorning-after

20. On Your Side

Some of the most depressing music ever.

21. Lose You
22. Paper Bag

Fiona Apple
When the Pawn…

23. The Way Things Are

Who can forget Fiona Apple. Don't have the new one, but this one goes through the entire range of hurt (mainly anger)… poor Auryn.

24. Get Gone
25. I Know
26. Goodbye, Goodbye

Jess Klein
Draw Them Near

ASHES TO ANGELS

27. Song for an Angel

28. Open Me
29. St. Teresa

30. Let's Just Get Naked

31. Crazy Baby
32. Wayward Angel

33. Saturated

34. Looking at the World from the Bottom of a Well

35. Unsingable Names
36. Busting Up a Starbucks
37. Sunken Eyed Girl
38. Your Misfortune
39. Wild

40. 5 ½ Minute Hallway

Another big-in-Boston singer/songwriter.

Joan Osborne
Relish
Damn radio overplayed "One of Us" and turned everyone off.

Kasey Chambers
Wayward Angel
An Aussie, plays somewhat whiney bluegrass.

Mike Doughty
Mike Doughty
The headman of Soul Coughing. Just got the album, and I think it's great.

Poe
House of Leaves
I often feel like I'm the only one in the world who owns this album. Poe is the sister of Mark Danielewski, so the book and album go together somewhat. The album contains some wonderful songs.

41. Not a Virgin
42. Hey Pretty
43. Could've Gone Mad
44. Amazed
45. Super Vixen

46. Heaven Is Wide

47. Not My Idea
48. Vow
49. Fix Me Now
50. The Trick Is to
    Keep Breathing
51. Dumb
52. Sleep Together
53. You Look So Fine

Garbage
Garbage
One of those bands that made its mark, faded out, and is back again. Don't have the new one.

Garbage
2.0

ASHES TO ANGELS

Chapter Thirty-three

Auryn:
"I Don't Know, It Must Have Been the Roses"

"How stupid could you be, a simpleton could see, that they're no good as wings, but they're the only ones the cops will see." Asher paced. This unwitting mistake could be solved, with some cunning and masterminded puppeteering. Enter the artist. He glanced at her. She looked too innocent. "That crack-whore you got for a sister has issued a search warrant. For you, for your wings. She claims *you* stole *your* wings." Suddenly Auryn knew: *I know who killed me.* He shook his head. "It's a scream, I tell you. The police are out looking for—" he snatched up the daily paper and scrutinized the fine print— "'an angel in devil's shoes, running around in a pair of fake authentic wings.'" He waved the paper at her. "You get it, angel doll? You can fake it for the papers, but they're on to you." He approached her as she lay back on the futon and stared down intensely into her wide eyes. "*I'm* on to you." He started picking up things around the room. "No scissors, no hooks and tacks, no thumbscrews, no pins and needles, no more playthings for you, my dear little masochist." He shoved all the kinky toys into a wine cabinet and locked it, so that the perverse menagerie was tantalizingly in sight behind the glass, but inaccessible because with a jaunty swing he twirled the key around his finger and pocketed it. Then his final instructions: "Don't show them your back. No public exposure. Plead the 5th and a ½: You have a right to remain clothed. We're lucky it's a bad tattoo job, but I'm not taking any chances on you. You're too vulnerable." All this time, she rather uncharacteristically hadn't said a word. Out of nowhere she flung a retort at his back as he was heading for the door.

"Don't let them see *your* back," she mimicked, adding an eerie warning to the clause, "cross the Patron Saint of Switchblade fights. You said. We're not celebrities. We spark and fade. They die by threes."[161]

He shook his head. "You're wrong. We *are* famous. 'If I thought I replied to one who might go back to the world,'" he nodded accusingly at Auryn, "'this flame should never move. But since – if what I hear be true – no one has ever returned from this gulf alive, I answer without fear of infamy.'[162]"

---

[161] My Chemical Romance.

[162] The epigraph to Eliot's poem is from Dante's *Inferno*, Canto 27, where the poet asks Guido to identify himself. This time, Asher has chosen to plagiarize in translation.

ASHES TO ANGELS

"Human passion *is* a flame that burns to its own destruction," Auryn quipped back at the mortal, to which the former replied, "Ah, our Lady of Sorrows, what ever are we going to do with you, my chemical romance?"

As he reached for the doorknob, he turned on impulse and asked, "Really, Auryn, what made you do it? Why make body art out of a missing body part?"

She seemed not to hear. She was solid gone, half underwater, high above the tree line, sitting crossed-legged on the ground[163], in love with her own chemical romance and a half biology that wouldn't let her come down. Distantly, she answered from somewhere else, giving the answer to a different question: "I don't know, it must have been the roses." Her vacant gaze seemed to refocus like a camera lens, and "I followed the fungus," she confessed suddenly.

THE ACID FEVER EVENT

There are ghosts behind my rib cage
trapped there like prisoners of war
I wage with myself each day
They rattle the bones demanding to be free
It's too hot so close to the heart, they say
I'm sorry, I am ONLY human!
my screams traverse the world,
then go back down the way they came,
a transfusion of color wheels having
a hard candy meltdown choking me
till I hear my soul coughing
and my reflection troubles me to magical hysteria:
my eternal complaint housed in two sunken

---

[163] Based on Ani Difranco's lyrics from her song "Studying Stones."

hollows in my face, two dark half-moons
cradling the orbs – does panic surface here
for air like camera lenses and photographs
they are truth-tellers. feelings of guilt
have been linked to vitamin B12 deficiencies.
My sign is vital, but my hands are cold –
did you drain all my iron will in one bloody kiss?
and suddenly I can't distinguish where you end
and I begin – I just wish
there was a body to go with it.

At his surprise, she continued without inhibition, "Angels are simply drug addicts." She felt like she was betraying the centuries-hoarded secret of her own kind, but she couldn't stop now she had the momentum and the nerve. "Or the product of a painful ecstasy. As agonizing as that fit of gut-splitting nausea was, I've never been higher. I'd do it again in a heartbeat. I am the last true masochist. I've turned the pain I've known in various forms my whole conscious life into a source of pleasure – I've turned life back on itself: life in terms of death becomes the beautiful experience others perceive when I take the elements of death and live off them. Here is the delicate line between you and me – mortal and supernatural – I've (literally) stumbled upon the soul between worlds: more than human but not quite free of death." When he still said nothing at the end of her monologue, she persisted, "Really! Ask St. Teresa of Avila; 'Her desire knows no pain…she hardly knows whether she is in the body or out of it.'[164] The spiritual animal is simply a union of the psyche and the earth."

Asher had stood there with his hand still on the

---

[164] Godwin 246.

doorknob, imbibing all her words with a drunkard's passion, and now he cleared his throat. "You know," he offered, "if you can live in the first 26 years of your life what most people only get in their entire life span, then you've got like two lives credited to one account – 2 for 1." He eagerly anticipated her affirmation of his contribution to the genius formula she had just exposed.

She nodded, still conflicted between her betrayal and her brainchild. "That's kind of a schism, I mean a split thought process, but then, I guess that's what you humans really are: two contradicting entities coexisting in one body."

He nodded furiously. "We are either oh-my-god brilliant, or I am gonna kill myself – perhaps there isn't much difference between the profession and the confession." He could feel the union of their greatness about to give birth to genius from the wombspace of her creativity. The product of their minds was this Daughter of a Poison Love, with her own specific

Recipe: How to Cultivate a Muse

1/8 psychedelic (this could be liquid PCP
sprayed on marijuana leaves to create angel dust)
+ 37.5 psychotropic (this could be Thorazine or
Zyprexa or Diazepam, or any of the 'pams)
swallow, rinse, and repeat
and watch your creativity mushroom
(if your rules and wisdom don't choke you first!)

But later that night, when Asher went out to see a friend, she wrote in red ink on the bathroom mirror 672 times

I am a brilliant and prolific liar.

I am a brilliant and prolific liar.
I am a brilliant and prolific liar.
I am a brilliant and prolific liar.
I am a brilliant and prolific liar.
I am a brilliant and prolific liar.
I am a brilliant and prolific liar.
I am a brilliant and prolific liar.
I am a brilliant and prolific liar.
I am a brilliant and prolific liar...
GLORIOUSLY.

It was worse than the 1980's, when a note on the bathroom mirror confessing "I have AIDS – and now so do you" the morning after a one-night stand said pretty much the same thing. Asher would have preferred the death sentence.

ASHES TO ANGELS

Chapter Thirty-four

Asher:
"It Must Have Been the Mushrooms"

(Ash trips)

"You were the savior who tripped and fell...
...You're the religion I should forsake"[165]

Asher left her that night. Dorian had got hold of some rather potent psychedelic mushrooms, and they split an eighth between them. He wanted to try out the new recipe for a muse, see if a good trip would bake up some creative inspiration. He was having a dry spell in more ways than just the writerly variety. Dorian took the opportunity to accuse Asher, "You

---

[165] Over the Rhine, "Who Will Guard the Door" from the album Drunkard's Prayer.

need her like a drug."[166]

"Hey man, love is a trip." Asher took a puff of the magic dragon. He passed the bong back to Dorian. "We all have our particular brand of morphine for this life."

"So your heroine is your heroin," Dorian prodded and punned.

"And the reverse."

Dorian furrowed his brow. "Wait – you're losing me. Are we talking about a lady or a drug?"

"She claims to be an angel – and angels, she further claims, are essentially the product of a drug-induced psychosis – so I can't even distinguish reality when everything is so ambivalent. Can't trust my senses. I only know a grand illusion, what most people think they know as life, but at least I'm on to the sham. It can't shatter me if I'm already living in fragments. Disillusionment equals invincibility." He tapped his notebook thoughtfully with his pen. "Better write that one down, I'll never remember it when I've come down."

"You and she – or it – are the perfect codependent relationship."

"But not even love can surpass its own tolerance level. Like any addict, I'll always be chasing that first high," nodded Asher.

"Chasing – or dodging?" Dorian queried. "Stop dodging bullets from her gun, man."

"But don't you see," Asher insisted, "it's alchemy. Pain *became* the morphine. It's simple chemistry, really, a practice of ancient mystics since the land before time. When you've withstood a pain so strong for so long,

---

[166] U2, "So Cruel," <u>Achtung! Baby</u>

you become immune, then beyond immunity is euphoria, when you start to feel beyond the pain, nothing at all, or things too good for this world."

"Your theories on love and morphine are profound, my friend," Dorian conceded. "Your philosophy is enough to blow up a meth lab."

"Or my head." Asher cradled his skull in both hands. "My own thoughts are too much for me. They hurt my head. Give me migraines that scream for the axe. It's all I can do keep from plagiarizing *Pi* with the ending of my own life story."

Dorian was too far out in space to realize the danger of being a writer. How literature made you morbid. How you basically had to sell your soul to become an English major. How all writers self-edit to their own destruction. Cut and paste, cut and paste, cut, cut, cut…writers and cutters. The marriage of heaven and hell might simply be a rationalization for the illegitimate child conceived of separate-but-equal strokes of genius and insanity – *part of brilliance* is *insanity* – William Blake may have had something there.

Asher hugged his knees to his chest. His face withdrew into the shroud of his sweatshirt hood. A string of lyrics wafted out of the cavernous hollow between cheekbones on a softly curling tendril of smoke. "What a wicked game you play, to make me feel this way. What a wicked thing to do, to let me dream of you." His voice rose to a wail matching his ghostly figure with each line of the chorus. "What a wicked thing to say! you never felt this way!"[167] Finally his tone slumped in defeat and self-pity. "What a wicked thing to do, to make me dream of you, Auryn."

Auryn, meanwhile, had her own blank page. Her

---

[167] "Wicked Game" by Chris Isaak.

candy heart was crack; or LSD in the teddy bear's tummy pocket. Either one was her own brand of

    Narcotic Love

    come sing to me where it hurts
    with your beautiful twisted mouth
    make me crescendo
    or better yet
    inflict the pain
    bleed like me
    and take me higher than i've ever been
    because i've been high on you, my friend,
    you are my drug of choice
    and i am your sole devoted addict.
    you are the best and worst thing
    that ever happened to me
    i'm still smoking the ashes of your memory.
    no wonder you haunt me,
    my morphine, my love,
    no wonder you hunt me,
    my hero, my heroin.
    i can't get off you
    i haven't been clean
    since you got me off
    all it took was one hit
    to send me tripping around the world
    looking for my next fix.
    if you withdraw,
    i am withdrawn;
    if you never come back,
    i guess my date with the dead
                      poets is still on.

ASHES TO ANGELS

Chapter Thirty-five

Like a Loaded Gun: Some Say It's Love

"I brought you my bullets, you brought me your love."[168] It was as simple as that.

> "Love me,
> Thrill me,
> Kiss me,
> Kill me."

Auryn said.

"Kill me: kiss me again," Asher said, giving himself up for dead. It was a rare moment of complete surrender. Helpless release of liability. And she was no guardian angel.

She told him so. He threw back his head, pleading

---

[168] My Chemical Romance.

desperately, "Kiss me with your teeth, oh please, I want to feel you break skin. Lovely vixen, you look so fine, I want to break your heart and give you mine."

"Are you sure?" she whispered, panicked now that the moment had presented itself. He was making this too easy. He was putting a gun in the hands of a suicidal. She wanted to push him till he said no, and then she would have an excuse, for a vampire cannot cross human thresholds unless she is invited in. She dropped her head on his neck, weeping at her terrible brilliance, her lethal love. He lay there waiting, breathing heavily, sweating sweetly, and his scent was intoxicating to her. She couldn't resist any more. She lifted her head a little and curled her lips just under his collarbone, and when she got enough skin between them, she bared her teeth and pressed slowly, evenly, hoping he wouldn't scream and make this harder for her. She would make this up to him; for a taste of his mortality he could do anything to her, when it was his turn. She rationalized like this until she finally pierced with her kitten-sharp incisors, but the faintest taste of human blood so shocked her she spooked and let go prematurely, leaving her great vampire bite the unfinished work of a cat's nip.

He gave a little yelp when she let go, more in surprise than pain, as she danced around in epileptic hysterics. She clutched at her mouth where a tiny dribble was all she had to show for her overwhelming effort, and she trembled as if in diabetic shock. Asher jumped up with his hand over the two tiny teeth marks above his heart and tried to steady her. She couldn't seem to stand in one place. Clearly this was more traumatizing for the sadist than the victim himself. He put his free hand on her shoulder, gasping, "Auryn!

ASHES TO ANGELS

Get a hold of yourself! It's over! It's okay. Gee, even I've tasted my own blood before, it's nothing."

She continued to shake violently, and now she had started mumbling incoherently to herself. When she was finally able to stand in place for a whole minute, Asher peered into her face between his hands and vaguely deciphered the words "Blood sugar" spilling off her lips. She repeated it over and over, "Oh the blood sugar, the blood sugar, it was the sugar, so much blood and sugar...." She refused to lick her lips clean of his blood stain, so he finally grabbed her by the shoulders, held her steady for one solid second, and then pressed his own lips firmly against hers, cleaning himself off her. He kissed her long and hard. Her mouth was sore when he finally pulled away, but at last she was silent and still. She stood there a long moment staring at him, both of them engaged in an eye lock, unmoving and unrelenting, while his two little spider-bite wounds clotted and scabbed over. Then he took her weak form in his arms and held her while she cried calmly and noiselessly. The tears dripped off the edge of her chin bent over his shoulder, and she could feel the warm spot she had marked above his heart. When it grew very late, he carried her ragdoll body to the mattress and buried it there six feet under the covers. He kept watch all night, by the light of the full moon flooding through the sky window, sitting up close by her head and smoking cigarettes in unbroken succession.

Stroke your skin,
There are teeth marks to be sure.
Maybe we're best close to the ground.
Maybe angels drag us down.
I wonder which part of this will leave the scar?[169]

NATALIE MCCOLLUM

X
"Karma Police, arrest this man.
This is what you get when you mess with us.
Karma Police, arrest this girl."[170]
X
Six shots fired (graffiti on a red brick wall)[171]
(petals on a wet black bough):
This is what you get when you mess with love.

---

[169] "Faithfully Dangerous," from The Home Recordings by Over the Rhine.

[170] Radiohead, "Karma Police," Ok Computer

[171] In the Oregon District downtown Dayton, Ohio.

ASHES TO ANGELS

Chapter Thirty-six

Pawning the Wings

Poe tried to sell her stolen angel wings in a cameo of Auryn's selling her soul[172] to the demon sister. The wings were feathery black now – demonized – and ragged from Poe's abuse. The pawnbroker hoarded the wing costume in the same shack in the Brooklyn ghetto where Munch's stolen painting *The Scream* was imprisoned in the form of the ghoulish-girl figure eliciting the title (Auryn's double existence as Auryn's Other). Alias "Plan B," the run-down pawn shop had all appearances of having gone out of business years ago (except to the crooked dealers who ran the underground like a narcotics ring). Poe sold her used

---

[172] "...but love separates all things from the soul." Meister Eckhart, German mystic.

costume – damaged goods – after her stint as a dancer at the strip joint. On the same afternoon, Auryn just missed Ash in passing, on her way into East Third Street Corridor Pawn Shop by Midnight Market while he was on his way out. She had come to buy back the wings, the original set that she cut and the Avatar vampirized, in desperation to get back some of her sanity, dignity, and *im*mortality. She had heard that Poe had finally ravaged them to pieces, until she was viciously satisfied that she fully "broke the angel," but Auryn wanted what's left of them. They were, after all, still her own body.

But Asher beat her to it. He had decided to do something special for Auryn, because he had a feeling this might be *the* night. So, to make her feel better about the whole wing loss, which she still insisted had actually happened, he went to the pawn shop to pick up a pair of costume wings for her to flit around in all sexy and kinky. He knew it wouldn't be the same, but it was definitely better than that nasty tattoo job she'd gotten in mirror images on either side of the long scissor-scar down her spine. He had no idea they were actually the real thing, especially since they were almost unrecognizable now to Auryn herself. But like a lost child from her own womb, Auryn could never disown them. Had they been like the burn victims in Shriner's burn unit, scarred and disfigured to disbelief, she could never not know they were hers. She would sense the connection, even without her extra sixth. All five human senses would do just fine, and it was here that she finally found her human-angel boundary, precise and provocative as a G-spot. In their corrupt form, the recovered wings could now afford her the fleeting lapse of vulnerability to mortality and biology

ASHES TO ANGELS

(like the very fleeting and specific time of the month when a woman is ovulating and able to conceive). Those defeated crooked wings were also what got her and Asher in that place "where I can scream from the bottom of my lungs in places that don't even exist and not care about anyone hearing" because there is no one *to* hear in the voided exchange of slices of mortality and deity, that negative space where "I could hear you, but I couldn't speak. So maybe we don't have to imagine: we have no heaven in exchange for no hell."

"Save your sanity for another night."

So. She did.

NATALIE MCCOLLUM

Chapter Thirty-seven

The Rape of an Angel

"I got you twisted round my finger, crawling round my legs."[173]

"Raven's on a vacation far away, come on and talk it over," he'd said to her reassuringly on the way. Choirs of angels seemed to say, *Dream, if you can, a courtyard, an ocean of violets in bloom. Animals strike curious poses, they feel the heat, the heat between me and you.* He'd scaled the fire escape like a sea nymph on acid climbing a wall in sunshine, to get in without being interrogated by the night watchman. *When I jab the sharpened object in,* her arms about his neck holding so tight after the fall that

---

[173] "Sleep Together" by Garbage, album <u>2.0</u>.

ASHES TO ANGELS

her nails dug into the skin, he set her down and regarded her from the other side of the tenth floor tenement, a bit doubtfully. "So many things that I wanna say, you know I like my girls a little bit older."[174]

The sign was somewhat telling of this perverse arrangement: "No room in the inn" left little merit to its name, "Hope's Hotel," but either the "p" had fallen off the letter-board or some kid thought it funny to spray paint it out, but…such was the state of Post-Postmodern Earth's most popular nook and cranny for the nooky on Christmas Eve.

She saw him standing behind her own shadow, which got in the way when she looked out the window. She drew a breath. *Vampires don't have reflections or shadows.* But the face she saw in the great oak dresser mirror was not her own; the thin line of his lips she always loved to stroke her skin, she thought, *there are teeth marks to be sure. Maybe we're best close to the ground. Maybe angels drag us down. I wonder which part of this will leave the scar.*

"Hey," gently, tenderly was all he said, simply. At the mirror she was taking down her hair, laying her jewelry, all the wrought-iron twisted rings and moonstones, the shiny stuff that attracts ravens, and everything reflective of a mirror that attracts suicides. She saw them all in there – her witch mother Lilith; Poe the Avatar; Adia and Luca the drug addicts; Izzy and Marley the blood-sisters; Teresa the tripping saint; Veronika, the girl interrupted, who jumped; and…*Mordren.* He knew EXACTLY what he was going to do her in the next two hours, he knew exactly that he had won, that love is blind, and this night he would take what was his by eternal right. "I'll take

---

[174] "Your Love" by The Outfield.

your soul out into the night, but I can't promise you won't go untouched."

Her hand was on the doorknob.

"You might get taken advantage of." *So I'm provoked.*

"So – what's your point?" *She's not backing down.*

"You won't make it through the night untouched." Grinding. Both of them could feel the fork in the gut. She had the advantage now; her answer could either keep it or allow him to take it – from her, and *of* her. Reading between the lines was imperative; a bad reading put more than just word choice on the line.

"So – WHAT'S YOUR POINT." It was 12:45 a.m.

"I might get attached." She advanced toward him.

"So – you just wanna *USE* my love tonight."

"I might not be able to let go." Her hand reached out.

"So – you don't wanna LOSE my love tonight."

It was 1:01 a.m.

She turned around slowly, then in a turn of aggression stomped her way over to him, shaking the boarded-up floor with her heavy trench boots. They reached mid-calf, stopping just below her knees to allow the fishnet knee-socks to take over until mid-thigh, leaving a pale white space of unprotected flesh between the red satin band hemming the nets and the frayed hemline of her army girl mini skirt, which by means of a chain-link belt complete with fob, hovered precariously just over her hips, likely the only thing keeping it there, exposing her somewhat bloated little belly hooked with a halo in the navel and then pale white space all the way up her mid-riff until the glittering silver and ruby jeweled metallic brassiere took over the eyes and the mind. Even as she came at him,

ASHES TO ANGELS

Asher couldn't help think what a pretty little piece of flesh he had just locked in this little rat-trap hotel by the freeway. The Insane Asylum for Love Addicts would never do the royal little slut justice.

When her hands made contact with his chest, digging her nails in as she barreled right into him, pushing him backward onto the bed, then crawling lusty bloodthirsty up the length of his legs like a rabid animal clawing its way up a mountain side then wrapping her own legs tightly around his midsection to pin him down. She leaned in for his neck like a wolf going for the throat. Asher backed up until he was hard up against the headboard with a hard-on, the little vampire still stuck on his neck. His arms flailed out the sides with the first surge of this chemical romance, then softened as his hand went up her skirt. He groped for a long time, until he felt he knew every inch of her under there, while her mouth was unflinching in its hold on his neck, her razor-sharp incisors sunk so deep into his aortic artery it twitched and writhed like the teeth were having sex with his vein.

"I want to see you."

At this she pulled away. A surge of hope had sent shock waves through her own chemical romance, though of a very different nature in regard to its origin: brain chemistry doesn't always mix with matters of the heart. They are highly reactive substances, easily abused by each other, and the slightest contact is capable of explosions of mass destruction totally extinguishing the human race in the throes of their own love crime by the hand of their own love child, that Daughter of a Poison Love marked on a little black bottle with skull and cross-bones. Somehow, this **WARNING!** label had been mislabeled, or torn off altogether, making lovers addicts, angels virgins, and poets sex offenders by they own Spoken Words.

"You want to see me? You want me now, yes?"

"I want to know you before I get in. I want to see where I'm going. You said you wanted me to see you. In your note, you wrote 'SEE Me.' So let's spread the Word."

At that, he peeled her legs off from around his sides, raised them up, and criss-crossed them around his neck. He lifted up her skirt, exposing her in the dimly lit room. He patted back the hair, then opened her up deftly with his knowing fingers. At the first invasive look at the swollen redness, he drew a sharp breath that pierced the liquid darkness like iron and cold roses. "The painting," he exhaled faintly, like getting a glimpse of an ancient holy relic so guarded not even god himself was allowed to look upon it, "you look just like the picture in the tattoo parlour–" at her confused look – "the cavernous womb-space. Post-modern surrealism, Salvador Dali inspired." He looked up, his eyes all aglow with wicked phantasm. He seemed not to see her disturbance, the war raging right on her face in epileptic spasms, and he looked back down to his as-yet untouched canvas and plunged right into the finger painting.

His slender bone inserted inside her made her spastically aware of places she never knew existed before. She cringed and cried, not recognizing the orgasm orbiting the breaking point of greatness, until she finally kicked so hard she kicked him off. She lay crumpled in a bruising bony heap at the end of the bed, sobbing like a little girl, while Asher glared at her menacingly and finally got up from the head of the bed and turned his back to her. His one wet finger, clenched in a bruised fist like a wine-stain behind his back, still glistened like iron and wine on the rocks spiked with cold roses in a bed of nails hammered to the floor boards.

"All right, okay, Auryn. This is it. I'm only hanging on to watch you go down…my love," he ended up pleading. Then he switched back to playing the patron saint of switchblade fights. "Do you want this or not? I haven't got all eternity – it's tonight or back to Never Land." He turned around, like scolding a naughty puppy. She saw the stone set in his eyes; he saw the thorn twist in her side. She was backed into a corner a fate worse than a headboard with a sick black rose crucified in its purple gift tissue on the mantelpiece above the busted lovers' busted heads.

"I…I, *do*…" how could she tell him she didn't know the difference between the two clauses in fine print she had signed away in her own fermented body fluids in the absence of holy blood holy grail, pawned off her wings and forfeited her soul, and it all came down to two words, one object, and a difference in meaning too easy for the highest paid stripper in free verse: a man who could **make** love to her without being **in** love with her? *Don't fuck with my heart – if you fuck me, it must mean you love me!* He was raising the stakes to the difference between sex and love, so dangerous was the polarity between the two unstable bedmates, and she was caught in a deadlock somewhere in that negative space. It was either jump or be jumped.

She was still sobbing while she let him lower her back to the bed. She was crying for every used girl, for every winter's rape of the flower on the vine, for every ravaged pair of soft pink clitoral wings as he undressed her. She was crying *yes* like pleading *no*. The last thing she remembered he said to her, before the first pain of penetration was, "Your hymen -- has never been torn?" And in a turn of former bullying, "Or *is there* even one to tear and bleed?"

"Sweetheart, you're so cruel." It was useless to argue the age-old point of contention between an atheist and an avatar; he was forcing the impossible existence of a virgin angel before the riddle could be realized with the first invasive thrust to the rhythm of her paralyzed scream.

The Scream that "leads you to an overwhelming question":

If we sleep together, will you like me better?
An Essay.
…and standing there at the cupboard, I realized the whole of what had only been in and out of my awareness in fragmented shards before now: like a shattered mirror pieced back together (has that EVER been done?) I saw it clearly without even any cracks: my life since ash, especially since February, especially this week, ESPECIALLY THIS DAY, has been writing out ashes to angels for me. Not, my character has become me – I HAVE BECOME my character! This person I created thinking she was fiction's problem, is actually me – her problems have cross-migrated and manifested, finding their full existence in what and who I am "how much truth is actually in fiction" – it's feeding off of a real life, it's <u>thriving</u> on the <u>trashing</u> of a human soul.

"We were <u>so</u> meant for each other, that it was <u>not meant</u> to be."

25.07.05

ASHES TO ANGELS

22 july 2005   I sacrificed my body knowing too well there was an extremely permanent chance that this was just to borrow my body to feed his carnal male hunger. But the forfeit was rather necessary. I now have a rough, minimal idea of what rape feels like. There was especially one particular moment when I actually remember a conscious awareness running through my head almost in words, of how he was doing more to me and to a greater, rougher, more violent and uncontrollable degree than I wanted or thought he would, and I was powerless to do anything about it – both physically, he had me pinned down so hard it hurt my legs, I thought my calf muscles would get Charlie horse and he would wake up from his alternative state of $^{sub-}$being, a mixed drug of intoxication and arousal, to my screaming under his bones, the echoes of my voice suffocated under his throbbing ^{beating} $_{(me\ up)}$ chest $_{(on\ me)}$ and breaking the sound barrier of his bones.[175]

Grade: F+++

Comment (sticky-noted):   Sorry if these comments are more than you care to know. I don't care to censor myself for you anymore.

---

[175] In the author's handwriting on the back of a typed response to a friend's first novel manuscript, 22 July 2005. No words have been changed since the original journal page. Line edits have been retained.

Feedback: "Let's Just Get Naked."

HOW TO: "You're gonna have to get a little closer than that. And naked. Actually, A LOT NAKED." (Ash)

"Make me hard and make me happy, *make me beautiful*!!!"[176] (Auryn)

Saints in Orgasm, Saints Tripping;
"We crossed the line – who pushed who over?" said Asher.
Rape of the Saints, Vampire Rape.
"It doesn't matter to you, it matters to me," said Auryn.

It was so cruel.

And suddenly, it was not the angel who lost her wings; it was the human on which they were borne: "two halves are equal, a cross between two evils" yields half-vampire half-angel in a moment of consent to the bite and bang theory on writing, sex, and suicide. He slit her wrist with the sharp end of the red-tipped blackened quill extracted from a wing, then blotted up the blood with his lips, which he then placed on her own, so she got a taste of her own momentary mortality. The brutality was so beautiful, it was like poetry assaulted, and it was like ballet as she writhed, thrashed, and strained gracefully on her way down to the floor, where all was quiet and still once she hit.

Cursum perficio[177]

---

[176] "Sleep Together" by Garbage.
[177] "My journey is over, my journey ends here." Enya, <u>Only Time: The Collection</u>.

ASHES TO ANGELS

Cursum perficio
Cursum perficio
Cursum perficio

Cursum perficio

Verbum sapienti
(eo plus cupiunt)
Verbum sapienti
(eo plus cupiunt)
Verbum sapienti
Quo plus habent

eo plus cupiunt
Verbum sapienti
Quo plus habent
eo plus cupiunt

Post nubila, Phoebus
Post nubile, Phoebus
Post nubila, Phoebus

Quo plus habent, eo plus cupiunt
Quo plus habent, eo plus cupiunt
Quo plus habent, eo plus cupiunt

Post nubila, Phoebus
Post nubile, Phoebus
Post nubila, Phoebus

Post nubila, Phoebus
Post nubile, Phoebus
Post nubila, Phoebus

Iterum
Iterum
Iterum

Auryn hit Earth just as Asher hit the brakes.

ASHES TO ANGELS

Chapter Thirty-eight

Angel Dust: Bleed Like Me, O Mortality!

And your face, I do know well.
Every breath breathes farewell.
It's so still, no soul could tell,
But one day like this the angels fell
And it's never quite what it seems.[178]

Why can't we see, when we bleed, we bleed the same.[179]

It was the end of the world
There was nowhere to go
No safe place to be

---

[178] Over the Rhine, <u>Good Dog Bad Dog</u> / The Home Recordings, 2000.
[179] "Starlight" by Muse.

Nothing to do
'cept make love to me
We thought maybe love could still save
as the world became a mass grave
Earthquakes around us
Fires licking the skies
I found you waiting for me
outside a shattering high-rise
As buildings went down, so did we
Sawdust on our lips
We kissed not as lovers,
but as the last human beings.

"I woke up in a motel in Las Vegas with seven new piercings!"

"I kissed your lips and I broke your heart, and you – you were acting like it was the end of the world."[180]

"Well, it *was* the end of the world, at an airport in Japan."

In the half-light of pre-dawn the morning after, she was stunned by an irreversibility more soul-selling than ditching heaven – now the 15-year-old Hebrew had conceded to her: a mortal, built to please in this way that at once most defines and defiles human dignity, was undefined by a man as immortal beings were incapable of the inconceivable, and somehow she had defied the laws of biology and, *done a human. Just a slob like one of us – Could millions of people have been wrong?* She turned on her heel and swept down the street in a spuriously conjured flurry of snow to get her thoughts and emotions together before she attempted to deal with this painful reality any further, but not before she

---

[180] "Till the End of the World" from U2's album Achtung! Baby.

ASHES TO ANGELS

had thrown an impulsively uncharacteristic "You're an asshole! Asher! Ash! Ass! 'Ashes to assholes!'" back at her inferior in all manner of dealings, except in the art of profanity. She didn't see him any more that day, which went on for hours and those very hours went on for days.

> The life I've left behind me is a cold room,
>
> the hotel room on the 10th floor tenement
> I've crossed the last line from where I can't return
> virgin mary bloody mary – *no they'll never catch me now!*
> Where every step I took in faith betrayed me
>
> every violation I agreed to in the bedroom
> and led me from my home and sweet,
>
> my wings the universe
> sweet surrender is all that I have to give.[181]

I finally surrendered to him what I had already surrendered to him.

> **The FBI estimates that only 37% of all rapes are reported to the police. U.S. Justice statistics are even lower, with only 26% of all rapes or attempted rapes being reported to law enforcement officials.[182]**

"Sweetheart, you're so cruel.[183] How can you leave

---

[181] Sarah McLachlan, "Sweet Surrender." Cited elsewhere.
[182] As printed in the "Violence Against Women and Girls" fact sheet in The Vagina Monologues program published for a university theater adaptation.

me standing alone in a world that's so cold? Maybe I'm just too demanding, maybe I'm just like my father, too bold. Maybe I'm just like my mother, she's never satisfied. Why do we scream at each other? This is what it sounds like when doves cry!"[184]

The girl who thought she was an angel spent the next three – days or hours, it wasn't known or very different, either way – in solitary anguish, nursing her stinging, smarting heart. People say she carried around cigarettes and a box of matches – cigarettes and coffee – coffee and 10 packs of sugar in a paper to-go cup held close to her heart, the heat pressed into the ridges of the depression between her breasts, the heat pressed into her heart, searing the skin where blood runs hottest where tears fall hardest, and dent. People say she forced the coffee cup into the crevice of her chest, below the collar bone, bare leg hanging out the car door, head thrown back like the whiplash got her neck, radio turned up to drown out all thought, feeling, emotion, and just drain…let her soul drain itself and leak out like the faulty faucet on the 10th floor tenement where she slept among bones, her pillow a pair of broken hearts she put her head in between the cracks of which so the soul could help the body die a double suicide, like putting a wounded animal out of its misery.

"Give me this moment! What you say to the universe to invoke its higher power, protection, and aid; what you say to the one you love so damnably that he played you for a fool to love. Give me this moment. A small voice screams world. Spoken Word.

---

[183] U2, "So Cruel."
[184] Prince, "When Doves Cry."

ASHES TO ANGELS

The terror and the beauty of being human. We can't change that we are human, but would we really if given a chance? What else is there? The race, people, is called H-U-M-A-N-I-T-Y!!! There's not much difference between that and the god-concept, god-terms, god-things. A 'forced suicide' is all this life really is. So give me this one moment, to feel the world twitch, give me this moment my glory in the ditch. All that's really down here is dirt and if our souls in afterlife are recycled atoms, then all that's really up there is somebody else's dirt. Inhalation of second-hand smoke."

"I can't keep holding on to what I got, when all I got is hurt!" Her innocent idealism had been shattered. The dramatized "new version" of herself that had promised love-story returns had rendered her merely a love-child of mismatched tragic heroes: the eternal and the evanescent. She had now conceived of something as far-flung as The Virgin's predicament had seemed to the carpenter and his people – what were they supposed to believe, that she had sex with god? It was no more believable that a man had sex with an angel, The Unvirgin – the unvirgin angel. She reflected on the long-ago warning, which in her manic obsession with Asher, she had brushed aside irreverently, about falling in love with a poet. Artists are very nasty people, the carpenter's son had once told her. Well, he was an artist all right – a con artist, who had conned her into impossible sex, according to the bite-and-bang theory of "vampire-rape." Anything is possible that's undefined; she justified the construct called "god" only being existably possible owing to the very fact of his being undefined. Merely a creative energy rush, at once contained within – and unchecked by – the cosmos, yeah? But like a smitten teenage girl, indeed like Lucy Westenra of the setting sun herself, she had let her enthrallment run away with her own spirit-given sensibility. She had become her namesake: Lucy a derivative of Lucifer the epitomic case of fallen-angel syndrome; Asher a pseudonymic variant on the gray feathery matter that covers up the wounds of burn victims, hyped up as what pop culture likes to call angels. It was a brainwashing; what's in a name can't change what's in its reference. Poe had failed just as miserably in their little scheme: altering her species name from "demon" to "avatar" after she bailed out of hell couldn't hold stolen wings onto the imp's back if they had been tattooed on with barbed wire wrought of the crown of thorns itself. After languishing in self-pity for a few days, her sorrow turned to an anger, rising exponentially at Asher himself, and finally, when it reached its peak when nothing changes, on New Year's Day she stormed like the fading star she still didn't fully recognize herself as being, and banged on Asher's door in the middle of the night, forgetting in her fury the human bio-rhythms and sleep cycle. Asher, groggy and tousled, opened the door half conscious of what met him there.

ASHES TO ANGELS

Chapter Thirty-nine

Pulvis et umbra sumus, or
Dust.

> *Human destinies
> are like the planets
> They meet in
> space only to
> disappear once
> again…*[185]

"How could you do this to me!" she shrieked in the dim hallway at the startled face before her. Her countenance displayed the almost comical paradox of what it looked like for a "good" angel to be overcome by that most wicked of emotions humanly possible: rage. *Against the dying of the light. I've got a stalker from heaven on my hands, worse than a vindictive ex-girlfriend on the man-hunt.*

---

[185] Edvard Munch, on *Encounter in Space*, 1899, color woodcut.

"What do you mean, what I did to you? You're the one who wanted to be with me," Asher, regaining his senses, shot back at her.

"You *made* me fall in love with you!" Now she really was shouting, and it was quite disconcerting, even to Asher, to see such a formerly sweet, pretty little thing so consumed with the darkness he was afraid to admit he recognized as his own.

"Hey, hold on there, I didn't even believe in angels before you showed up," he took up the defensive. "How could I lead you on if I didn't even know you existed?"

"You act like it never happened, and you want me to do the same!"[186] she answered a different question. "In Tokyo you were playing the part, you kissed my lips and broke my heart. Your capacity for understanding the mind of an angel kidnapped me, the poet's envy. Don't you understand? Damn it, Asher, *FINISH WHAT YOU STARTED!!!*" Now she was in tears, making Asher very uncomfortable to see an angel weeping like a damned soul. Wringing her hands, she started pacing up and down the shadowy hallway like a ghost condemned to suffer eternal agonies for the choices and actions committed in a former corporeal life.

Her crazed behavior was now really starting to freak Asher, even for someone who himself was wont to psychotic episodes of disillusionment. Her hysteria was beginning to bring on a state of panic to his already unwell mind, and he thought desperately what he could do. He finally knew what he *wanted to do* with this unsolicited slut from heaven: He wanted to make

---

[186] U2, "One"

ASHES TO ANGELS

love to her like she had wanted him to for the past twenty-six-six-six years, give or take a few dirty digits. It was backwards, sex pre-cursing love, but this was the way the world ends, Eliot said: *not with a bang but with a whimper.* The poet before him was enough justification for the poet in him. As her screams continued to pulse through the night, he began to realize, *she's showing through like a mortal, she's being contradictory,* but in her complete rage, *how unearthly beautiful she looks,* and for the first time since he had been involved with her, he suddenly *wanted her.* Her rage at him made him want her more, and her love for him made her hate him all the more. *You never **looked** like an angel – till now.* But before he could act on these raw, troubling feelings, she was gone as mysteriously as she had come, angel in devil's shoes tapping down the shape-shifty hall, leaving behind a pair of gothic black lug-sole combat boots filled with coal rather than food for the dead who had been starved obscenely almost exactly two months earlier to the day on November 2, All Souls Day. An eerie violet-gray mist heavy with cinder filled the halls and haunted Asher like a pair of wings for the rest of the night that was to be left of him.

NATALIE MCCOLLUM

Chapter Forty

Ash.

Ring around the thorns,
Pocket full of pins,
Matchsticks, matchsticks,
We all sing sin.[187]

*   *   *

Human passion is a flame that burns to its own destruction,
but

> *Only few meet in the one*
> *tremendous flame —*
> *where they both can*
> *be completely one*[188]

---

[187] Line based on the song title, "We Sing Sin" from the album <u>I Have Supped Full on Horrors</u> by Romance of Young Tigers.
[188] Edvard Munch, *Encounter in Space*, 1899, color woodcut.

ASHES TO ANGELS

Her madness had irrevocably shaken his own unstable, highly reactive condition. He too began to pace-prowl around his apartment, unable to return to sleep. But sleep was not to be, except in the eternal sense. With badly shaking hands he lit a cigarette in the dark, but could not smoke it. His guilt at being the cause of the fall of an angel drove him to the realization that somewhere they had traded places – he was the rebellious angel banished to fire, and she was the unsaved human soul consumed by fire. But boundaries are relative – were they really the same person? Was his name really hers? Was he inventing this occurrence, writing this poem under the screams of his direst dead poetic fan, to justify the staging of a pre-meditated death wish? If it's not suicide, how can the murderer also be the slain? By virtue of "The Vile Rape": no sadistic penance could ever reverse the fallout conceived by fucking an angel. Their two worlds could not totally transcend the last unsound step into the other's body – even in an embrace, the arms are still an impassable barrier to the person on the other side. You can't break it, even if you can touch it...how then could mortal words ever be powerful enough to hurt a being that thinks in poetry? Some things, *not even poets know*, he thought of Peter Mulvey's rock lyric poetic lines, *I'm going down*. He'd had his hands on the devil before, and finally he knew there was only one place he would ever be able to help her fulfill her dream that lay in the ashen ruins of a pair of wings now. It was not quite heaven, not quite hell; *I'm going down, / down to where / my angels live*...he would meet her halfway. *Alright/OK, Auryn: I will be with you again.* At that confession, he finally threw up his hands in surrender to hand-me-down love laid bare: the body of ash out of which Auryn was pulling his soul.

He winced at the pain of her nimble fingernails, razor sharp as kitten's claws as they plucked it in pieces, one by one like forfeited feathers of her sold-out wings, which disintegrated to dust as soon as they touched air. *It's not the spark that caused the fire; it was the air you breathed that fanned the flame,* she shot back in defense of her methods. It was almost like she was attempting to regain her soul by ravaging – and ravishing – his. *What you thought you solved with violence? Turned out to be an orgasm – You either face your fear or spend your life with one foot in the grave.* Well, she would know. The trashing of a human soul was being executed by the Sixth Angel like performance poetry. *God she's good.* He realized that all the erotic sensations being triggered by having your soul helped out of your thrashing body was exactly what his greatest fan always wanted. A dual reality, a co-authorship. The Angel fanned him with her wings. *Her* wings. *Wings.* He saw them for the first time, tainted and crooked and corrupted as they were after their stint on the demon. In all their fallen misshapen distortion, like an unrecognizable accident victim so horribly disfigured not even corrective surgery could restore, never had anything looked so freakishly beautiful. He didn't care if he was tripping, or having a relapse, or hovering in the zone of pre-dead. For the first time, he asked, with uncharacteristic wavering voice, "Are you an angel? Am I already that gone?" She responded with her own direct question she had always wanted to ask him, posed with uncharacteristic boldness and a version of straight talk as close to the human language as metaphorical beings could dangerously get without setting off like dynamite the end of the world and thusly the extinction of the entire endangered species, never having otherwise gotten a completely lucid answer as to why he had called it off between them in the first place:

"Tell me, tell me, where do all the poets go?"

But it did.

Her millennialist thinking, his apocalyptic dreaming, collided in Armageddon between two forbidden worlds marked with a crude, massive X on one body. Like an ancient burial map it said, "…WAS HERE" but neither Asher nor Auryn could tell whose name it was because the script in blood was so smudged as to be indistinguishable as a really bad tattoo job scratched on with dirty nails or a very phallic looking dagger.

At that, like a bullet through a butterfly he was smashing pumpkins 5 ½ minutes down the cinderblock hallway where dead poetica was waiting to get high with, and go down on, Writer #5 ½, the Sixth Angel, The Scream, the Poet's Muse. He saw them both over there, the schizophrenic poet and the raped angel; they fit each other too well. **Where body yielded 2 souls split from ashes to angels he couldn't tell.** *What the hell; I WILL BE YOU again.* Eyeing his lighter as he donned the wings, his last thought went to ashes, like her, scrawled longhand in quill tip on the back of a pay stub. It read:

I want to go be with Ash. Wherever he is, on the other side. But how do you get to the Other Side? And even if I did make the cross-over, how can I know that's where I'll be?

I'd go to hell if it meant I could just have a second chance to be with him. I don't care if it's Hell, though I don't think it's there. He was a good person, not a good mortal, but a good human. If his one good deed and contribution to humanity was his trade-off to mine, an organ

donor of mortality so an immortal could fall, not rise, that is worthy because – falling *was* the best part. The soul, taken from the rib of an atheist, behind his rib cage is where our race of angels was born. I feel like I was kind of mean, I know he wanted me, the Sixth Angel counting down the rib cage, writing down the bones, but I let my fears and scars and distrust of the whole human ½ of the race hold me back from giving him the word, and when I finally did decide to risk it on him, to respond to his unforced invitation and go for it with him, it was too late. His last words to me, "Let's go get some Starbucks" – so laden with heavy situational irony, and my surrender of inhibition came too late.

When I finally did call him, I knowingly left a message to a dead man.

His name's still in my phonebook.

I'll never completely recover from this. Any dead poet I'm with has to know that I wrote us into being. U and I verse the world.

An eating disorder is one thing. "Are we to surmise that in the Middle Ages angels had come down to earth and suffered from anorexia?"[189] But love is entirely a disorder far worse. Inadvertent clairvoyance: People ask me the poem on my wrist: Suicide isn't just death, It is love too.

That's what it means.

His own means settled, Asher added his own signature and postscript to the suicide note written in a love letter, or love letter written in a suicide note

---

[189] "Evolutionary Feathers" section of <u>Angels: An Endangered Species</u> by Malcolm Godwin, page 246.

ASHES TO ANGELS

(because are not they both really just the same thing). A double suicide, mutually assisted, half-failed, each one forced by the other, and so forth the reciprocal impossibility, left behind in the moment between the swallowing and the waking.

> "We hope that you choke,
> That you choke.
> We hope your rules
> and wisdom choke you."

~~Human passion is a flame that burns to its own destruction.~~

(Right away she had gotten something hard in her expression – she loosened her hair – let it fall down over her shoulders – then threw it back with an impatient movement – she was so beautiful now – looked like an offended queen...

She had never before stayed as long as this with him – he begged her not to leave – he was more ardent than ever before – he wanted to, had to embrace her again feel her kisses again – when they got up the glow was once more extinct –

She stood straight and fixed her hair with the posture of a queen

There was something in her expression that made him feel fearful – he did not know what it was –)[190]

Storms in Africa[191]

---

[190] Parenthetical material is the writing of Edvard Munch, on *Ashes*, 1894, oil on canvas.

[191] "There are two versions of "Storms in Africa", one in Gaelic and one in English. The Gaelic version is our personal favourite, which we have included here. Both versions were realised as a single in 1989." Enya, Only Time: The Collection.

NATALIE MCCOLLUM

Cá fhad é ó
Cá fhad é ó
Siúl trí na stoirmeacha
Dul trí na stoirmeacha

Cá fhad é ó
An tús don stoirm
Cá fhad é ó
An tus go deireadh

Tóg do chroí
Siúl trí na stoirmeacha
Tóg do chroísa
Dul trí na stoirmeacha

Turas mór
Tar trí na stoirmeacha
Turas fada
Amharc trí na stoirmeacha

When I jab a sharpened object in, choirs of angels seem to sing[192]: "Thus with a kiss I die."[193] She took one of the longest, slender, sharpest points of the black feather from her wings and started gutting him with it, first in the lower abdominal region like some form of medieval torture, like disemboweling though she knew not how to do this, and then taking her cue from the banned body piercer she pierced his left side with the quill tip like tiny swords, and finally ended with a scissor-leg laceration jaggedly slashed into the corresponding left thigh to match the long-ago jump at the demon

---

[192] "Bad Habit" by the Dresden Dolls.
[193] Romeo and Juliet, Act 5, Scene 3, line 120.

ASHES TO ANGELS

sister and her deal. In a fleeting moment of vulnerability akin to the mortality her wings exposed to both biology and violability, they also exposed her brutality in a similar shocking human vein. She was no more ½ vampire than she was at precisely the moment she was ½ angel. No doubt she cried as she did this, forking him in the stomach cavity as the closest proximity to the vagina made possible only through a rape, making her painfully conscious in toxic shock of the womb-space unoccupied by her unborn children and the birth canal made carnate only by a cold metal clamp being plunged up a hole she wasn't supposed to have. With each driving force of the feather like a syringe being plunged without mercy, she wept. "It's my life!" she screamed. "Don't you forget!" And just to make sure that he didn't, she yanked the quill tip out of him, and while it was yet dripping in his own blood, she wrote in the words of *The Scream* down the length of his whole torso, beginning up at the chest and ending just above his hip bone:

I felt our love
lying on
the ground like a
heap of ashes[p.106]

When you left me over
the ocean it was as if
fine threads still uni-
ted us it tore as
in a wound[p.111]

…Fine threads of her hair
are still attached to his

NATALIE MCCOLLUM

*heart – it bleeds – and
hurts
as an eternally open
wound*~p.115~[194]

The Jesus-freak murder-rapist had finally met his match: his own victim. This time, the Sixth Angel had the serious god-complex, making the sick motherfucker her fourth victim in three months.

Her work nearly complete, she gathered up the remains of loving him – her wings – and in a retrospective of her thwarted suicide attempt, the badly tattooed wing job, and finally all the way back to the beginning – wing-clipping and the (sub)sequential fall through space and airlift from hell – she stepped up to the window, seeing, as promised that day the sky was falling, pictures of her own death in slow motion as she wrestled the universe on the way down. Turning to look back over her shoulder at her bloody masterpiece still lying spread-eagle like a Da Vinci anatomical sketch on the floor, she tossed the crucifix of the black rose ripped in shards of purple tissue with the tacks still driven in at his feet as she choked, "Missed me, Mister, now you've gone and done it! Hope you're happy! In the county penitentiary – SERVES YOU RIGHT, FOR KISSING LITTLE GIRLS!!!"[195]

---

[194] As printed on said pages of <u>Emunch: Words and Images of Edvard Munch</u> by Bente Torjusen. The words describe the images of *Ashes*, 1896; *Separation II*, 1896; and *The Girl and the Heart*, 1899, respectively.

[195] A very telling line let slip in a moment of self-consciousness, by the speaker in a song about a pedophile from the viewpoint of

ASHES TO ANGELS

"Wait – don't jump." He lifted his head.

"Bleed like me, O mortality!" she spat, part the cynic, part the romantic.

"How can an immortal commit suicide?! You're either already dead or faking fatality! You can't die, you can't even *bleed!!*" She caught his reference to the bleeding lessons, said somewhat with nasty condescension in a flare-up of his earlier atheistic disdain for the concept of anything with claims beyond humanity. She summoned herself. He was still an atheist in love with the divine.

"I was only trying to bleed
because if I can bleed like a mortal,
Bleed like you,
then I can *be* a mortal,
be like you.
And if I can be mortal,
I can have human biology too,
and if I can be biologically human,
I can logically sleep with you.
And if we sleep together,
You will love me better.
Right?"
Pause.
"I was not trying to die;
I was checking for vital signs,
Looking for Signs of Life –
signs of mortality –
Signs of love."
(As an afterthought,)
"(I did not *mean* to commit suicide
I did not *mean* to do it by your side.)"

Asher's face clouded over, and his brow furrowed in grave recognition of the gravity of the situation. He

---

the young girl. "Missed Me" by the Dresden Dolls: an interpretation.

was only hanging on to watch her go down, he knew that now. For once, words were too much for the poet. So she choked him out of his writer's block with a prompt to die for. "If this isn't love, then it doesn't exist any more than I do!"[196]

"Well, if that's love, then it's all semantics. The most significant parts of the human experience, the eternal sense of mortality, all come down to semantics. Language, and the meaning we attach to abstract words. Life and death based on a unit of sound?! No wonder our existence is so *un*sound," was all he could muster in the wake of her retort:

"Maybe love can't exist without mortality…'And in the end'—" she shifted her heavy wings over her heavy heart— "'the love you take'—" he had started to crawl toward the window sill— "'is equal to'—" she rose up on the tips of her devil's shoes—"'the love you make.'"[197]

She spread her wings and jumped—

---

[196] "Remember that the angel cannot be separated from the witness." <u>Angels: An Endangered Species</u> by Malcolm Godwin, page 15.
[197] The Beatles: "The End."

ASHES TO ANGELS

Chapter 40 ½

P.S.

—Back.

[*Note to Self: Writer #5 ½ self-edits. Do not stop here. The editor is programmed to self-destruct. Writers are cutters that edit to their own destruction. The pen is mightier than the sword. The pen, the poison.*] ~n. (for narrator)

He caught her by the heel, pulling himself over the floorboards and yanking her back. "No."

Blind-sided, she caught herself mid-takeoff and turned slowly around in indignant shock.

"This isn't how the story ends."

She glared at him.

With much effort he pulled himself to his unsteady feet, hanging onto her shredded wings for support. "We both go down together."[198]

Cautiously, he took her left hand in his. Still limping, he helped her step up to the sill once again, a punked-out princess and her fallen warrior. "Don't let

---

[198] As in the song, by The Decemberists.

me go," he said, squeezing her hand and staring fiercely into her eyes.

"You're gonna have to hold on, you're gonna have to hold on,— to meeee," she warned holding the note of the last word. Then the two of them stepped off the ledge and fell that way.

The world he sees— Auryn, knowing her consequence for choosing to give herself away to the love that called her to the things of this world, had made a humble last request of the Emperor of the Sea, that he might send her former rival, the six-wingéd Raven, Priestess of the Air, to salvage the ashes of her fallen counterpart from the little velveteen coin purse sewn round her neck and scatter them in universe's womb, as Asher had forfeited his chance of ever seeing the alien galaxy of her misbegotten displacement. He only saw her on the way down. Like a silent picture movie reel, he experienced herstory from the vantage point of her wings, the greatest story never told.

U aNd I verse the world.
. . . .
Blessed be the womb.[199]

The Footnotes, The Voices – The deal/the Dealer; the soul-swapping/wing-clipping; the Fall-out while the sky was falling; the busted angel in a hospital ER; the coffee shop mortality, the rock opera, the Brain Trust bugged for *every poem ever written*, the Playlist; the Commune and its residents and the finite escape from Mantua; the suicide letters and the various failed

---

[199] Saul Williams, 1996 journal entry in The Dead Emcee Scrolls: The Lost Teachings of Hip Hop.

ASHES TO ANGELS

attempts and the disappearance; the screaming fans as the cast of Voices in his head; the vampire bedroom fantasies, the abusive love-making and –mutilation; the re-union on separate-but-equal sides of the bars at the gate of the Embassy; the drug addiction, eating disorders, domestic violence, suicide survivors, and rape victims; the bad tattoo job as a poor substitute for scissor-back wings; the pawning of the wings; the Rape of an Angel. *That was this story!*

The world she sees— Her descent into the underbelly of the trans-World was justified by the one in whose arms she finally found refuge for a terminally ill heart, while something like outer space above was dusted with the ashes of an angel's illicit love.

> *They were called humans before angels got wings.*
> *No, no, they were called angels before humans lost wings.*

> *So, which is it, Auryn?*
> *I don't know, Asher:*
> *The sign just said,*
> *"Leave your wings at the door."*

When the paramedics found them later, the dead giveaway to the double suicide was two clasped hands. The wings were gone, the only evidence of their existence being an indentation in the cement, like the fossil of some prehistoric animal. Scientists still have not been able to identify it.

Finis.

Exit Music: The Playlist
[insert "Songs for Asher and Auryn" mix tape]

Acknowledgments

To be fair and, in keeping with the nature of this book, uncomfortably honest, what you hold in your hands was supposed to be my master's thesis, the irony being that I dropped out of grad school, among other more personal reasons, to finish my first novel. As such, this novel with thesis origins would not be the realization of a dream without my thesis advisor, Jimmy Chesire, whose role took variations of editor, devoted reader, literary critic, and at times, counselor/therapist who listened not only to the words but also their author in the darker moments inevitable to the writing of this story. Jimmy supported the project from its initial conception as a ten-page story to the first awkward attempts at writing the first chapter, a daunting task – how do you even start a NOVEL?? – and even after I broke with the program, his guidance stayed with me till the last line on the last page. I've had the honor of being mentored by a master of the craft.

I also thank my personal readers: people both in

and outside of the university who have read versions of the manuscript in its various manifestations and developmental stages. These fans, friends, and other "voices" have made my novel a collaborative work through their intellectual contribution and emotional patronage. This includes Gary Pacernick, who has read and critiqued nearly every original poem in these pages at some point in some creative writing workshop; Brian Leingang, for his musical compilation of "Songs for Asher and Auryn," the mixed CD which has become the soundtrack to the story; and James Brubaker for his insightful readerly observations directing me to similar works of art in film and the recording industry that served as a reference for my own creation. Art feeds off art. To the artists, musicians, and poets I have known both casually and intimately who lent voice to characters, setting, and scenes; to random strangers in public places like coffee shops, bars, and subways whose conversations I overheard and fictionalized from "real life" into believable dialogue. And finally, to Dan O'Donnell, loving friend, confidante, and respected fellow writer, for randomly stumbling upon the publisher who gave me not only a job but also my first byline on a bookshelf. None of this, not even this sentence, would be in a book if you hadn't been idly surfing the Web.

Made in United States
North Haven, CT
29 December 2023